A Tale of the American Clustertruck
Fump's Fiendish Plot

Adal Smith

LEAD-BASED BOOKS

CONTENTS

PROLOGUE..VII

CHAPTER 1...1

CHAPTER 2...19

CHAPTER 3...45

CHAPTER 4...59

CHAPTER 5...107

CHAPTER 6...147

CHAPTER 7...177

CHAPTER 8...203

CHAPTER 9...225

EPILOGUE...255

Prologue

It was a cold, late January night in Washington DC. Deadly wolves howled at the new moon and vultures swarmed around the soon-to-be rotting corpse of an old man who had a mental condition parallel to a great American hero who once went from big-time movie star to President.

The newly-crowned Emperor Fump sat in his easy chair, which sagged, bent and cracked under every slight movement of the girthy ruler. He cackled maniacally into the perturbing, slightly-nightmarish darkness as he thought of his succeeding efforts toward the destruction of the United States as the world knew it, as well as thinking about the 8-year-old girl he had espied just the other day. All the lights in the Oval Office were turned off, and all the staff had long since been sent home for the night, aside from the usual security outside the White House doors. The room had an air of abandonment. Nothing appeared to be in use (except for Fump's easy chair) like a house abandoned. There were no cobwebs or dust, however, as spiders were too weary of being eaten by the gargantuan Emperor Fump (who quite enjoyed snacking on spiders) and dust mites too steered clear of the room – unable to stand the odor of the orange-skinned man-like beast.

Fump says to himself aloud, "Only 11 days in and already my first 26 Orders of Evil are set to be carried out throughout this country which I can once and for all call my own! Oh, I can already smell *Kroshechnyy Von Chlen's* cologne..."

Prologue

Fump closes his eyes and reaches his right hand into his pants. With his index finger and thumb, he begins to rub himself.

He doesn't continue this for long before he stops, opens his eyes and continues his monologue, "But before I get to that; let me call my faithful apprentice..." Fump hisses as he enunciates the "s" sound in "apprentice", "Lord Junkie, and see how he's faring in the Midwest."

The Emperor presses a miscellaneous-looking button underneath his desk and a blue, life-size hologram image of Lord Junkie appears in the center of the Oval Office, slightly illuminating the previously blackened-by-night room. Lord Junkie appears to be smoking some sort of controlled substance through a glass pipe.

"Lord Junkie!" Fump calls in a commanding tone. Lord Junkie drops the pipe and faces the Emperor, who continues, "Why are you smoking when I'm trying to fucking call you?"

Lord Junkie stammers in startled, submissive reply, "Shit, I ain't mean nothin' by it baby; jus' lookin' for a taste. Not this meth is any good anyways; what I really wants is-"

Fump cuts him off when he shouts, "What you want doesn't mean a damn thing to me you crackhead! I understand you've been working with the United States' government for a long time now – distributing hard drugs to the blacks and the Latinos – but now you answer to me and I hate the blacks and the Latinos more than I love making money off of them! That is why I have formulated a plan to rid this country of them forever; especially the Latinos! Now, there's a small problem brewing right in your area and I'm gonna need you to take care of it."

"Anything for you massa," chimes Lord Junkie.

"Good apprentice," chortles Fump. "We'll wait until August to carry this plan out, but I will tell you of it now."

As Emperor Fump tells Lord Junkie of his evil plan, the temperature around the crack-addict seemed to grow even colder. The blackness of the night sky grows more menacing, the faint ring of light where the moon should appear appears to have a red hue to it. Lord Junkie gets the feeling that the plan he is currently being instructed to follow will indeed, once and for all, lead to the end of the United States of America. A small, long-forgotten part of him wants to retaliate; to stand against Fump and his wicked ways, but the drugs in his system have long turned his brain into a malleable heap for stronger minds to form and shape into whatever they please, like clay. So he merely listened closely with the intent to carry out his master's terrible plan.

Fump finishes explaining his plan, and then says, "I would have you do this all now, but there are some minor complications... too many eyes on this particular problem right now. So until August, don't leave that fucking shithole you call a castle or I'll sodomize you with a Coleman flashlight! Got it?"

Lord Junkie nods rapidly like a cartoon character and says to Fump, "Oh yes massa Emperor Fump, I's gonna do jus' whachu say baby."

Emperor Fump presses the same miscellaneous button underneath his desk to end the hologram call and proceeds to continue cackling into the night as his fiendish plot quickly approaches his unsuspecting target.

Chapter 1:
The Explosion and the Ballz that Come With It

Once upon a time not long ago when tyranny ruled the land and voters were slow. When stupid laws were passed and justice was dying; and some people celebrated while many were crying: There lived a young man named Adam Ordell in a Northern Midwest town called River End.

Adam was a giant at 6 feet and 5 inches tall, and was 195 pounds of pure, lean muscle. His complexion was something between golden brown and high yellow. He had arched eyebrows which often made his soft face look angry, and wide, topaz-colored eyes. Something Adam couldn't understand since he first became aware of it at age 9 was why on Earth his luscious lips were raspberry pink rather than brown or a light fleshy color like most people with his complexion.

The young man had two identities: One the name his parents had given him, Adam Ordell. The other, the persona he created for himself: Ardell Johnson, the author.

Though only 20 years old, Adam had made a career of writing books. So far, he had only written and gotten published two books, with a third on the way. The first one had not done very well (as first books typically do not), and the second had only done well enough for the young writer to live frugally off its profits, yet this made Adam very proud of himself, and his parents even more so.

Adam enjoyed his life as a humble author, living in his $800 dollar a month, run-down studio apartment in his hometown of River End. He partook in various hobbies and activities he thought were fun, such as antiquing, walking various nature trails, tinkering with his old Chevy truck, going to the beach and either walking along the water's edge or sitting under a black umbrella, reading a book, visiting his local record store to see what strange old 12s or occasional 45s they had to offer in the dollar bin, and, of course, Adam loved to read. Two things that many young people did that Adam could never bring himself to do, however, were drink alcohol and do drugs. He believed there was no point in wasting life away with such trivial, momentary pleasures when he could be out enjoying life for the long term; doing one of the various things which he liked to do and which wouldn't kill his brain cells or break down his young, virile body.

Despite his comfortable life of self-identified luxuries, the author still yearned for more out of life. He wished to travel the world one day; he wanted to see all sorts of different modes of life, cultures, architecture and everything else that comes with the open road.

That is why Adam was working twice as hard on his upcoming book (which still lacked a title). He decided that it would have to be this book that would finally make his dreams come true. He wanted to make something fantastic; something so unique, incredible, and unheard of that not only would he capture the hearts of his own readers once again, but the hearts of everyone in America – if not the whole world.

It was seemingly just another late, mid-August morning; the time was approximately 11:30am. Adam Ordell had just rolled out of bed a half hour earlier. This is how many of the author's summer mornings started: late. Adam was not slothful, however, he was in fact a very self-motivated person with a work ethic which rivalled that of even the late, great Emile Zola. For his entire life, in fact, the young writer had always strived to complete tasks with the upmost efficiency – no matter how trivial or how urgent. From homework and tests when he was in school, to grocery shopping as an adult living on his own, Adam prided himself on doing everything fast as inhumanly possible. He attributed his growing success in the writing world to his own diligent work ethic.

Yet the studious young man often found it impossible to wake up at any decent time in the morning. The only times Adam could ever motivate himself to raise out of bed before 10:00am was when he had an important appointment (such as one with the doctor) or if he had something exciting planned for the day ahead (such as a trip to the beach, which required the somewhat shy author to arrive early so as to avoid being surrounded by too big of a crowd for too long). But the thought of getting out of bed simply to be productive, such as he was supposed to be doing on this fine morning – it was his plan to finish writing an entire chapter of his next book today – just wasn't enough to pull him away from his comfortable, extra-long twin mattress which was situated on a box spring without a frame to raise it off the floor.

So, at 30 minutes from noon, a time most first-shift factory workers spent either eating or counting down the last half hour until they could finally eat their lunch, Adam was in front of his tiny bathroom mirror; wrestling with his kinky-curly afro before brushing his naturally-white teeth. He then proceeds to dress himself in his normal summer attire: A pair of black cargo shorts and a black graphic tee shirt with some obscure logo belonging to either a band or pop-culture character long forgotten.

Once dressed, Adam finally sits at his desk, which is situated against a wall directly across the room from his bed, facing toward one of two windows in his entire apartment. He turns on his laptop, opens the manuscript containing his next book, and with a crack of his knuckles and saying aloud to himself, "Let's knock out an entire chapter today," Adam resumes typing what he is sure will be his magnum opus until his fourth book surpasses it.

The ambitious author did not count on what would become of his life next, nor could he have ever guessed or anticipated it. For, as he worked studiously, almost mechanically typing the manuscript for his masterpiece, a set of events was getting ready to take place which causes our tale of tyrannical trouble and comical folly to unfold.

Perhaps if the morning-detesting author had gotten up just a few hours earlier, and thus started his work earlier, he would be out to his favorite sandwich shop for lunch by now. Maybe he would have written enough of his upcoming book to justify allowing himself to go take a look around his favorite antique stores or take a walk around the state park just a mile from his apartment; it was after all a very nice day to enjoy the outdoors. But instead, he had slept in as he usually did, and what was to happen next did indeed happen.

Unbeknownst to Adam, just down the street from the apartment complex he lived in, in the center of the always-busy intersection of Rollins Road and Fox Drive, a junkie sat enjoying his blissful trip in peaceful basehead tranquility. Nobody dared hit the junkie, nor did they honk at him for sitting in the center of a busy intersection; for this was no ordinary junkie – this was Lord Junkie.

Lord Junkie was well known around the quiet town of River End as the king of all junkies; one whom possesses powers of voodoo. It was unknown where and when Lord Junkie came from, but everybody in the know knew, and most people were in the know, that it was suicidal to disrupt his peaceful junkie ways. Thus, Lord Junkie was able to sit in the middle of a small town's most busy intersection getting fried without being disturbed.

Meanwhile, even further east from Adam's apartment down Rollins, in a blind spot corner of the town's mall parking lot, a sick trick who had gotten an anonymous tip about something scandalous was sitting in the driver's seat of a brand-new, matte-silver Messla coupe. He was rolling down his window and whispering to the dozen prostitutes standing there, "Hey uh, I've never done this kinda thing before." As the sick trick said this, beads of sweat the size of golden tortoise beetles rolled down his fat face and neck.

To contrast his fancy and expensive car, the sick trick was best described as an out-of-shape, homely-looking, middle-aged man with a horseshoe of shoulder-length, graying-burgundy hair around his scalp and a meek little face, too small for his head, that seemed to wear an expression of constant hidden shame.

"But, um," the sick trick continues, "I'm looking for a *pit plum* if you know what I mean?"

One of the snickering prostitutes slowly approaches the fat, balding, pasty-skinned, beady-eyed, overgrown neckbeard having crusty-lipped, suit-and-tie-wearing organic stain upon the Earth and says, "Motherfucker! Don't be comin' 'round none of us lookin' for no sick shit like that! Some of us have daughters we're trying to raise to never have to encounter a filthy sub-creature like you unless they the prosecutin' lawyer or judge handing you your death sentence! Now if you don't get the fuck outta here real fast like–" The sick trick speeds away with blue in the crotch of his pants.

He reaches the other side of the mall, where all the teenagers, dreading the upcoming week when summer break would end and they'd have to return to their miserable lives as schoolchildren, resided. The sick trick's eyes light up as he espies a metallic-red, 1964 Impala SS dropping off a young girl with a dollar sign hanging around her neck. He pants in heat as he barrels the Messla toward the girl.

The sick trick rolls his window down once more and says to the girl, "Hey, uh, are you... working?"

The girl is clearly no older than 16 years of age, about 5 feet and four inches tall, slim but not anorexic, wearing a black, pleated skater skirt hiked up an extra inch or two, with black Converse high tops, and a bright-pink baby tee with the words, "Looking for a Cupcake?" written on it in black, glittery letters. The glittery-pink lipstick, black mascara, and dramatic-winged black eyeliner with a little tightlining only added to the effect of the girl's presence and appearance on the sick trick.

The girl bends her head down so she was now at eye level with the sick trick as she says with a childish giggle, "Of course, silly! I don't just dress this way for anyone – I knew someone like you would turn up sooner or later." The sick trick beams with excitement as she continues, "And I know that you'll pay big money to spend time with lil' ol' me... especially nowadays when I could easily get your precious balls cut off for the same shit men like you have been getting away with for far too long now..."

The sick trick stammers, "Feisty, I like it! I'll pay whatever you want – and all I want is a little *French*."

The young girl laughs the way an innocent child who has found a new rebellious game to play laughs and replies, "Okay cutie. If *all* you want is some *French*, then give me ten grand. And remember, if you don't give it up or if the cash is fake, then you'll be getting your cute little butthole reamed out for the rest of your miserable life."

The girl may be a prostitute, and she may have only just recently started, but she's smart. Most men who approached her only asked for as much as this latest sick trick, and the few who asked for more than that got a slap to the face and the act of a girl not turned bad by unfortunate circumstance – that is to say the girl would scream at the top of her lungs until someone came to her aid or the sick trick would flee. That is what made her so perfect to set off Fump's evil plot. She knew this desperate bucket of cat piss would shell out all ten thousand dollars right then and there, and, of course, he did. The mention of being used for anal sex for the rest of his life had seemingly made him more excited, as he hastily pulls the cash from a brown paper bag from the bank. The girl takes the money, carefully counts it all with her back turned to the sick trick, stuffs it away underneath her skirt, and proceeds to get in the passenger seat of the Messla.

"Alrighty then," the girl says cheerily, "let's get somewhere with more privacy now."

The sick trick quickly pulls out of the mall parking lot, and booms the Messla down Rollins Road, headed west.

The girl waits until they're a little ways down the road, then says, "Oh, you know what – I think you're a little more brave than most. Maybe you'd appreciate my company while you drive?"

The sick trick, in complete shock, can only nod frantically with a disgusting, eager look on his face. What happens happens, and next thing the sick trick knows he's headed for the intersection of Rollins and Fox going 90 miles per hour. He pays the intersection no heed, however, and keeps going; almost hitting Lord Junkie. In fact, he would've ran the junkie king straight over had it not been for Lord Junkie's super basehead reflexes, which allowed him to move out of the way at such a high speed that it appeared he had teleported a mere millisecond before the speeding Messla made contact with his body. The near miss angered the junkie immensely, as he thought he had been enjoying his junk on his own front lawn.

"Shit, this motherfucker done fucked up now baby!" Lord Junkie vociferates to himself. He proceeds to pull an Uzi from his waistband and quickly chants, "Baby butts oh baby butts! Little sick trick dick and exploding nuts!" before unloading the entire 32 round clip of the Uzi in the general direction of the speeding Messla; which at this point is nothing but a little silver dot, growing ever smaller in the distance ahead.

Because of the voodoo magic with which Lord Junkie had laced his shot, all 32 bullets miraculously hit the sick trick directly in the back of his fat-roll covered head, barely missing the occipital bone and instead shattering first the parietal bone and last the frontal bone – of course, splattering the corresponding lobes of his mostly-unused brain all over the front windshield.

The sick trick's carcass' arms jerk the wheel of the Messla to the right, causing the car to veer off the side of the road and into an unsuspecting house; the residents of which were thankfully not home at that moment. The young girl, having been in similar situations before since becoming a 16-year-old prostitute, barrel rolled out of the car just before the car made its impact with the one-story home. Both the car and house erupted in a violent explosion which shook the ground around it. This also just so happened to be the house next door to the apartment complex Adam Ordell lived in.

The time was now 12:45pm, and the author had just gotten into a good groove, writing line after line of literary gold. But of course, the sound and extreme vibration of the ground from the explosion just outside his apartment jolted him to his feet and made him ask aloud, "What in the fuck?" And as Adam says this, a pair of shriveled-up testicles (previously having been attached to the sick trick) splat against his east-facing window. The author looks away from the window, but a moment too late as he projectile vomits onto the black bookshelf he kept to the right of his desk.

"Motherfuckin' sonofabitch!" Adam yells. He looks down at the little bookshelf, which contained his most precious books, and watches with frightful dismay as vomit drips down the bookshelf, instantly ruining most of its contents. The devastated author started to cry as he thought of the memories he had of reading *Mama Black Widow* by Iceberg slim. He thought also of Truman Capote's *In Cold Blood* (which he had stolen from his high school years ago), *The Tropic of Cancer* and *The Colossus of Maroussi* by Henry Miller, *The Autobiography of Malcom X* as told to Alex Haley, the service manual for his truck – all now soaked with vomit.

The now enraged author stomps his right foot, and spins around – swinging his fists around violently; as if he were fighting some invisible foe. He stops flailing around and stomping after 45 seconds of the tantrum, looks back at the window with the dislodged testicles sliding down it, and begins taking deep breaths – trying to think clearly enough to form a rational plan of action.

As Adam begins to cool off and starts to grab some cleaning chemicals, a trash bag, and a sponge from his little bathroom to clean the vomit from his bookshelf, he sees out of his window, walking away from the pile of burning rubble which used to be a house and a car, a teenage girl. She was looking gaily mischievous, with her right hand barely covering her ear-to-ear grin, and her head bobbing and shoulders shaking with laughter.

Somehow, Adam knows that this girl has some connection to the amputated pair of testicles which had now slid from his window all the way down to the ground below, leaving a slimy trail of ooze behind. And so the flame of his rage is once again ignited as Adam throws on his pair of black Nikes and runs out his door, down all 5 flights of stairs in great bounds and leaps like a majestic gazelle, effectively going down 4 stairs at a time.

The furious author reaches the street, and, determined to learn the truth, he dashes toward the teenage girl. He intercepts the path of the girl's walk and she simply goes around him, and also begins speed walking.

He follows after her, calling, "Hey goddamnit! There's a nutsack on my window and I'd like to know just why that is!"

But the little prostitute ignores the slightly-terrifying man of over 6 feet as she continues speed walking down the street – giggling the whole time. Adam continues walking and calling after her, so she pulls out her cellphone and texts her pimp that she needs to be picked up; some guy was chasing after her.

After another minute of patiently walking after the girl, Adam's irritation takes over him and he runs after the girl, jumping in front of her path and now standing with his legs apart wide enough that she cannot simply step around him without going into the knee-high weeds on one side of the sidewalk or the traffic-filled road on the other side.

"Okay, look," Adam starts, "I'm not going to hurt you or any shit like that. I just wanna know why in the fuck a car done blew up a house next to me, and how there came to be a pair of wrinkly old nuts on my apartment window!"

The girl just laughs like a drunk baby, giving no response to Adam's interrogation.

"Come on now, look! I'm an author, and I'm trying to finish writing my next book because it's only half-way done and it's running behind schedule and I ain't never gonna get it finished with all these damn distractions! Not to mention the fact that seeing those nuts splattered against my window made me throw up all over the bookshelf with all my favorite books! Please, just tell me whose ass I gotta kick for this shit and I'll be on my way! Or, if this shit's your fault then just admit it and I'll leave you alone okay! I ain't gonna hit no little girl."

Adam's demeanor had returned to being calm and collected, and the girl was no longer worried this strange man would hurt her. She only remained standing in front of Adam out of pure amusement; humored by this tough-talking soft giant who didn't want anything from her but the truth about the house that blew up just outside of his window. The young whore was actually about to tell the author about what had happened out of her growing sympathy for this man who probably didn't have much other than his writing and his now-ruined bookshelf, but instead couldn't help but break out in a fit of laughter once more as she noticed her pimp's metallic-red, 1964 Impala SS coming down the street behind Adam.

Through her laughter the girl chortles, "Ooo you're in trouble now! That's my daddy coming up behind you!"

Adam turns around, and sees the six-four Impala speeding straight toward him. The driver is obviously not planning on stopping before hitting the author, so Adam stands completely still until the car is mere moments from colliding with him, then lunges into the tall grass to his left. He lands hard on the soft grass, as the Impala comes to a screeching halt, with the front, passenger-side tire ending up on the sidewalk. The once-again enraged author jumps quickly to his feet, anticipating a fight with some hulking behemoth of a gorilla pimp who is surely behind the wheel of the four-door car.

Instead, a five-feet-and-one-inch-tall middle schooler with a little strip of almost imperceptible peach fuzz on his upper lip steps out of the car. The kid couldn't have been above the age of 13. He wore a suit with a purple velvet sportscoat and matching pants, platform shoes, and a fedora. Underneath his coat he had on a white dress shirt and a yellow tie with a circular, silver pin on it. The band of his fedora appeared to be real cheetah hide. The little pimp also donned gold-rimmed locs with dark-purple tinted lenses, a solid-gold cane with a spherical handle covered in purple velvet, with some kind of big blue gemstone on top, diamond stud earrings, and a golden ring on his left pinkie finger which read in bold letters, "Ohio Playas". His skin was olive brown, and his shoulder-length, jerry-curl-processed hair was midnight black. When he opened his mouth, the kid pimp revealed a singular golden tooth in the very front of his upper row.

"Bitch, where's my money?" were the first words from his mouth.

The young girl promptly reaches a hand up her skirt (as Adam politely looks away) and pulls out the big wad of bills she had gotten from the sick trick. The apparent chili pimp smiles as his whore hands him the money.

He stuffs the cash in his coat pocket and says to the girl, "Now get your fine ass in the car while daddy handles his business." Adam turns back toward the pimp as the kid asks, "Whatchu doin' with my bitch, big nigga?"

The author looks down at the child-turned-pimp and pities his mother. He smacks the boy across the face with three quarters of his full strength, which causes his hat to fall off as he stumbles to the ground.

Adam then picks the mini pimp up by the lapels of his sports coat, and screams at the top of his lungs, "Now just who the fuck you think you talkin' to with all that bass in your voice? Where your momma at boy? And why ain't yo' lil' ass in school? Or ain't it started yet? And just why the fuck you got some trick's balls flyin' at my goddamn window? Huh? Speak up motherfucker!"

The middle schooler starts bawling his eyes out and begging Adam for mercy. The author decidedly puts the child down, who is now urinating in his pants. The baby pimp runs down the street away from Adam, terrified into almost becoming a square, the $10,000 falling out of his pocket as he takes off. The young girl gets back out of the Impala and scoops the money up off the ground.

She then looks at Adam, holding the money out toward him and asks, "You want this money, daddy?"

The author quickly responds, "Woa woa woa kid! You got the game all the way fucked up! This ain't no kinda cop-and-blow situation you got goin' on here. I ain't no pimp and if I was, I *damn* sure wouldn't be out here pimping no babies. You keep that money; I still just wanna know why the fuck yall out here runnin' cars into houses and shit!"

"Oh, that," the teenage girl responds, a disappointed tone in her voice, "Yeah, I was just taking care of that sad little two-inch piece of disgusting, wrinkly old skin while the trick was driving, and out of nowhere he gets shot in the head and the car spins out of control and into that house there." She points to the still-burning pile of rubble. "Kind of a shame about that house, and I'm sorry about your window and your bookshelf. Kinda wish he woulda got shot sooner though – the inside of my mouth tastes rank as hell! Hey, you got some gum or mints or something?"

Adam thanks the girl for the information, and tells her that he doesn't have any gum or anything on him. The teenage prostitute shrugs and gets back into her pimp's Impala before starting it up and driving away.

Adam too leaves the scene, and as he walks back to his apartment he can't help but wonder about who shot the sick trick and why (other than because of the fact that he was worse than a monster). Adam thought that maybe the little girl had a real daddy out there, somewhere, who found his baby girl in the car of a sick trick and let rage consume him before thinking things all the way through (as any half-decent father would do).

But what Adam wasn't thinking about, because he hadn't noticed it, was the little easter-egg blue Ford Pinto parked on the opposite side of the street from where Adam had confronted the young girl and scared her pimp. The car had seemingly materialized out of thin air from the very first moment Adam had arrived on the scene. Within the car sat two agents working for the Man.

"Okay, so it looks like we got what we needed then," says the agent in the driver's seat.

"Yep," replies the one in the passenger seat, who's holding an archaic, professional-grade camcorder from the 1970s. "But are we sure this is really enough to put him away?"

The agent in the driver's seat laughs and replies, "Oh don't worry – we have some top-notch editors back at the Complex. Hell, we've put away fellers with his complexion with a helluva lot less 'evidence' than this before. With this video, it's a cinch like women's jeans. Nobody would ever suspect a thing."

Both agents laugh as the one turns the key in the ignition and slams the Pinto into drive; burning rubber a block down Rollins.

The unsuspecting Adam returns to his 5th story apartment, and proceeds to try and salvage what he can from his vomit-soaked bookshelf. In the end, all he could save were two books: Dante Alighieri's *Vita Nuova* and *The Naked Soul of Iceberg Slim.* The next hour and a half he spends getting rid of the ruined books, bookshelf, and thoroughly cleaning the carpet at the foot of where the bookshelf had been. Afterward, Adam finally gets back to working on his next book. He spent the rest of the day writing, in fact, and only took a handful of breaks to stretch, use the bathroom twice, eat once, and shower before bed. Despite the author's incessant insomnia, as soon as he laid down on his bed at 10:43pm, he fell fast asleep; having been quite satisfied with his incredible progress on the book that day.

That night, Adam has a very abnormal, nightmarish dream. He dreamt that that he had been set up to take a fall for a monstrous crime by a villainous criminal. All signs pointed to a mysterious man wearing a beige-colored suit with horns on his forehead as being the one who had sold him out as a scapegoat to the unknown villain.

The author decided immediately that he would find and beat the man blind. A figure shrouded in blinding light comes to Adam like a deity in an ancient Greek tale and strongly advises him against seeking out the man and instead finding the villain who had put him up to the fiendish plot. Adam ignores the advice of the deity, however, and continues forth with his plan to find the man. Once the author finds the beige suit wearing man, he loses his temper completely and miraculously procures a knife, which he uses to stab the man in the neck. The dual-horned man explodes into dust, and a hissing laugh not unlike the sound of an angry goose can be heard. Adam doesn't get any time to process what's going on, however, as he's abruptly awakened from the strange dream by the sound of a battering ram caving his door in.

Police storm into the run-down studio apartment, flashing bright flashlights in every which direction and they shout, "Adam Ordell, you're under arrest!"

Adam glances at his illuminated alarm clock; it reads 12:00am. "Ah fuck," Adam murmurs aloud, only half awake, yet able to mostly grasp the severity of the situation at hand.

"Don't resist!" shouts the officer in front of the sounder of six other police officers. "We have the place surrounded! One funny move and you'll be shot!"

Adam slowly and drowsily gets up, his hands held high above his head as the low ceiling of his apartment will allow him, and responds, "Don't worry officer, I have no intentions of–"

The top hog cuts Adam off by shouting, "He's resisting! Beat 'im good boys!"

Adam is then jumped by seven police officers, who attack him with billy clubs. The author is unconscious within a matter of seconds, and one younger officer of the group begins to worry aloud that they'd accidentally killed the man they were ordered to arrest:

"Uh, hey. I think we might've broken this nigger," the young cop says.

Another officer slaps him on the back and says, "Oh, young buck, haven't you read the whole manual yet? This is a code 2-6-11 Break-a-Nigger!"

The young officer stares at his older comrade in disbelief, so the more experienced police officer pulls out a pocket-sized handbook from his righthand cargo pocket and flips through it until he finds the page containing code 2-6-11. (The spine of the book has a severe crease directly where the page is, and the page itself has significant wear at the edges.)

"See," the officer says, "right here on page 8: Code 2-6-11 Break-a-Nigger."

The younger officer leans in close to get a good look at the page, and after reading its contents for himself he sighs with relief.

The sounder then drags Adam's barefooted, pajama-wearing, unconscious body out of the apartment and throws him into the back of a squad car. The police officers then all load into their own vehicles and drive off into the blackness of the early morning.

Chapter 2:

The Trial and the Imprisonment

Adam awoke hours later, propped up in a wooden chair. His arms and legs felt like lead, his spine hurt, and his jaw was swollen where one of the officer's billy clubs had struck him. He looks down at himself, and notices that he is miraculously dressed in one of his many black graphic tee shirts, khaki cargo shorts, his black Vans, and his Casio watch; whereas his last memory was of him being in his pajamas in his apartment.

"Well, at least wherever I am, I'm dressed," Adam thinks to himself.

The pain grew as the author shook himself all the way awake, becoming also fully aware of his surroundings. The drowsy author realizes he is inside the main civil courtroom in downtown River End when he notices the judge's stand: a grand varnished oak table elevated 2 feet off the ground, standing about five and a half feet total.

The presiding judge sat behind the stand, seemingly glaring at the dazed defendant with his large, oval-shaped eyes, and his appearance made it difficult for Adam to contain his laughter. He had an abnormally large chin, similar to a blonde-headed cartoon character from the 1990s which the silently chuckling author had fond memories of. His nose was long and slender like that of Carlo Collodi's character Pinocchio – which Adam figured was fitting for any government official. His salmon-pink lips were so thin that the only reason they were even perceivable was because of the way they were terribly chapped and scabbed-over where they bled due to the extreme dryness of his mouth. The judge's ears were large and round like an elephant's, and his hairline had receded to the very crown of his head – yet he tried and failed at hiding this fact with a comb over of his decaying brunette hair. The diagonally-striped, yellow and blue tie sticking a quarter of its total length from underneath his black judge's gown only added to his comical impression; at which Adam had to bite his tongue in order to stifle his laughter.

Adam begins to look around the courtroom and notices the grimaces on the faces of the ancient-looking jury members, as they sat at the coffin-looking jury stand. All but three of the members of the jury were old men, while the remaining three were old women who reminded Adam of witches – the entire jury was white.

At the prosecution's stand sat the 16-year-old prostitute, wearing the same outfit as when Adam had seen her last, only now her hair was in complete disarray and the collar of her hot-pink baby tee was torn in the center – as if she had been attacked. The girl was softly sobbing beside her lawyer, a man of about 30 with his hair solidified with pomade, round-frame silver glasses and a smug smirk on his face as if he was aware of something everyone else was not. His beige suit and pocket watch on a silver chain only added to the effect of college education which his character exuded in abundance.

Now the author looks to his immediate right, where he sees at last his court-appointed public defender. The public defender looked to be only a little older than Adam, maybe aged 25. He was a thin, short, pale man with the tendency to fidget with his thumbs and bite his lips.

When looking at this skittish, pathetic excuse for a lawyer, Adam immediately lost all hope for his situation and thinks to himself, "Ah fuck. The Man done got my ass now and there ain't shit I can do about it – not with this damnable *rent-a-lawyer*."

"Oh thank god; you're awake now," the public defender says with a hint of relief in his voice. "I think the trial is about to start so listen up."

The bailiff to the right of the judge's stand then says loudly, "Court is now in session, Judge Composé presiding, in the case of Janie Fagen versus Adam Ordell on one alleged account of sexual assault and rape. The prosecuting attorney is Dr. Colin Hochstedler, and the public defender defending Adam Ordell is Mr. Jacob Browning.

"Now, Dr. Hochstedler, would you please step up to the stand and give your opening remarks?"

The cocky lawyer with the price-tag doctorate jumps up and with a hop and a skip makes his way to the podium. Once at the podium, Dr. Hochstedler begins his opening remarks:

"Your honor, I believe this will be a quite swift and efficient trial. The defendant, Mr. Adam Ordell, is beyond even an unreasonable doubt guilty of both sexually assaulting and raping poor little Janie Fagen as I shall soon prove to the fine court today. The victim of Adam's monstrous crime knew nothing of sex before he got his hands on her..."

As the lawyer continued his opening remarks (which rambled on for far too long to the unconcern of the judge) Adam sat at the defendant's stand, burning internally with deep-seated ire and a great sense of confusion.

The author was furious at the accusations being thrown at his name, and he couldn't wrap his head around the predicament he was currently in. Why was the young girl he'd met yesterday now accusing him of rape and how was it that he could already be in court the very next day after having met her? Why was this happening to him? How was he going to get out of this situation? And would he ever finish his next book at this rate?

While the angry and distressed novelist turned these questions over in his head, searching for a logical answer and a way out of his terrible situation, the bailiff calls for the defendant's opening statement and the rent-a-lawyer whispers to Adam before walking up, "Wish me luck up there; we're going to need it."

At the stand, Jacob, the public defender, says with a tremble in his voice, "Your honor, th-the d-defendant, Mr. Adam Ordell, w-would l-like to plead not g-guilty to both charges brought a-against him. Mr-Mr Ordell is a humble writer of t-two books and is known as a p-peaceful man among those in h-his tight-knit circle of f-friends and family. Th-thank you your honor."

The rent-a-lawyer walks on shaking legs back to his client. He sits down with a sigh of relief and Adam looks at the anxious little man with a look of total, crushing disappointment.

"How did I do?" the public defender asks.

Adam responds honestly, "Man, that was fucking terrible."

The rent-a-lawyer, shocked, asks, "That wasn't good?"

"No nigga no!" the author responds in a low, furious voice. "Matter of fact, how the hell are *you* the lawyer, the professional at this shit, asking *me*, the average joe shmoe, how the opening statement went?"

Tears form in the corners of Jacob's eyes, and Adam decides to let off as he attempts to convey his feelings in a more calm way, like one would do to a small child that has done something wrong which they did not know was wrong.

"Look, it's just that you gotta be more assertive up there! I mean, all that stuttering shit–"

But the author is cut off by the booming voice of the bailiff, who calls out, "Will the prosecution now please present their evidence?"

Dr. Hochstedler stands up, retrieving a VHS tape from his inner jacket pocket as he does. The lawyer nods at the judge, who taps his desk with his finger once. Shortly after, an old CRT television with a built-in VCR is carted out and placed in front of the witness stand.

Before placing the tape into the player, Dr. Hochstedler says to the court, "All the evidence this prosecution needs to prove their case will be found on this tape." The high-dollar prosecutor pauses, then puts on a face of fabricated disgust as he continues, "Though I must warn you all – its contents are quite disturbing."

He finally turns the television on, switches the input to the VCR, puts the tape into the player and hits play. On the television plays an ingeniously edited recording of the scene of Adam speaking to the 16-year-old girl from yesterday. It begins just as things actually happened, with the author simply speaking to the young girl. But before the young pimp drives up in his 1964 Impala, the tape appears to go off track for a second, the whole screen goes gray, and then it shows the same location except with some other man who is clearly not Adam standing where the innocent author had been previously. The man is two shades darker than Adam, appearing to be old enough to be Adam's dad, with a poorly-adhered afro wig on his head. The actor pretends to pin the little girl down to the ground, as she writhes in pretend struggle. The actor proceeds to touch the girl in similar fashion to how a certain billionaire claimed to do to women back in the year 2005. Adam grows once more furious as the hideous scene plays on.

"This is fucking bullshit," he thinks to himself. "These cocksuckers done got some other punk, bitch-ass-motherfucker-ass Oreo trick who don't even look nothin' like me to pretend to be me and do all that fuck shit to that baby!"

Adam looks over at the jury – all 12 members of which are glaring at him with murderous intent. "Man, and these dumb motherfuckers believe this shit? Ah but that's right; all us niggas look the same to everyone else in this fucking country. Figures."

Of course, everyone includes Adam's court-appointed lawyer, Jacob Browning, who had been previously crying softly about the author's previous harsh remarks, but now only stared at the television screen with an expression of horror across his face and his already pale skin was now almost translucent.

"Oh no," the public defender whispers, "This is it man, we're fucked! Only my first ever case and we're fucked! They have you on video Adam! There isn't anything I can do to disprove that!"

The beyond angry author responds through gritted teeth, "You dumb motherfucker! That isn't me; it's clearly an actor! Just prove that shit to the court and everything will be okay."

The rent-a-lawyer regains his composure somewhat, looks closer at the screen, and notices that his client is indeed correct. The man on the tape is a completely different person, not even resembling Adam remotely. He then looks at the jury, who clearly haven't had this same epiphany.

"But how do we prove it?" Jacob whispers.

His client is about to respond when the tape ends and Dr. Hochstedler shouts, "This footage here we find self evident! That is to say," he pauses, looking around the courtroom with a determined facial expression, "good, rational people of the court, that this grotesque tape is as stated previously: all the evidence needed to prove that Adam Ordell is guilty of the horrific crimes he is currently being tried for."

Adam wears a poker face of calmness and tranquility, while inside of his mind all his thoughts are of hanging the wrongly accusing lawyer from his expensive-looking tie. The reaction to such blatant lies, which most certainly will ruin a man's life, was somewhat normal. But this mockery of justice was taken as a personal, specialized and calculated plot against him. Not necessarily because of the specific lies being told, but because the simple fact that lies and false accusations were being made against the author at all. It was the author's deep-seated hatred for those who tell lies about others which made him feel so hostile.

For almost his entire life, Adam had been completely intolerant of any false truths told about him. This was because of something which happened to the author at the tender age of 6 – something which he could never let go of.

When Adam was in the first grade, he had been punished for a crime he did not commit. At lunchtime, the lunch ladies claimed that everyone was being too loud and rambunctious, so they made all of the children sit in the hallway rather than go outside for recess. Once lunchtime was over, and the children's teacher came to escort them back to their classroom, the lunch ladies decided to pick a couple of especially-troublesome kids out from the rest – Adam was one of those kids. This came as quite a surprise to the 6-year-old not-yet writer, who always sat alone at lunch and hardly ever spoke to anyone. He got lunch detention and a report sent to his mother, who did not believe him when he told her that he hadn't done anything wrong.

Though the injustice had happened so long ago, and was in hindsight not so terrible, Adam had swore that never again would somebody lie on his name and get away with it.

This vow was at the front of Adam's train of thought as he sat in court, helpless against the American judicial system, and watched as his name was slandered and buried in the ground in front of a jury of so-called peers who hated him from the moment they laid eyes on him.

Dr. Hochstedler sits back down next to little Janie Fagen, a look of complete satisfaction painted across his face, as the bailiff asks, "Will the defense now please give their testimony?"

The public defender, befuddled, scrambles to stand up and stammers, "Y-your honor th-th-the defendant–"

"Guilty!" one of the jurors shouts abruptly. The juror who spoke out was at least 80 years old, with a gray toupee leaning to one side of his head, a glass eye in his right eye socket and wearing a dark-green suit like a leprechaun's. "That motherfuckin' nigga is guilty!"

The judge bangs his gavel and yells, "Order! Order! Sir, you have to wait until the jury is allowed to deliberate!"

"I don't *need* to deliberate!" the juror responds. "We all saw the goddamn tape! That boy is a goddamn rapist like two pack! I say we just take 'im out back an' shoot 'im!"

The judge looks at the elderly man with much compassion in his eyes and says sincerely and soothingly, "Sir, I know the nigga is guilty – everyone in this courtroom got eyes can see that! Hell, I'm supposed to stay impartial, and I've already decided what *I'm* going to be saying at the end of this trial.

"But we have to play along legally. You know, hear the nigga's asinine little speech of lies, then we quote-on-quote, 'deliberate', then I sentence the nigga to life without parole; let Big Bubba and the gang getta hold of him everyday for the rest of his life."

The juror, satisfied with the answer given by Judge Composé, stays silent for most of the remainder of the trial.

The judge looks Jacob the public defender sternly in the eyes and says, "Go on now! Get on with your plea!"

The rent-a-lawyer, looking scared as a five-year-old child confronted by the boogie man in a dark room full of mirrors, continues his testimony: "Th-the defendant is not the man o-on th-that tape y-your honor. T-to p-prove this I, I would like to ca-call Mr. Ordell himself t-to speak on his own be-behalf."

The pitiful public defender looks at Adam so pitifully that Adam can't help but feel a little sorry for him, though he remains furious at the rent-a-lawyer, as he slowly gets out of the defendant's stand and approaches the witness stand. Once there, the bailiff makes the author swear to tell the truth and he does so through gritted teeth.

Jacob the public defender then asks his client, "So, um, M-Mr. Ordell, did you co-commit these heinous crimes le-levied a-against you?"

Adam closes his eyes momentarily, takes a long, deep breath, cracks his knuckles (which he has always had a terrible habit of doing when he's extremely irritated) then proceeds to say carefully into the microphone before him: "Simply put, no. To explain further – and I say this without malice toward the courtroom nor the prosecution, both of whom are clearly and simply mistaken – I am not the man who did those awful beyond words things to that poor child.

"If you look closely at the man in the tape recording, you'll notice that not only is his complexion noticeably darker than my own, but his facial features differ quite extremely from my own both in genetic attributes and to the effect of his advanced aging. Perhaps one may become confused because of the afro wig the man in the tape wore, but if you look closely at that too you will notice how his hair is indeed a wig, whereas my hair is naturally grown from my scalp. I have only one more thing left to say to the courtroom before the prosecution begins their cross-examination: You have the wrong man; Adam Ordell is *not* a rapist."

Dr. Colin Hochstedler, eager to discredit Adam since the very moment he stepped up to the witness stand, pounces at the author like a hungry jaguar onto his prey and points out a seeming fallacy in Adam's defense: "But Mr. Ordell, how can you deny that you were at the scene of the crime when your wallet was found on the sidewalk where it took place?"

The high-price lawyer produces Adam's wallet from an inner jacket pocket and the jury gasps dramatically.

The astonished author can't believe what he's seeing. He knows for a fact that he couldn't have dropped his wallet on the sidewalk yesterday for the simple fact that he hadn't had it on him when he ran out to question the girl.

Adam starts to reply, "But Mr. Hochstedler–" but is cut off by the prosecuting lawyer, "It's *Doctor* Hochstedler."

The enraged author cracks his knuckles once more and continues with a furious tremble in his voice, "*Doctor* Hochstedler, I did not deny that I was there, I simply stated the truthful fact that I did not commit the crimes this court levies against me."

So you admit you were in fact at the scene of the crime?" the prosecutor asks.

"Yes but–"

"So you see," Dr. Hochstedler bellows, "honorable people of the court, Adam Ordell is clearly guilty, and has even attempted to commit perjury in this very courtroom! That will be all, Mr. Ordell."

The jury once again glares at the author with eyes full of hate and start screaming out, "Guilty" "Liar" and "Nigger" before Judge Composé bangs his gavel and yells, "Order! Order!" The courtroom once again grows silent.

"Now, does the defendant's lawyer have any more questions for Mr. Ordell?" the judge asks. The public defender meekly says no and Adam is dismissed from the witness stand. The author returns to his seat at the defendant's stand and the prosecution is called to bring a witness to the stand.

Dr. Hochstedler calls for someone named Lynne Brown to come up to the witness stand. A middle-school-age black kid stands up from the gallery and begins to approach the witness stand. As he passes Adam, the author realizes that Lynne Brown is the 1964-Impala-driving mini pimp from the day before.

"Goddamnit," Adam thinks to himself, "they must have this kid in on all this bullshit too."

The young pimp, now dressed in a plain-looking black suit like the kind someone would wear to a funeral, his hair combed straight back like Billy D. Williams, takes his place at the witness stand and is promptly sworn to tell the truth.

Dr. Hochstedler approaches and asks him, "So, Mr. Green, were you present at the time and scene of the crime in question?"

"Yes," Lynne responds.

"Would you please describe to us in your own words what happened on the day in question?" the prosecutor asks.

Lynne looks over at the author piteously and silently mouths the word "sorry" before giving the account which he was being forced to relate in court: "I was walking down Rollins Road, when I came upon Mr. Adam Ordell sexually assaulting a teenage girl. I then proceeded to confront Adam, and he pulled a gun on me and forced me to record what was shown on the tape with a camcorder he had there on the ground. After the incident, he told me to keep the tape while he took the camcorder; also threatening to kill me if I were ever to take the tape to the police."

"As you can see," announces the crooked prosecutor, "the evidence from the tape, along with Mr. Lynne Brown's testimony proves that–"

"Objection!" shouts Adam, now standing, no longer able to sit idly by and listen to the lies. "The witness' testimony is in direct contradiction with the so-called 'evidence' you've presented on tape! How could Lynne Brown have witnessed the alleged assault in progress before recording it, when the recording starts before the assault?"

"Order! Order!" bellows Judge Composé with a few bangs of his gavel. "Ni – uh – Mr. Ordell, you can't make an objection like that! You have to wait for your lawyer's turn to cross-examine the witness so that question may be posed. Another outburst like that, Mr. Ordell, and I'll hold you in contempt of court!"

Adam clenches his jaw and sits back down. The high-price prosecutor announces that he's done questioning the witness and the bailiff asks the defense if they have any questions for Lynne Brown. Adam lightly kicks the rent-a-lawyer in his shin so that he knows to answer "yes".

So the public defender rises to his feet on shaking knees and answers the bailiff, "Y-yes. I, I would l-like to cr-cross examine th-the w-witness, M-Mr. Lynne Brown."

The rent-a-lawyer walks up to the witness stand and begins his feeble attempt at a cross examination: "S-so M-Mr. Green, you say y-you witnessed m-my c-client at the scene of the c-crime…"

The public defender looks hopelessly lost, as he turns around to look for help in his defendant's furious eyes. Adam angrily and silently mouths the words, "my objection" to the pitiful lawyer, who then turns back toward the witness and continues his cross examination: "So, uh, h-how c-could you have wi-witnessed the crime st-starting a-and at th-the same time b-been forced to re-record it before th-the crime a-actually started?"

The prosecutor interjects, "Objection! That question is irrelevant to the actual matter at hand here – thereby the witness doesn't have to answer that question, your honor."

Judge Composé promptly responds, "I agree. Motion sustained!"

The bailiff then asks if the defense has any other questions for the witness. Jacob, the public defender, stammers that he does not and sits back down next to Adam. Lynne Brown is dismissed from the witness stand as Dr. Hochstedler announces that the prosecution rests.

"Does the defense have any more evidence or witnesses to call to the stand?" asks the bailiff.

Adam looks at the rent-a-lawyer, who's already standing and saying, "The defense r-rests too y-your honor."

The author, in furious disbelief at the words of the public defender, grabs Jacob by the lapels of his suit jacket and asks, "Now what the fuck did you go and do that for?"

The rent-a-lawyer whimpers in response, "I, well, w-we don't ha-have any more evidence or–"

"You fucking idiot!" Adam yells. "You could have got some character witnesses or something goddamnit! Hell, I always date and time my writing so you could have tried to use that as evidence! What about finding a police report from when that Messla crashed into the house next to my apartment? Goddamnit! Now they're definitely gonna–"

"Order! Order!" the judge shouts to the sound of his gavel once more. "I swear to god, Mr. Ordell, one more outburst – just one – and I'll hold you in fucking contempt!"

The juror who called Adam out as guilty earlier shouts, "Hold the nigga in contempt right now!" and nobody says anything in protest.

Colin Hochstedler stands up, approaches the jury and says to them, "Ladies and gentlemen of the jury, I trust your deliberation will be swift and correct in its ultimate conclusion. The evidence against Mr. Adam Ordell speaks for itself and without a doubt proves what we all know is true." Then, turning towards the judge he says, "That will be all, your honor," before returning to his seat next to the 16-year-old prostitute.

Jacob the public defender then stands and without approaching the jury (due to his cowardice) he stammers, "Um, m-my client i-is clearly b-being mistaken fo-for someone else a-and so I, I trust in the j-jury's b-best judgement."

The rent-a-lawyer sits back down and Adam has to look down at his own feet, pretending the public defender is not indeed within arm's reach, to avoid strangling him to death.

"Members of the jury," starts Judge Composé, "you have heard all of the testimony – asinine blathering and truth together – which concerns the case. It is now up to you to determine the facts. You and you alone are the judges of the fact. Once you decide upon the obvious facts which can be easily drawn from the evidence, you must then apply the law as I give to you the facts as you find them: You are to deliberate on whether or not Adam Ordell is guilty of the sexual assault and/or rape of 16-year-old Janie Fagen.

"Momentarily, the bailiff will take you to the jury room to consider your verdict, which I trust will not take much time at all. There, you will select a foreman to preside over your deliberations like a chairman in a meeting. It will be the foreman's duty to sign the verdict form when you have agreed on a verdict. Whatever verdict you render must be unanimous; and of course I'm sure it already is. The bailiff will now escort you to the deliberation room."

The bailiff leads the jury to the deliberation room, and after 60 seconds they return to the stand.

"Have you reached the verdict?" asks Judge Composé.

The green-suit-wearing foreman responds, "We have, your honor."

"Well, say it then," prompts the judge.

The foreman smiles ear to ear, and with a giddy giggle in his voice he reads from the signed paper in his hands, "We the jury, in the case of Ms. Janie Fagen versus Adam Ordell, find the defendant guilty as hell of the charge of sexual assault and rape."

Judge Composé smiles warmly and says, "Thank you, jury, for your service today. The sentencing day will be exactly 30 days from today, at 9:00am. Court is adjourned."

The jury and the few people sitting in the gallery begin leaving the courthouse. The prosecutor, Dr. Colin Hochstedler high-fives his client, Janie Fagen, who is then approached by Judge Composé.

The judge whispers something into the ear of the 16-year-old girl, and she giggles and says just loudly enough for Adam to overhear, "For you? Why, only 8 of course."

The author recoils with disgust as the bailiff, accompanied by a previously hidden-away police officer comes to take him away to jail.

"You ain't hear nothin' nigger, got it?" the police officer asks rhetorically as he jabs the helpless author in his ribs with the butt of his billy club.

The wind knocked out of him, Adam falls into the two servants of the court's arms while trying to nod his head "yes". He is then dragged outside to the same police cruiser as he'd been abducted into the night before, thrown in, and driven to the River End Country Jail. Upon arrival, Adam is thrown violently into a filthy cell with rust on the bars.

The door is slammed and locked behind the author as the police officer who threw him in says with a sarcastic snarl, "Enjoy yer stay, boy."

The doomed writer now finds himself locked in a single cell with a schizophrenic man sitting in a wheelchair in the far-right corner. He's facing away from the bars, shivering, though the temperature of the cell is hot and humid.

The man was saying quietly to himself, "Oh how I want to go home. Don't wanna live here; I'd rather feel Krohme split my dome. My wings have been burnt off because at my success the god of jealousy had scoffed. But now a lesson is learned to communicate with the One and I've been chosen because I'm god's son."

"And I'm the retarded one," Adam finds himself saying abruptly.

The schizophrenic stops rambling and turns his wheelchair around to face Adam. The author takes a good look at the wheelchair-bound prisoner. His skin was a reddish brown like Redd Foxx. His eyebrows were large and expressive, with almond-shaped eyes that were a brown so dark they were almost black. His nose was tall and wide at the base. The man also had chiseled cheekbones and a chin well-defined by his salt-and-pepper full goatee. The lines by his mouth suggested a tendency to smile, while the lines between his eyebrows and on his forehead suggested a tendency to spend long periods of time thinking about life and death as well as reflecting on past adventures.

The wheelchair-bound man wheels closer to Adam and asks, "What'd you just say?"

Adam answers, "I, well, the last thing you said reminded me of something I think I heard a long time ago."

A pleasant expression shows on the prisoner's face, like that worn by an old man when meeting a friend for the first time since the days of their youth.

"There's only one explanation for this;" the schizophrenic says abruptly, "you are the chosen one."

The man pauses and Adam, with cynical intentions, asks, "What do you mean, 'chosen one'?"

The man laughs softly and replies, "Look, you need my help and I need you. Just trust me; do as I instruct, and you'll be out of here in no time – on a quest to clear your name and save more than you know."

Inside his mind, the author thinks, "Meh, fuck it. This poor old man is clearly gone insane so I'll humor him."

So Adam agrees to do whatever the man needs him to and the schizophrenic proceeds to introduce himself, as well as explain the ritual they must both complete: "I already knew you would agree; though reluctant and cynical you may be. To start with, let me introduce myself: My name has been many different things throughout the decades. Like many, my first title was bestowed upon me by my beloved mother. I received my second name from Emperor Helios a short time into my life, when I first became anointed in this shit; it is unimportant to mention now. A few years later, at the age of 19, that name evolved into a title I would wear for many decades later – I still sometimes go by it now. There were various other aliases I took on during my lifetime so far, but none of them are of any concern now; for I have ascended all previous names and am simply referred to now as 'The Grandmaster'."

Adam stares in bewilderment as The Grandmaster continues, "Yes, The Grandmaster, because I have gained through my years and experience a supreme mastery of the arts which I now control.

"Anyway, in order to get outta this cell, tonight at exactly midnight we must chant the sacred seance which The Prophesy foretells will bring upon the beginning of your quest, in turn, allowing you to escape this cell."

"What is the seance?" asks Adam, now intrigued by the fairytale imaginings of his insane cellmate.

"You'll know when the time comes," replies The Grandmaster. "Rest of now and we'll convene in the center of the cell later tonight."

The Grandmaster spins his wheelchair around and wheels himself back into his corner, where he resumes his schizophrenic babbling: "Tick tick time is short, bitten by the edge of a razor. Stupid-ass mouse chewing on the corpse of a traitor. But that was long ago; now a half a decade dead. The public will never know just what was said and why it's still floating in my head."

Adam tuned the sound of The Grandmaster's voice out and, not believing in his words or his ability to help Adam to freedom, the author begins to think of how he might really escape his current predicament.

"Goddamnit all!" his mind silently screams as he begins to lean against the cleanest-looking, green with mold and moss, wall of the cell. "I'm really fucked now. I can't survive in prison for a week – let alone the rest of my life! I'll be shanked or else I'll hang myself before even a month passes. Not to mention how difficult it must be to write and publish a book while in prison."

Adam finds himself looking over at The Grandmaster, who's still spitting out past-tense verbs and nouns in a strange, methodical pattern.

"I somehow get the feeling he'd know how to successfully produce and publish a book from prison," the author thinks to himself. "But really, no, I can't think like that. By next week, I have to have found a way out because there's no way in hell Adam Ordell is going out like no punk!"

The author then remembers Iceberg Slim's account of escaping prison back in the 1950s, and how he remained on the lam for several years before he was recaptured. Invigorated, Adam resolved that he wouldn't go down that way – though Slim did go on to write some of the greatest novels in American history – Adam would escape and never be recaptured. He would straighten his hair, learn to speak Spanish, and move down to Mexico before he allowed himself to rot in prison for a horrendous crime he did not commit!

He continued to lean on the moldy wall, daydreaming about ways to escape for the next couple of hours. A couple times during this period of deep thought, one of the correctional officers would stop by and ask Adam just why it was he was standing against the wall like that, wearing that funny face. The author would ignore them until they'd hit the bars with a billy club and startle an answer out of him:

"Oh, I'm just trying to chill – awaiting my eternal damnation from god's fine nation," he would reply and the officer would walk away murmuring angrily to himself.

Once the clock on the wall perpendicular to the cell struck 11:55pm, as if he had eyes on the back of his head, The Grandmaster spins his wheelchair around and says quietly so he doesn't garner the attention of any correctional officers, "The time to speak the seance is upon us!" He wheels himself to the center of the cell and continues, "There isn't much time left for us now; Iblis the Charming Devil whom precedes the world's digitized tears is upon the Earth now and the special herbs which once sealed away his gauntlet are forever lost now."

Adam stares blankly at the so-called Grandmaster; thinking that he must be at least seventy-five percent within some sort of schizophrenic state of delirium.

The Grandmaster looks past the author's blank stare, as he continues his apparent babbling: "Adam, I will now begin the seance. After I finish my part, you must chant your half – understand?"

Adam nods but asks, "Yeah alright. But first, how did you know my name? And what am I supposed to say for the seance?"

"To answer your first question," starts The Grandmaster, "your coming was prophesized – name and all. As for your second question... The words will come to you in the very moment; like putting pencil to paper."

Adam still had questions about this so-called prophesy, and he wanted to know why The Grandmaster used the simile "like putting pencil to paper" in that instance. Does The Grandmaster know more about Adam than he's saying? But he doesn't ask any further questions in that moment, as The Grandmaster begins his part of the seance:

"I check mate in the game of life like the EP. So many kids hear of me from the old Operation and call my flow creepy. But the Bottom Line is that these rhymes are mine and they're more than fine. And what these candy-sounding mumblers with beats that sound like rock tumblers will never know is that:"

The Grandmaster motions for Adam to begin his part of the seance, and after a silent 10 seconds the author blurts,

"Out in the streets, if you ain't got drumz then you ain't got beats."

At first, nothing happens. A few minutes pass, and just as Adam is about to go back to his wall to continue contemplating, there's a flash of red light and a tiny man the size of a giant hawker dragonfly appears floating mere inches from Adam's face.

The mini man has blue skin, an awesome, slick-back black mohawk, gray-and-white stubble peppering his face, medium-size black earlobe gauges, and little black wings like a tiny bat. He wore a long, black leather trench coat, black Dickies pants, and a pair of shiny leather Doc Martins boots. Adam thought that the little hovering man was the coolest person he had ever seen, but also wondered how he was able to get name-brand clothing his size.

"Yo!" the little blue man shouts. "I'm your fairy godfather motherfucker! My name is Derrick White, but real niggas just call me D – so that's what you can call me. But anyway, I'm here because you successfully completed the sacred seance, which means you're ready to start your Epic Quest to save America from–"

Adam stops the so-called "fairy godfather" right there and says, "Hold up, wait a second, what you mean, 'Epic Quest'? The Grandmaster said some shit about a quest but he made it sound like it's just a quest to clear my name. But save America? Man, that's impossible!"

"Calm yo' ass down boy!" commands D.

Then The Grandmaster says, "Adam, I did say that on this quest you'll be not only clearing your name, but also saving more than you know. You just did not pay attention to that part because you did not believe in my words. That is a bad trait that so many of those who write have – you end up saying more words than you listen to."

"Look," the fairy godfather chimes in, "it's either you go on this quest, or, well, there's a reason they call it the _penit_entiary. *Butt*, I mean, if that's your thing I ain't judgin' you–"

"Alright alright alright!" Adam quickly interrupts. "I'll do the fuckin' quest man, fuck it! Just tell me what I gotta do."

D the fairy godfather grins and begins his explanation of what Adam must do: "That's what I thought! Now, in about 20 minutes a big black girl the size of the Titanic gonna come and unlock the door to this here cell. She gon' be wearin' a CO uniform, but she really work for us.

"Actually, now that I think about it, she kinda look like Lizzo except less pretty. Like, I'd do Lizzo over her – not to say that's the only way I'd do Lizzo – I do like a little meat on my women. But to be honest, probably not now anyway. When I was younger, I wasn't too picky and I'd definitely do a girl like Lizzo; most young guys would. But nowadays–"

"Nigga," The Grandmaster cuts in, "get back to the point!"

D clears his throat and says, "Oh, right. But like I was sayin' before, this girl gon' come and get you outta here. She gonna set you up with a car to get away from here too. And from here, to get to the first destination on your Epic Quest, head straight west down Example Street (the street right in front of the jailhouse) until you reach Peanut Drive. Take a right on Peanut, then go about two blocks north until you reach West Douglass Boulevard. Turn left onto Douglass and go straight until it dead ends. Now, unless you go blind between here and there, you'll see a big ol' abandoned building there in front of you at the dead end. The front has big-ass letters on it that says, 'River End Paper Company'.

Go in there in the morning and I'll help you figure out the rest then. And of course, you know you can't go back home until you clear your name – that's the first place the piggly wigglies gonna go lookin' for you."

Adam, somewhat confused by his fairy godfather's instructions asks, "What's up with this Paper Company building?"

A slight grimace comes across D's face as he once again clears his throat and responds carefully, "That building might not look like much, but it's really a palace... Lord Junkie's Palace."

"Who's Lord Junkie?" asks the author.

The Grandmaster chimes in, "Lord Junkie is the baddest junkie you'll ever see; king of all junkie kind with mystical voodoo powers he learned down in Louisiana."

"In fact," D says, "he's the reason you're in this little predicament. He's the one done shot that sick trick and sent his cursed balls at your window."

Adam, now angry, asks, "But why fuck with me?"

The Grandmaster answers first, "Because you're the chosen one motherfucker!"

Then D the fairy godfather answers, "But it's really just coincidence – ain't no way Lord Junkie somehow knew the sick trick he shot was down the way from your apartment, and that his balls would hit your window and spread his voodoo curse to you."

Just then, the three hear Godzilla-sized footsteps coming from down the hallway.

"Alright," says D, "that's the plant CO. I'll be around later when you need me – sassafras!"

And all of a sudden, the fairy godfather disappears in a puff of angel dust. Thirty seconds of Earth-shaking footsteps later, the luxury cruise ship sized, dark-skinned woman finally reaches Adam's cell.

Adam takes one look at her, with her shoulder-length, naturally curly, midnight-black hair, round face with hypnotizing green eyes, and luscious red-brown lips and thinks to himself, "Damn; maybe she's less pretty than Lizzo but she ain't bad at all... But no! This ain't no time to be getting distracted!"

The woman unlocks the cell door and says to Adam, "I will never ever ever ever ever ever ever ever ever, *ever* be your side chick."

Adam almost laughs as he asks, "What?"

"I dunno nigga," responds the woman. "I just felt like sayin' some random shit. But fo' real, lets get you outta here."

And as Adam exits the cell with the huge imposter correctional officer, he turns his head to tell The Grandmaster "Thank you" for aiding in his swift escape, but finds the wheelchair-bound schizophrenic had disappeared.

The woman led the author out of the jailhouse with ease, the other officers not thinking about it twice when the apparent correctional officer with Adam passed the convicted writer off as another black man to be released at 12:30am.

Outside, she shows Adam to the getaway car: a kitchen-yellow, 2011 Chevrolet Aveo LS sedan. The author was too relieved and happy to be free to complain. So with a simple "Thank you" to the big woman, he crammed his six-feet-and-five-inch frame into the little disgrace of a car, put on his seat belt, started it up, and sped off toward Lord Junkie's Palace.

Chapter 3:

The Meetup with Lord Junkie

As Adam sped the little yellow car down the dark and desolate street of downtown River End, racing to reach Lord Junkie so he may clear his name, he began to philosophize aloud to himself over the Epic Quest on which he had just started:

"Ain't this a motherfucker. I went from putting down ill-ass lines into my laptop computer to being on trial for some fuck shit I ain't even do to being on the lam from the law; partaking in some kinda 'Epic Quest' with fairy godfathers and junkie kings and who knows what the fuck else. At this rate I ain't never gonna get any real progress done on my book... Well, I guess that's my turn."

The deep in thought author puts on his right turn signal and makes his turn onto Peanut Drive.

"I've always wondered why people call this area of River End the hood," Adam thinks aloud. "I mean, sure; this is a low-income kind of place but I've never seen anything bad whenever I roll through—"

Adam's soliloquy is interrupted by the sound of gunshots. He looks to his right and sees a toddler in a Tommy Hilfiger brand pull-up diaper firing a Tek-9 at another toddler – this one wearing a Polo brand pull-up diaper – who's loading the clip of a 44 millimeter so he can return fire.

"Damn," Adam says aloud, depressed by what he is witnessing. "I guess I never saw anything bad here because I've never been around when it gets dark outside."

After another 5 minutes of cautious driving, Adam reaches West Douglass and though it's pitch-black outside, aside from a few streetlights and the dim-with-fog headlights of the Aveo, the author can clearly see the massive, abandoned factory building which serves as Lord Junkie's Palace standing before him. The details of the ghetto palace were hardly discernible, but Adam could still clearly see the big bold lettering across the front which, just as D the fairy godfather had said, read "River End Paper Company".

Adam stops the car in front of the building and looks for somewhere to park the car and wait until daybreak, not being able to return to his apartment. He notices what appears to be an old delivery gate and driveway tucked behind some overgrown hanging foliage to his left, and decides to pull the car into it, obscuring it behind the hanging foliage.

Despite his being exhausted, Adam fights to stay awake – paranoid of one of the toddlers he'd seen coming and robbing him if he were to fall asleep. However, an hour after parking in the abandoned drive, the author finally falls under the spell of the sandman and doesn't wake until daybreak.

The first thing Adam does once he's awake, is check his watch – it reads 9:15am.

"That's the earliest I've been up in a while," says the author to himself.

Then the scorching temperature of the inside of the Aveo hits the author like a tidal wave and he stumbles out of the little yellow car to get some fresh air. The mid-August morning air is refreshing compared to the inside of the car, yet it still feels about 80 degrees outside already. Now that the sun was out, Adam could clearly see all the details of the faux palace which were previously hidden by the midnight shadows.

The River End Paper Company was an ancient-looking, dilapidated three-story building that obviously hadn't seen any industrial use for a number of decades. The side which faced the street had no siding, showing the crumbling, reddish-brown bricks the building was constructed of while the right side, where it appears an employee parking lot once was, has white, metal siding held on with rusted screws which had made streaks of red and brown all along the length of the building. The adjoining used-to-be parking lot was so overgrown with various vegetation – such as tall grass, juvenile trees, and thorn bushes – that it was beginning to look like a tiny forest.

In fact, it looked to Adam as if nature was reclaiming the old abandoned factory from humanity. Long, healthy vines grew up and down its walls. The cracks in the faux palace's foundation were all filled with different kinds of weeds – some of it looked like poison ivy, others looked suspiciously like hemp plants.

The front of Lord Junkie's Palace contained many windows and rectangular holes where ventilation fans once were, and it made the building look a lot like a project apartment building. Most of the windows of the upper two levels of the building were missing glass, others had plywood boards or tarps covering them. Curiously enough, most of the windows on the first floor were still completely intact except for one. The intact windows were all heavily fogged, some graffitied, but somehow not broken nor even cracked.

The front doors were boarded up, so Adam figures that unless he can find a special arachnid to bite him and turn him into one of his all-time favorite childhood superheroes so he could scale the building and climb in one of the third-floor ventilation holes, then he'd have to enter through the conveniently circular-shaped hole in the first-floor window closest to the boarded-up front doors.

So he locks the doors of the little yellow Aveo and begins to approach the window, when D the fairy godfather appears out of thin air behind him and yells, "Wait!"

Adam almost jumps out of his skin, stops, and says to the fairy godfather, "Man, don't be just appearing out of nowhere like that! And what is it?"

"Your hair motherfucker!" D replies with a laugh.

Adam goes back to the Aveo and looks at himself in the passenger-side door mirror.

"Oh shit," the author says, "I got bedhead like a motherfucker! But I ain't got no pick on me, so what do I do?"

D the fairy godfather chuckles and answers, "That's why I'm here boy! Just hol' on a second."

D waves a hand before his face and a plastic pick appears in the author's hand.

"There you go," says D. "Now you can fix that fro before you meet Lord Junkie so you don't look like just some other junkie to him... Welp, sassafras!"

And with that, the fairy godfather once again disappears in a cloud of angel dust. Adam proceeds to unlock the doors of the Aveo, sit down in the driver's seat (with the door open so as not to overheat himself) and pick out his afro. His hair fixed, the author finally approached the broken first-floor window.

The concrete foundation of the old building raised it 3 feet off the ground, making the base of the window about 6 feet off the ground. This was no problem for the young and agile author, however, as the foundation was stepped just enough that he could use it to raise himself up so that the window was only 3 feet above his feet. Adam was then able to put one leg through the broken window. But the author hadn't realized that he had stepped on some loose debris inside of the palace, and slipped. He almost fell, but was able to catch himself in time; the crotch of his shorts a mere half inch away from the razor-sharp edge of the broken glass of the window.

"Whew!" Adam sighs with relief. "That was almost my ass – or rather – my nuts!"

Once fully inside, the author coughs as he tries to breathe in the rank and mildew-smelling air of abandonment around him. The room Adam had stepped into was surprisingly well lit by the sunshine coming in through the broken window, as well as being lit by the fogged-over windows.

The room likely used to be some sort of front office waiting room, with a few old vinyl-wrapped chairs scattered about. The floor of the room was concrete, with only a few old tiles of the old flooring remaining scattered about. Both the walls and the ceiling were constructed of bricks, many of them crumbling, others turned white by limescale. There are two doors within ten feet of each other in the far-right corner that perhaps used to lead to restrooms. The back wall of the room was adorned with graffiti, each tag likely done by the same "artist". One tag was of what Adam perceived as a big face made of a big red arrow as the mouth, which pointed to red letters that said, "ACAB" which served as the left eye, while the right eye winked and the nose was an equilateral triangle. To the right of the face was a tag which read in all capital letters "FUCK THA POLICE", and above that was a tag which simply read "Tits" in black letters. The rest of the wall was adorned in similar such graffiti.

Once he was done looking at all the tasteless graffiti, Adam noticed just how large the room he stood in actually was. There were I-beams in neat rows going down the length of the room, meaning it perhaps wasn't a waiting room in its past life after all but a few offices divided by walls. Other than the chairs and tiles, other debris laid strewn about such as crumbled drywall that looked more like sand and dirt in its current state, snack food wrappers, plastic soda bottles, beer cans and soda cans, old buckets both plastic and metal, a plastic milk crate containing old VHS tapes, an old toppled-over desk, and other such signs of long-since abandonment.

Adam thinks silently to himself, "Okay, so what do I do now?"

And as soon as he thinks this, poof! D the fairy godfather appears before the author's very eyes once more.

"You wonderin' what to do now, ain't you?" the fairy godfather asks.

Adam, once again startled by the sudden appearance of his fairy godfather, flinches slightly and D begins to laugh.

"Oops, did I scare you? Hahaha! But I'm sorry. So like I was saying–"

Adam cuts him off: "Nigga don't just be poppin' up outta nowhere! Goddamn almost gave me a heart attack… But, uh, yeah. Where do I go from here?"

"Well, like I was about to say," D says, slightly offended by Adam's outburst, "all you gotta do now is summon Lord Junkie via a simple chant: Just yell 'Motherfuckin' Junkie; show yourself!' Then you'll hear his voice asking you why you're here, you tell him you're here to clear your name, and he'll appear. Simple."

Adam responds with a smile of relief on his face, "Shit, that's alright. I get the motherfucker to show up, threaten his life if need be, make him lift the voodoo–"

"Nah nigga that ain't gonna work!" D cuts in.

"Why the hell not?" Adam asks.

D answers, "Because Lord Junkie is a goddamn junkie – ain't afraid of shit – and he's got junkie superpowers plus voodoo to boot! You ain't gon' be able to get him to lift that curse that damn easily. You gotta work with him and shit man!"

Fuck all that!" Adam yells back. "I ain't negotiatin' with no fuckin' junkie – superpowers, voodoo or whatever the hell else! That motherfucker *will* respond to pain."

The frustrated fairy godfather shrugs his shoulders and says, "Suit yourself nigga. Sassafras!" before disappearing in a cloud of angel dust.

The determined by his own fury author then clears his throat and yells the magic words: "Motherfuckin' junkie; show yourself!"

Fifteen seconds pass, and Adam hears the voice of an old-school basehead say, "I welcome you to my palace. What business you got wit' me baby?"

The author thinks for a second about how he should word it, then responds, "You've slandered my good name and I ain't takin' that shit from you!"

Another fifteen seconds pass, then a flash of blurred, super-speed movement passes from a door in the far-left corner of the room in front of Adam, and the author feels something tap his left shoulder. He turns to his left, and there stands Lord Junkie.

Adam is first taken aback by the putrid stink of the junkie king. Lord Junkie smelled like a day-old dead skunk that had been baking underneath the hot Arizona sun in the middle of July, and was then dipped in sewage from underneath a Taco Bell restroom.

His presumably once ebony-colored skin now has the disgusting yellow hue of diseased flesh, with pockmarks of almost black and red spots all over his body, in a pattern similar to vitiligo. His body was extremely malnourished, his eyes sunk in and his cheekbones pronounced so that his face looked like a skull tightly wrapped in leather. Lord Junkie had 5 teeth missing total from both front rows and what teeth remained in his mouth were near festering, most of them brown, two of them black, one yellow: all practically hanging on by the gums. The junkie king wore a blue tee shirt with an unrecognizable brand logo over the right breast that hung over his skeletal frame like a poncho, with holes and stains all over it. The gray sweatpants he wore were 3 sizes too big, with stains all over like his shirt, and were held up by a clothesline tied around his waist like some sort of makeshift belt. Lord Junkie also wore a pair of ancient-looking brown loafers, a Carhartt beanie that perhaps used to be brown but had been poorly spray-painted gold, and a big, old, tattered American flag tied around his neck like some sort of cape.

Lord Junkie chuckles a little at Adam's expression of pure revolt before saying, "It looks like you's gotta problem wit' my scemell baby. Butchu fuckin' 'round in *my* palace now! So if you can't handle the heat–"

The author regains control of his senses and bellows with much bravado, "Look here you junkie punk! I ain't got no time to be playin' games with you! You put a voodoo on a sick trick just the other day and now that shit done fucked over me! So I'ma tell you what: you gon' lift this shit up offa me and I'ma go on about my business and leave you to do whatever it is you junkies like to do during the day – especially if that means killin' more sick tricks. *Capisce?*"

Lord Junkie cackles maniacally and chortles, "Nigga shit, I don't see nothin' in it for me if I gives in to yo' demands."

Adam's patience with the junkie king had long run out, and so he jabs a hand out to grab the cause of his extreme anger by the throat but before his hand can touch the basehead, he disappears in a flash of brown.

"Missed me baby!" Lord Junkie antagonizes.

Adam looks around in front of him, but can see no Lord Junkie.

"Behind you nigga," he hears and turns around to find Lord Junkie standing a few feet behind him with a grin on his face. Adam lunges at the junkie, but once again, he disappears in a flash.

"Goddamnit junkie bitch!" Adam calls out. "Quit runnin' and face me like a man!"

Lord Junkie cackles from an unknown location within the palace and says, "If you wanna fight baby you gon' hafta catch me first!"

As the junkie king continues his cacophonous cackling, the author closes his eyes and listens close to determine where the noise is coming from – thus discovering the whereabouts of Lord Junkie within his palace. A few seconds go by and, his eyes still closed, Adam points in the direction of the hideous laughter. He opens his eyes and sees he's pointing to a door in the far-left corner of the large room. The author dashes toward the door, and once he's through it he stops cold.

Adam now finds himself standing in what likely used to be the factory production floor, where paper products from the River End Paper Company were actually produced. There are a few old, broken-down and very long conveyor belts running along the edges of the room, with piles of garbage – mostly old snack food wrappers – on top of them. In the far-left corner there's a big pile of rotting wooden crates that the author can smell from 100 feet away. Like the rest of Lord Junkie's Palace, the walls and what was left of the ceiling were constructed of crumbling bricks, while the floor was deteriorating concrete. The ceiling was caved in in the center of the room, with a large pile of rubble and bricks underneath the large hole – most of the bricks blackened by mold. Strewn around the rubble pile, which served as a grandiose centerpiece to the disastrously disarrayed room, were discarded needles, glass pipes and other junkie paraphernalia, old, distressed articles of clothing, beer cans, CD's of various albums from such artists as Carti B, Future, Playboy Carti, and other such trifling trash of which nobody has any use for.

The gaping hole in the ceiling went through all the way to the roof of the abandoned factory, allowing sunlight to enter the room – especially shining down on the pile of rubble underneath it like a spotlight on a stage. Adam wonders to himself if this is what preachers mean when they refer to heaven "shining down".

All-of-a-sudden, as the author scans the room for Lord Junkie, the junkie king himself appears, sitting on top of the large rubble pile where sun shines upon, grinning wide and mocking Adam with an unbothered look in his eyes. The author looks down at the ground, locates a dislodged brick amongst many near his feet, picks it up and swiftly hurdles it at Lord Junkie with all his might. Lord Junkie once again disappears and reappears standing beside the author. He taps Adam on the left shoulder again, and the infuriated author swings around with a right hook, only to find Lord Junkie has disappeared once more.

He's sitting atop his rubble pile throne once again as he says to Adam, "Shit baby, you fuckin' with the kid! You can't catch me in your wildest dreams 'cause I'm the Gingerbread Man!"

Adam screams out in rage, "Fine! But I know you's just a junkie-ass motherfucker, Jack, and all junkies got the same weakness – junk! So I'll tell you what: I'll get you some meth, and you lift this here voodoo offa me!"

Lord Junkie only cackles maniacally and responds, "Shit, that weak stuff? Baby, I got so much drugs in my system; meth don't even do *nothin'* for me. I'm from the old school young nigga. I remember sippin' crack out the bottle while cuddlin' in my momma's arms; oh how I miss those days…"

Lord Junkie looks off into the distance, a glint in his glassy eyes as if his tear ducts actually functioned.

"Goddamn you junkie punk!" Adam bellows. "If you don't lift this voodoo up off me then I'ma torch this place tonight!"

The junkie king then chortles, "You torch *this* place? Baby, these walls got so much asbestos that motherfuckin' napalm couldn't burn it down! Besides, like Richard Pryor I'm immune to being burnt to death. But, I'll tell you what: you bring me what I *truly desire*,"

Lord Junkie disappears and then reappears standing three feet before Adam, "than I'll lift that vex offa you."

Adam attempts to drop kick the junkie king, but once again he moves out of the way at super speed and the author is left flat on his behind. This time Lord Junkie has moved to the second floor of his palace, standing at the edge of the hole in its floor, looking down at Adam and cackling some more.

D the fairy godfather poofs into existence before Adam's face and says, laughing, "Boy I tried to tell you; you ain't gonna be able to get things on your terms like this. And this whole entire Epic Quest is gonna be like that too – almost none of it on your terms. Sure, it would be nice to get shit all your way; make life a little easier, make the quest a little more enjoyable. But sadly, that just ain't how this shit works! You gotta work with assholes and dicksmacks like this until you reach the point in your Epic Quest when you can start playing by your own rules all the time – you'll know when that time has come. But for now, you just gotta work out a deal with him, *on his terms*. Sassafras!"

And with that piece of familiar advice, D once again disappears in a little cloud of angel dust.

"Better listen to the pixie," chortles Lord Junkie. "Bring me what I want and I take that vex right off ya."

Adam, feeling quite defeated and desperate, finally says, "Fine goddamnit! Just what the hell do you want then?"

Lord Junkie smiles ear to ear, then sits back down on his rubble pile throne and chortles, "What I require is 5 Sacred Items. I haves a list here for you which tells what these items are and where to find 'em."

Lord Junkie procures a reproduction copy of the United States Constitution for classroom use. It appears to be part of the Bill of Rights. The junkie king miraculously floats it down to Adam, as if controlling the paper with his mind (which the author knows is impossible, since Lord Junkie's mind had to have been next to melted by decades of drug use and abuse). Adam grabs the tattered piece of paper, flips it over to quickly look over Lord Junkie's list, and grimaces at what he sees.

"This looks like a lotta shit to go through junkie!" Adam says. "You better be good to your word!"

"Always baby," responds Lord Junkie. "Now go! Or be vexed forever and locked away like Romell Broom!"

Adam folds the list neatly and puts it in his right-side front pocket as he exits Lord Junkie's Palace. He unlocks the doors of the Aveo still parked outside and gets in. The author pulls Lord Junkie's list back out of his pocket.

"Don't know why I bothered to put this away," he says to himself, "knowing damn well I'ma need it to know where I gotta go. Now, lets see where we gotta head to first."

Adam unfolds the paper, notices the list is conveniently numbered, and decides to go follow it in numerical order.

Upon reading the first item's location, Adam grimaces slightly and says, "Well okay then. It looks like first we'll get the Sacred Text of Happiness from the LGBT's hideout over at the abandoned Burroughs High School building."

Adam pauses thoughtfully for a moment, stone faced, before saying nonchalantly, "Shit, I hope they don't recognize me for my books somehow. I know there's probably some kind of misunderstanding between us over the one poem I wrote in my last book."

With a shrug of the shoulders and an "Oh well" Adam proceeds to buckle his seat belt, start the little yellow car, throw the shifter into drive, and the author starts off toward the abandoned Burroughs High School building to retrieve the Sacred Text of Happiness from the plucky yet fearful LGBT's.

Chapter 4:

Happiness as Told by the Gays

As Adam drove down Gate Road on his way to the LGBT's hideout, he began to reminisce about his own time being a high schooler, back before the school was shut down and taken over by the refuge-seeking LGBT's.

He thought of all the time he spent not in school – riding his old BMX bike around town, sitting at home doing anything but learn what they wanted him to learn, sleeping until 12:30pm and staying awake until 3:00am – those were some good times. But it wasn't always like that, and so the author also remembered the bad parts of high school:

He recalled the endless hours of homework (some of it due to his not showing up to class) the tests which caused him so much stress, maintaining a 4.0 GPA just in case he decided later on to go to college, the hours of torment dealt by the Calahoochi, the isolation he felt from the other students (with whom he felt no connection) and all the time he spent sitting on the stairs, practicing his literary skills by writing down his pain in various notebooks.

Thinking about his writing reminds the author of his upcoming book, as he says aloud to himself, "Dammit!

Through all this I'm almost forgetting about the impending deadline for finishing my third book! Shit man, I gotta finish this 'Epic Quest' and quick before I miss that deadline and get dropped by my publisher! They're already actin' funny because I don't have a title picked out for this book yet, *and* I'm on thin ice after that stunt I tried to pull with my last release..."

Thinking aloud, fretting over his next book, and trying to lay-out in his mind the entirety of the second half of the book (which he has yet to write) the author absent-mindedly turns off Gate Road onto Lake Street, then Rollins Road, then finally he turns onto Saturn Drive; where the image of the abandoned Burroughs High School building begins to come into sight.

Even though the building is still a quarter mile down Saturn from Adam, he can see clearly the vines growing all around the building – which the author finds strange because the school has only been abandoned for 2 years. Adam draws nearer, and notices how the bricks of the building are turning a rainbow-array of colors from a variety of vegetation growing up and down the building. As he pulls into the parking lot, he sees how all the cracks and crevices of the asphalt were green with overgrown weeds and wildflowers. The shrubs around the flagpole, once nicely kept, were now overgrown like wild bushes growing in a forest untouched by man. The vines the author had seen while driving down the road were thick with little pink roses.

Adam parks the little yellow Aveo close to the front entrance, in a parking spot with a name of a girl he recognized from when he was in high school painted on it. He proceeds to exit the vehicle and begins to approach the doors with slight caution – not sure of who or what the

LGBT's might be using for security. Drawing closer, he notices the metal door frame has gone from black to green and yellow with moss. Upon reaching the doors, Adam hears a flamboyant voice yell, "Halt!"

Before placing his hand on the door before him, Adam heeds the command and looks around him to see who has told him to stop. The entrance of the Burroughs High School building was recessed in between the gymnasium to the right, and the front offices to the left; creating the effect of some sort of courtyard in front of the school. When looking around, Adam sees a person clinging to the wall to his right like a certain superhero the author idolized as a child. On the opposite wall clings another person, identical to the first.

"Oh I see, so these two B-listers get cool powers and shit and I don't," Adam grumbles to himself.

"You can't go in there," the person on the right says.

"Unless," the one on the left continues, "you can answer this one queer question."

The two leap down from the parallel walls and Adam turns around to see them standing a few feet behind him. Both of them have their hands on their hips, and they're dressed in pink-metallic, long-sleeved, hooded unitards with a little rainbow flag on the right shoulder. The hoods of the unitards were aqua blue with a white stripe running across the top and down the entire length of the unitards. The two guards had identical facial features – chiseled jawlines with well-defined cheekbones, narrow and small noses, small black eyebrows and pine-needle green eyes. They both stood about 5 feet and 9 inches tall, and Adam assumed they were twin brothers, though he wasn't quite sure if they were men or not. They both had thin waists and hips that were slightly wider than their waists, and their chests protruded slightly, but it was impossible to tell if it was lean muscle or fatty breast tissue.

So Adam decided "fuck it" and asked before either of them got to ask their queer question: "I'm not trying to be offensive or anything, but are you two men or women or something else entirely? Not that it really matters or anything, I just don't want to call you the wrong thing because I ain't tryin' to start no shit–"

The unitard-clad person on the right interrupts Adam by answering excitedly, "*That's* the queer question! You must guess what gender we are. And to make it easier I assure you, we both identify the same way."

The one on the left continues, "And if you guess incorrectly," the two then say synchronously, "then you must never come back to this place!"

Adam remembers what his fairy godfather had told him about playing by other's rules for the remainder of his journey, and so he begins assessing the two with his eyes: "Their faces appear mostly masculine," the author thinks to himself, "but with feminine touches in the way their eyes and noses are shaped. Their hair is completely tucked into the hoods of their unitards – so there isn't any answer there. Their eyelashes are pretty long, but then again, so are mine. I don't see an Adam's apple on either one of them..."

Then Adam decides to ask them a question directly: "What brand makes the best eyeliner?"

The sleuthing author asks this, thinking that no man would have an opinion either way – regardless if the man in question has ever worn makeup or not. So this question would narrow things down, or so Adam thought.

"Our sister swears by Elf," they both answer in unison.

"Damn," Adam thinks. "That really tells me nothing. Sure, the fact that they both remembered the name of the makeup brand that makes their sister's eyeliner could mean they're both female, but they didn't actually have any personal insight either way."

The twin on the right then says, "Also, you may only ask us a total of 3 questions before guessing our gender. That was the first."

"And remember," chimes in the one on the left, "you're to guess our *gender*, not our sex. There is a distinction between the two, you know. It isn't so black and white as what we have between our legs."

Adam reflects on this for a moment, then asks his second question: "Would you suggest purchasing a vehicle with a 1.4 liter motor, combined with a continuous-variable transmission?"

The author feels confident in this question, thinking that no man would be able to resist flexing what mechanical aptitude he does have by answering with wide eyes, "Avoid that car like the plague," while a woman would either say that she's heard bad things about that motor, or that it depends on what kind of car.

The twin on the left sneers and responds, "You fool! It's like you didn't hear a single word of what I just told you! Gender isn't so black and white; yet you ask such black-and-white questions. And besides, such stereotypical gender-affirming questions as that are meaningless. Don't you know that in today's age a woman can be more mechanically inclined than a man, and a man can be completely clueless about anything to do with a car?"

Both twins take a moment to laugh mockingly before finally answering in unison: "As a personal preference from experience, we would both avoid a car like that. But if you want it then go ahead!"

"Another completely useless answer," Adam thinks to himself. "Sure, they knew to avoid a car with such a terrible combination for a drivetrain, but that opinion was from 'personal experience'. Besides that, the twin on the left seems to be real insistent on telling gender from sex, and how gender isn't a this or that kinda thing – so I gotta rule out them identifying as either men or women; which only leaves, like, infinite other options."

As Adam thinks, he sees the two twins hold their hands low in front of themselves with their palms facing down, and both examine their nails with a bored look on their faces. This action didn't necessarily mean anything, but it leads Adam to begin formulating a hypothesis in his mind.

He thinks of the subtle clues both twins had left; such as their voices, for instance. Both spoke flamboyantly, stereotypically gay or feminine, but with a slight forced rasp which sounded somewhat masculine. Their voices, Adam theorized, would sound perfectly feminine if toned up a pitch or two. Their voices, in fact, would likely sound neither feminine nor masculine if disembodied, such as if heard over a phone call. Even the way in which they both had jumped down from the walls seemed like a clue. It was a movement without gender expression, yet the argument could be made that the way in which they came down like acrobats was feminine enough to be considered gay for a man, but not feminine enough for a woman to have jumped down the same way. And now, the way they both looked at their unpainted, medium-length nails: such disinterest could be found in their eyes. Though the fact that they thought to look at them at all, even out of boredom, means they have to had cared for them somewhat.

And so Adam formulated one last question he felt he didn't even have to ask, but which he did anyway just to confirm his suspicions: "What is a typical, everyday outfit for either of you – aside from your unitards?"

Both twins grin and answer simultaneously, "Oh, typically we like to wear long, black trench coats, tight-fitting tee shirts, baggy jeans, big hoop earrings, and steel toe boots. Now guess our gender!"

Adam lets out a confidently-triumphant laugh before he says, "I know exactly what you two are now! You were both assigned female at birth, however, you are actually bigender. You express both male and female characteristics; though you both prefer to lean slightly more masculine."

The two bigender twins clap and say in unison, "Congratulations! We are indeed AFAB, bigender individuals!"

The twin on the left then says, "And *I'm* quite impressed you picked up on the fact that we lean a little more masculine than feminine – since you were struggling there in the beginning. So tell me, how did you know?"

"Well," Adam replies, "I knew you were both bigender by the mixed-message body language you display and by the way you kept throwing me for a loop with your answers to my questions. Your fashion sense only confirmed my suspicions, as well as tipping me off to the fact that you prefer to present slightly more masculine than feminine – since you didn't mention wearing any specifically female clothing other than the big hoop earrings."

The twins bow and say, "Very well then, you may now enter this sanctuary."

As they say this, the twin doors directly behind Adam open by themselves. The author turns around to see the open doors, then turns back around to thank the twin guards – but they're already gone.

"Welp, guess I'll just head on in then," the author says aloud as he enters the seemingly-desolate main hallway of the abandoned high school building.

Inside the building is pitch black, aside from the light shining in through the glass doors behind Adam. And as soon as the doors close behind him, the author is confronted by another member of the LGBT's.

This member was a 5' 6" black woman with long, fried-straight and dyed-green hair. She wore black butterfly frame glasses, a rainbow-striped crop top tee shirt which barely covered her large breasts, a black leather miniskirt, fishnets, and round-toed, black pumps with white soles. She was perfectly plump, not at all like the skeletal models seen in magazines. Her face was kind looking yet stern, with smile lines and permanently furrowed eyebrows.

The middle-aged woman, maybe 35, says to Adam, "Greetings traveler. They call me Kai the Guard, but you may refer to me as simply Kai. To have made it here in the first place shows you must have a great deal of sensitivities for the LGBT's. But I sense you are not one of us so I must ask: Why do you come to this place? Are you merely a supporter on a goodwill mission? Is my intuition wrong? Are you a lost member seeking refuge? Or is there a reason for your coming that I am not seeing?"

Adam responds, "Kai, my name is Adam Ordell. I am merely an outside supporter of your kind on an 'Epic Quest' which leads me here to obtain the Sacred Text of Happiness."

Kai the Guard looks at Adam with a raised eyebrow and says, "Ah, so you are indeed here for our prized Text…"

Kai pauses for a moment, looking off into the darkness of the hallway – as if reflecting on this newcomer and his quest – before resuming, "I thought you might be here for that, but I didn't want to say it first in case you were unaware of its existence. But if you already know of the Sacred Text of Happiness, then your quest is righteous.

"Very well then, I will start you on the path to our Sacred Text… On this path you will face 3 trials which will challenge your spirit and prove your merit. But beware! For these trials are not simple tests of the purity of your heart nor the prowess of your physical abilities. They are complex tests of which the failure to pass will result in the end of your so-called 'Epic Quest' – for it would prove fatal. And once you start on this path, there is no returning to the outside world unless you reach the end. Will you still proceed or will you turn back?"

"I will proceed," Adam replies. He feels uneasy about the impending trials, but the author knows that if he doesn't accept the grand task set before him then his efforts thus far would all be for naught, and his good name would be thrown into the gutter.

Kai smiles warmly and instructs, "At the end of the path you will find the former den of the fearsome Calahoochi, which is now the throne room of our fearless queen; she holds the text you seek. The torches will light your way."

Kai gestures to her right, where a line of torches along the walls suddenly light themselves.

"I wish you luck in your quest, Adam Ordell," Kai the guard says.

"Thank you," the author responds. "But real quick, tell me, why is it so dark in here? And where are the rest of your people?"

Kai replies with a straight face, "It is dark in here because it's so damn hard to see the light of tomorrow anymore. And as for everybody else, they are here, but they're tucked away – not wandering these depressing halls. You will only encounter a small fraction of them on this path."

Kai the Guard then disappears in a cloud of turquoise smoke and Adam thinks to himself, "Alright then; I guess disappearing in clouds of whatever the hell comes standard with this mythical shit."

And so Adam begins his journey down the hall. He treads carefully as he walks, staying hyper aware of the familiar yet changed surroundings so nothing can take him by surprise. The torches along the hall lit the environment well enough to discern the deteriorating ceiling tiles, the cracks in the floor tiles, and the peeling paint on the walls as well as the corroding lockers.

"Damn man," the author says aloud, "this place has gone downhill quick! I mean really, what the fuck is going on here? This place wasn't pretty when I had to go here, but it didn't look this goddamn bad. It's like everything's gone from fucked to absolutely fucked without a damn chance of getting better in an instant."

The author continues down the hallway, turning right at the end of the main hallway where the lighted path continued. In this familiar location, Adam began to reminisce about his high school days once more:

"Man!" the author exclaims. "This is the hallway where that crazy-ass girl tried snatching my hand like I was her boyfriend back during sophomore year!"

Adam laughs to himself and continues, "But shit, I kinda hate to say I'm sleazy but I like it when they tease me and I don't go for nothin' that seems too easy."

Then, to Adam's shock and dismay, the girl whom he had just referred to appears and says, "Oh so you think you Tupac now, huh? Rhymin' about girls and shit; nigga who is you?"

The girl is now a full-grown woman, much larger than Adam remembered, with a bad blonde wig atop her head, too much makeup, and wearing clothes two sizes too small.

Adam scrambles for a response as he says, "I, uh, girl I was just bullshitting! I didn't really mean that shit I just said I was just–"

"Just nothing!" the girl yells. "I was only fuckin' with yo' sorry ass 'cause I wasn't acceptin' my true sexuality yet! And now you coming 'round here talking nice like you some kinda Mr. Bitches or some shit. Nigga fuck you!"

The girl goes running away down some dark desolate hallway and Adam says to himself, "Okay, note to self: don't go mentioning no more ghost stories around this place."

The torches lead Adam into what used to be Burroughs High School's auditorium. The door closed and locked itself behind the author, who guesses this must be the first of the three trials.

The auditorium is still intact, with a few improvements made by the LGBT's: The walls have been painted with murals of rainbow skylines with little white cumulus clouds, butterflies, bumble bees, birds and other happy-looking imagery. The seats have all been upgraded from the uncomfortable, old-style theater seating to modern-style leather recliners with settings for heat and for cool. The audio system had been upgraded with very expensive looking equipment made by BOSE and the house lights looked new as well. Adam thought it was all very nice, especially since the old look of the desperately under-funded auditorium was distasteful and depressing.

The new curtains (colored with three horizontal stripes of varying shades of orange on the top half, a stripe of white in the middle, and three stripes of varying shades of pink on the bottom half) were drawn closed and the house lights were on. The renovated auditorium appeared to be empty, as Adam walked down to the row of seats closest to the stage and walked along them, thinking maybe he could simply escape the auditorium and whatever trial lay in wait for him by exiting out the door on the other side.

But Adam is stopped by the abrupt sound of a magical-sounding ballad coming from the speakers and the sudden appearance of people (mostly women) filling the seats of the auditorium turned theater. Not knowing what else to do, the author decides to take the one available seat to his right and watch as the curtains on stage slowly draw open.

Once the curtains are fully open, a tall, athletically-built woman can be seen slowly descending from a rope tied to the fly tower above the stage. The woman is fair-skinned, with loose-curly red hair cut in a pompadour. She's wearing an orange sports coat over a white dress shirt with a purple tie and gray slacks with orange-dyed alligator loafers. The house lights dim until they're off completely as a spotlight focuses on the woman descending from the fly tower. The people in the seats (whom are clearly her adoring fans) cheer and applaud the performer. The woman has a cordless microphone in her right hand and a single, red rose in her left hand. Once her feet touch the floor of the stage, she throws the rose out into the audience, before cupping the microphone and beginning to sing in one of the most beautiful voices Adam thought he had ever heard:

"How 'bout you bring that ass here?
And watch your panties disappear
Just thinking you're straight,
When baby you ain't
Just let me strap on and take a ride
Like Lou Reed I'm the Wild Side
I'll make you come over, and over
Just like your name is Rover
'Cause I'm hardcore lesbian!
I fuck girls like a man
So don't fret
'Cause I'll bet

...
You're already wet."

The entire crowd erupts in a roar of applause, except for Adam, who can't help but break out in a fit of hysterical laughter. His uncontrollable laughter is so loud, in fact, that it could be heard above the sound of everyone else's adoration of the performance.

The house ceases their applause and the author continues laughing for a moment, before the performer on stage demands, "And just why are you laughing at my performance?"

Adam almost chokes as he tries to hold his laughter back, wipes a tear from his eye and responds, "I'm just laughing because, man, that song was fucking *hilarious*!"

The performer scoffs and retorts, "Oh how simple-minded you men are... So tell me, what's your name?"

"Adam," the author responds, still with a giggle in his voice.

"Well, Adam, my name is Lily Green and I'm the first out of the three Trialmasters on this path. And unluckily enough for you... I'm already not impressed by what you've shown me so far."

The giggles leave Adam's system instantly as he inquires, "Why do you say that?"

Lily laughs cynically and chortles, "All of you men are the same – especially you straight, cisgendered men. You dare to laugh in my face – despite the fact that I'm a figure of high authority here – just because I'm a woman."

At this remark, Adam got angry. Lily's misinformed remark did to the author what had been done to him multiple times throughout his life – it put him in a box with a general label on it.

"Just hold on a second," Adam starts in rebuttal. "I think you must have the wrong man here goddamnit. Adam Ordell is no misogynist, okay. Look, I laughed at your song because I genuinely think it's funny. Even if a man would've sang it I would've laughed."

"Oh really?" Lily asks rhetorically. "So do you laugh when DJ Quik talks about feeding his 'nine-inch digity digity dick all up in' a woman?"

Adam opens his mouth to respond, but Lily continues her accusations before he can speak: "How about when Ant Banks talks about 'doing the same shit to a different bitch every night'?"

Again, Adam begins to respond but is swiftly cut off by Lily: "See, you can't say that you do now can you?"

Adam, now infuriated, says, almost yelling, "Man, those are different types of songs!"

"But how? They talk the same kinda shit I was just singing about."

Adam digs through the crates of records in the back of his skull, until he finds one he thinks will prove his point: "Well then, how about track 11 on *The D&D Project* LP: *Nine Inches*? That's a sexual song featuring a female artist, Juice, on the rhymes and I didn't laugh a single time she was rapping on that track because I was too busy admiring how articulate and clever her lines were."

"Irrelevant," replies Lily. "She's speaking from the perspective of a straight woman. You only accept that as how a woman should talk about sex... pig."

The audience applauds and Adam thinks to himself, "This bitch! How the hell is *she* gonna go and tell *me* how *I'm* really feeling? She's just basing all her opinions of me on the chromosomes found within my cells..."

As Adam finishes his furious thought, an epiphany comes to him about the situation in which he finds himself.

The author takes a deep breath, closing his eyes for a moment, then opens his eyes and says to the Trialmaster, "I'm sorry, I've been insensitive. I realize now that what you just did to me is what has been done to women since the beginning of time. Society is quick to assume a woman makes this or that decision without care. Labels are placed on you at birth and justifications for contradictions to your own words in court are made based on superfluous details such as 'what signals you gave off'. Your very words are discounted because you think with your heart and not with cold calculations. Again, I apologize for my insensitivity."

Lily smiles in approval and the entire audience once again roars with applause. The crowd quiets down, and the

Trialmaster says to Adam, "Congratulations! You have passed this test flawlessly."

She nods to the doors Adam had been making his way to before Lily's musical number had started, and they open as the Trialmaster says, "You can go on ahead to the next trial."

But before Adam walks off toward the door he asks Lily, "I have a question real quick before I go."

"Go ahead, ask," the Trialmaster responds.

"How come your trial only really has to do with women's rights in general? I kinda thought all these trials would be specifically tailored to LGBT problems."

Lily sighs and responds, "Meh, after a while you get tired of giving the same old lessons over and over again. I mean, truly, I'm supposed to give a lengthy trial on the gross sexualization of lesbians in society and all that jazz. But, like, half the people that come through here are women so they pass the trial real easy like and then also, everybody ought to know by now that just because you see two pretty women holding hands in public doesn't mean you have the right to go and yell obscenities at them. And of course, I just assumed you knew anyway, right?"

"Right," Adam swiftly responds. "Well, thanks for giving me a more enjoyable trial then, and maybe I'll see you again sometime in life!"

As the author starts toward the exit, Lily yells after him, "I'm wishing you good luck on your journey, Adam. But be careful out there; the rest of the Trialmasters aren't as cool or as easily persuaded as me. Especially the next one you'll come across; he's kind of a stereotypical diva type."

The author waves farewell and yells back, "Thanks for the warning!" before finally exiting the auditorium and continuing the path laid out by the LGBT's for anyone daring enough to want for their Sacred Text of Happiness.

The torch-lit path led Adam next to what was once the school's cafeteria. All the tables had been taken out; leaving the white room mostly desolate, aside from various LGBT paraphernalia lining the walls. Paraphernalia such as a small, black-and-red-colored wooden shrine to Freddie Mercury with a picture of him and an old, tattered copy of the LP *A Day at the Races*, life-size, rainbow-colored decals of unicorns plastered across the walls, a flag that looked to Adam like a toothpaste flavor, with two stripes of different shades of mint green across the top, a white stripe in the middle, and two stripes of different shades of aqua blue at the bottom, and a poster of 50 Cent, shirtless, with the title "50 Men" written in white bubble letters at the top of the poster. The letters were made to look like they were made of some kind of slimy liquid that ran down the length of the poster.

Adam looked around the room in a state of reminiscence. Despite the absence of the cafeteria tables and the new decor, the author was still reminded of the time he brought his Nintendo 3DS to school and he and his best friend spent all of their lunchtime making the most monstrous-looking Miis they could think of; all the while laughing until tears ran down their eyes.

While still deep in his state of remembrance, Adam hears the doors he came in through shut behind him.

"I knew this was gonna be the next trial," Adam says aloud.

"You can betchya tight ass honey," someone gaily responds.

Then, the ground begins to rumble and the direct center of the former cafeteria the floor opens to reveal a large black cylinder rising from underground. As the black cylinder slowly rises up out of the ground, Solange by Tobi Lou starts playing from the intercom in the ceiling.

Once the black cylinder has fully emerged from the ground, an elevator-style door opens with the ring of a bell and a slender man emerges. The man who emerges from the black cylinder is at the pinnacle of unique elegance and style. His multicolored suit exudes a level of eccentricity unlike any other Adam had ever seen with its hot-pink jacket and pants, black waistcoat with golden buttons, gold-thread shirt, iridescent, rainbow-stripe tie, and gold loafers with pink laces and black eyelets. The man also wore a magnificent, chameleon-color stole that changed from pink to orange to blue to green to yellow, as it seemingly danced in rhythm with the man's every movement.

The man steps out of the cylindrical black elevator, moving exaggeratedly as he does, and proceeds to place his left hand – manicured fingers spread apart – over his heart as he flings his right hand up toward the ceiling and announces flamboyantly, "Hello dear traveler and welcome to the second trial! My name is Larray; and yes, that's pronounced *Lair-ay*, not *Lair-ee*, and I'm the master of this trial! Before we start though... honey, what's your name and why have you started on this path?"

"Adam, Adam Ordell," the author answers. "And I have ventured into your domain and begun on this path for the Sacred Text of Happiness because I am on an 'Epic Quest' which dictates that I do so."

Larray lowers both his arms to a neutral position at his sides and says with a little scoff, "Alright then, *Adam Ordell*, on your *Epic* Quest; let us have a little bit of fun then."

The ground begins to rumble again, but this time more severe, like an earthquake. The entire floor of the cafeteria begins to slowly rise as the ceiling opens up to reveal the bright and blue sky above.

"You might want to get down on the floor for this one honey," Larray says as he lays down on the rising ground beneath them.

Adam begins to ask what's going on, but is thrown back by the sudden jolt of speed which the platform begins to rise with. The author is thrown violently to the ground, almost falling off the rising platform, and he begins to think that this is how he's going to die.

"Yep," Adam thinks to himself, "this is how I'm gonna fuckin' die. These crazy motherfuckers really about to shoot my black ass into the sun or some shit for their so-called 'second trial'. Man that's some fucking bullshit!"

But before Adam can scream out any final curses to humanity, the platform shoots just past some cumulus clouds and stops. Adam is thrown a foot into the air, then lands on his back. He finds it impossible to get back off the ground. He can't feel anything from his eyebrows to his toes, and every time he tries to breathe he gets the sensation of a ballon trying to inflate with a pinhole in it. Any air he can gasp into his body is evacuated the moment it enters his lungs.

As the author lies on the floor, helpless, coughing and wheezing in a state of misery, Laray the Trialmaster stands over him and laughs at his discomfort.

After laughing awhile, Larray finally says, "Darling, just take very short breaths. In for a second, hold, then out for a second until your lungs can get used to this thin air... And try not to hyperventilate either."

Adam does as the eccentric Trialmaster instructed, and within five minutes he's able to breathe at least somewhat normally. The strength returns to his limbs (though his body still feels quite weak) and he stands up, though he has to with his legs far apart to maintain balance.

"Dizzy eh?" Larray asks sarcastically. "That'll happen after traveling this high so fast. You'll regain your sense of gravity soon enough; just don't look over the edge of the platform. We are now 6,000 feet in the air.

"This has very little to do with the trail though – other than the fact that if you fail, you will be thrown off the edge of this platform. To be quite honest though, I just wanted to make my trial so high in the air so I could be closer to the birds – I've always admired them. The sky is their domain and it belongs to them only. Up here, they get to be whatever and whoever they want; they get to be free. It's a type of freedom that ground dwellers can never experience."

A tear starts falling from Larray's eye and he pulls out a pink satin handkerchief and uses it to wipe the tear away. "But anyway, let the trial begin!"

Three men poof into existence in a cloud of rainbow fog, standing behind a podium – as if in some sort of television game show. All three of the men are dressed in the same outfit – a white, long sleeve button up shirt tucked into Levis 541 blue jeans and white Nike running shoes with a red check mark and black soles. Each of them was about the same height, about 5 feet and ten inches, but all three differed in the characteristics of their faces and their ages.

The leftmost man, who looked about 20 years old, was very pale skinned, with a scraggly beard attached to a handlebar moustache and his black hair poorly tied into a sad-looking man bun atop his head. He had little gold hoops dangling from his earlobes and a gold hoop in his right nostril. He wore thick-framed glasses that almost looked like props and had a facial expression one has when they've won an argument; though he hadn't spoken a single word since he appeared. Adam instantly knew what this creature was that stood before him: a hipster.

The man in the middle looked to be in his mid 30s, with white skin tanned from being in the sun, with neat brunette hair cut in a medium-length fade. He was clean shaven with a long, thin face.

The rightmost man was clearly the oldest of the three, likely aged between 45 and 55, with graying hair in a crew cut and three distinct lines across his forehead. He had a round face with plump cheeks which made him look jolly, with the corners of his mouth slightly upturned, and a long, silver goatee.

Looking over the men for a moment, Adam says confidently and somewhat absent-mindedly, "Okay, I scc. I'm supposed to guess which one of these three men is gay and if I guess correctly then I can proceed and if I don't–"

"Bitch I know you did not just steal my line!" Larray interrupts with explosive anger.

Adam begins to angrily reply, "And I know your rainbow, unicorn-hugging ass did not just call *me* a bitch," but before he can say the words he's formulated in his mind, D the fairy godfather appears and yells, "Timeout!"

D flies over to Larray and says, "Let me introduce myself right quick: My name is Allen and I'm this fool's fairy godfather. Look, I'm sorry this nigga done gon' an' said some shit like that but just give me 1 minute with the boy and I promise I'll straighten him out."

Larray, still offended, flails his arms and responds, "Okay whatever! Just make it quick!"

D flies over to a corner of the platform and motions for Adam to follow him, which the author promptly does.

"I thought you said your name was Derrick before?" Adam asks.

D quickly whispers in response, "Shush up nigga! That *is* my name boy! I just gave that fool a fake name because ain't everybody be needin' to know everybody like that."

Adam nods in agreeance as D continues his scolding: "Look man, you can't be playin' that shit with these people while you in they house! It's like I told you, you gotta play by other motherfuckers' rules on this Epic Quest. Just go with the flow and don't rock the boat!"

Adam, somewhat confused and still irritated replies, "Alright, I guess."

Just then, Larray yells from afar, "I'm *waiting*!"

"Well alright nigga," says D, "you seem like you get the point so I'ma catch you later. Sassafras!"

The fairy godfather disappears in a puff of angel dust and Adam walks back over to the Trialmaster and the three men.

"I'm sorry," Adam says to Larray. "I was getting ahead of myself there; go ahead and say your lines."

Larray smiles and retorts, "Well you better be sorry honey! And I'm not gonna say my thang now; you already get the point. But I will explain this trial in a little further detail:

"So, as you've already deduced, you have to guess which of these three fine specimens – well, two fine specimens and one specimen – is indeed homosexual. Similar to how the Twins of Confusion's riddle was, you are allowed to ask each or all of them questions which will aid in your deducing which one of them is gay.

"However, instead of limiting the number of questions you may ask, you are limited in the amount of time you have to ask them your questions. You'll have 3 minutes to ask them as many questions as you'd like."

Larray pauses for a moment, allowing Adam to think to himself, "This oughtta be a cinch – since I can ask as many questions as I want. Hell, that's *all-right*."

"But," Larray says suddenly, "there are a few things you can't ask, like their sexuality (obviously) if they've ever had sex with another man and if they liked it, or if they've ever had sexual thoughts about other men. And no questions about partners! Basically, keep it to lifestyle questions that don't have anything to do with sexuality. Got it?"

The author nods and Larray pulls a little pink Barbie kitchen timer out of his back pocket.

"Ready, set, ask away!"

He starts the timer and Adam immediately asks, "What's your favorite TV show?"

The man on the left with the man bun and handlebar moustache and the man in the middle with the clean-cut hair and no facial hair answer simultaneously: "I don't really watch TV anymore."

The rightmost, oldest-looking of the three answers thoughtfully: "I used to really like Seinfeld back in the '90s, The Chapel Show in the 2000s (which was way funnier than Seinfeld) and lately I've just been watching whatever catches my eye on Netflix."

Adam thinks to himself, "That doesn't help me at all; but whatever…"

The author thinks deep for a few seconds, then asks, "What's a typical outfit for you and how much care do you put into how you dress?"

Adam figures this question will reveal which among them is gay; like how it revealed the gender of the Twins of Confusion.

But instead of the men answering the question, Larray chimes in, "Oh no honey, oh no! That's two questions in one, honey, you should've already known it's supposed to be one question at a time. Therefore, they don't have to answer that and you can't ask either of those questions separately as punishment!"

Adam wants to argue that a rule defining how many questions he could ask at one time had never been mentioned and therefore he shouldn't have to follow it, but he knows he's running low on time, so he formulates another question and asks it:

"What musical artists do you listen to on a regular basis?"

The leftmost answers, "Lately I've been listening to a lot of Ariana Grande and Harry Styles. I also like this band called the Deftones, and I'm also a big Swifty!"

Adam grimaces at the man's absolutely terrible taste in music (especially disgusted to find out the man likes the Deftones) but then grins wide as he thinks to himself, "Aha! I don't even need to hear the other two's answers – this motherfucker done already spilled the beans!"

But then, the middle man answers and all of Adam's thoughts of victory were terminated:

"Well I'm also a pretty big fan of Ariana Grande and Taylor Swift, but I don't care for Harry Styles and I've never heard of the Deftones. I do also really like Lady Gaga though."

The rightmost man begins mechanically listing off a plethora of different artists he enjoys as Larray says to Adam, "Honey, most men – gay, straight or whatever – listen to something that society might be inclined to label as gay. Musical taste isn't a good tell at all!"

Adam is reminded of his own appreciation of the singer Sade's music and mumbles to himself, "Damn; he's right."

"And better hurry and ask another question, honey. You only have 30 seconds left on the timer!"

Adam scrapes the back of his skull, trying to put together another question which may reveal the gay man, but finds it impossible with the droning on of the oldest man – who's still listing off various artists he enjoys listening to.

"Okay, you can stop answering now," Adam commands.

The man stops and now in silence, the author is able to quickly think of yet another question for the three men. But before he can open his mouth to ask it, the Barbie timer dings.

"Time's up honey!" Larray announces. "Now, with all your questions answered in full; guess who is the gay man!"

Adam, frustrated, thinks to himself, "Goddamn man, I really don't know which one of them is gay. I mean, visually, the older one of them is probably straight. But I oughtta know better than anyone that looks don't necessarily mean shit..."

The author peers deep into the eyes of each man, hoping desperately to find an answer in one of them, but to no avail.

"Man this is some ol' bullshit," Adam thinks. "You can't just tell what the fuck someone is by looking at them or by asking a few lousy questions."

With that thought, the author comes to a revelation and proceeds to say aloud, calmly and courteously, looking in no specific direction, "You can't tell someone's sexuality from their looks or their lifestyle choices. Being gay, straight, or whatever the hell is just a mere molecule in a person's whole makeup."

Adam then looks Larray dead in the eyes and says definitively, "I refuse to tell you which of these men is gay on the grounds that it isn't any of my goddamn business who any of them fuck. As long as it's with consenting adults – and none of these men look like priests, christian youth group counselors, police officers or certain United States government officials so I ain't too worried about that – then why should I or anyone else give a flying fuck who they fuck?

"And whether or not anybody wants to wear their flag on their sleeve is their business, and no one should ever have a problem with it. You'd think it wouldn't take this long to come to this conclusion in the 21st century, but I guess that's the fucked-up times we're living in now. But enough of this rant and back to my point: Larray, I will not tell you which one of these men is gay because I do not know and I do not need to know either."

Larray, with tears welling up in the corners of his eyes, claps with his hands held in front of his face like an elementary school teacher clapping for their students at their first recital.

"Oh my god," Larray manages to say through choked-back sobs. "I couldn't have said any of that better myself. Bravo, Adam Ordell, bravo!"

The eccentrically-dressed man takes a moment to compose himself, then says to Adam, "Congratulations honey; you've passed this trial. I wasn't sure about you when you first came here, but you're more than alright with me now."

The three men then disappear and the platform begins to descend at the speed of a department store elevator. And as it slowly moves back toward the Earth, Adam begins to grow impatient.

"So, uh, this doesn't go fast when it's going down?" asks the author.

"Well you don't want to go flying off, do you?" the Trialmaster asks in rebuttal. "There isn't exactly a roof to keep us in or anything you know; just be patient."

After a few minutes pass, the platform is just below the clouds and Larray asks Adam, "So, what do you do when you're not doing Epic Quests?"

Adam absent-mindedly responds, "Oh, I'm a writer."

"Ooo!" Larray reacts excitedly. "Anything I might of heard of?"

"Oops," the previously incognito author thinks. "I shouldn't have said that. If this guy figures out that I'm really Ardell Johnson, the author of *Literature to Go*, then he might just make sure I reach the ground before this here platform does!"

Adam responds, "Probably not; I've only ever done little news articles and the like until now: I'm writing my first book."

"Okay okay," Larray says. "What's the book about?"

"Sorry," the author responds, "but I'm trying to keep the plot under wraps; you never know who's listening."

As always, Adam was paranoid that someone was trying to plagiarize his hard work. It was because of this paranoia that Adam never released any details about his books until they were copyrighted. The author wouldn't even allow his publisher to advertise a book's existence until it was ready to be released. His friends and family never even knew what his books were about until they had a copy in their hands.

Larray, disappointed, insists, "Honey, trust me, I don't have a single bone in my body which compels me to write a whole entire book – even if the idea is given to me. And there ain't no one up here to hear us talk. Come on, let's not go down the whole way in silence."

Adam considers what Larray had to say for a moment, then responds, "I suppose. But you can't go tellin' no damn body about what you hear, alright?"

Larray grins and says, "Honey, I keep secrets that would cause murders to happen. I can handle not telling anyone about your book."

By the time the platform is back inside the used-to-be school cafeteria, the sun has moved from the center of the sky to the west half, preparing for its descent below the horizon, and Adam and Larray have discussed the plot of the author's upcoming book in its entirety.

"I'm definitely going to buy your book when it's out," Larray tells Adam as the ceiling seals itself above their heads.

"Oh, thanks," Adam responds.

"Of course!" continues the Trialmaster. "And I just love that one character you've written about! And the level of cynicism you employ throughout the entire narrative – it's so funny yet almost intellectual. You should try using that cynicism for the greater good of the people someday."

"Yeah, maybe," the author replies.

The cafeteria door on the wall perpendicular to the one Adam had entered through opens and the continuation of the path to the LGBT's Sacred Text lights itself on the other side.

"Oh but don't let me hold you up with my ramblings; carry on to the third and final Trialmaster," Larray says.

Adam bids the eccentric Trialmaster farewell and promptly exits the former cafeteria.

The black, cylindrical elevator which brought Larray to the surface begins to rise out of the ground once more as the Trialmaster thinks aloud to himself, "Maybe I should have warned Adam that no one has ever actually made it through the next trial, and that if I really wanted, I could have just taken him on a shortcut to see the Queen since I had a genuine connection with him."

Larray shrugs then steps into the elevator and says to himself, "Oh well! Shoulda coulda woulda. Hopefully he can beat the odds and become the first ever to make it through the final trial without being driven insane by Recto-Verso."

The torches lead Adam from the cafeteria room to what used to be the school's library. Standing just outside the wide-open entrance, the author prepares himself mentally for what he knows will be the third and final trial of the path through the LGBT's hideout.

"Alright goddamnit," he says to himself. "I'm gonna go in here, complete whatever ridiculous fuckin' trial is inside, and finally get my hands on that Sacred Text of Happiness. Hopefully it ain't much harder than the last shit either, 'cause I'm really ready to move on to the other 4 parts of this Epic Quest so I can clear my name and get back to writing my next book."

Feeling aptly prepared and mentally sound, Adam enters the library and is shocked to see all of the bookshelves are missing.

"Who knew the dismantling of the Department of Education could affect even a school that's been shut down since before the Emperor took over?" the author quips with a snicker.

He walks over to the librarian's desk: the only remaining piece of furniture which once made the big room a library, aside from the podium in an adjacent corner from the desk and a single faux-wooden table surrounded by chairs in the center of the room.

Looking down at the faux-wooden librarian's desk, Adam says to himself, "You know, I think we had like 3 different librarians come and go throughout my 4 years in high school."

Just then, the intercom comes on with a "ding" and a voice says, "Congratulations on getting past the previous two Trialmasters... **THE PUSHOVERS**."

The voice went from light and feathery – like the overly-courteous voice of someone who has social anxiety – to heavy and obnoxious – like the overly-assertive voice of a Marines veteran, high-school football coach – when it spoke the words "the pushovers". The intercom goes "ding" once more and the man who had been speaking through the intercom appears, standing behind the former librarian's desk.

He was tall as Adam, maybe an inch taller in fact, with a good build with well-defined muscles which shaped the clothes he wore. His skin was a rich brown like premium coffee beans. He had a medium-low Caesar cut with a fade, which was dyed two different colors in equal halves, split down the middle of his head. The left side was dyed a royal blue, while the right side was a cerise pink. His thin eyebrows were dyed some sort of dark magenta which appeared to be a mixture of the two colors on his head. He had a clean-shaven, chiseled, diamond-shaped face and azure eyes.

Like the other two Trialmasters, this man wore a suit. Though not as eccentric as Larray's and not as striking as Lily's, his suit was just as strange in its color scheme. It was a modern-style two-piece suit, color coordinated to match the man's dyed hair. The entire right side of the suit, from the right-side lapel of the jacket down to the cuff of the pants and even his right loafer was colored the same cerise pink as his hair. The left side was the same royal blue, and his tie was the same magenta as his eyebrows. All over his jacket and pants were little, magenta-colored question marks in a polka-dot pattern.

Adam had to bite his tongue as he thinks to himself, "Ha! The Fiddler!" which is an inside joke he and his brother – who is currently studying abroad – shared over a cartoon supervillain.

The multi-colored man continues his introduction: "My name is Recto-Verso... **AND I'M THE KING OF THIS MUTHAFUCKIN' TRIAL, YA HEARD?**"

Recto-Verso momentarily breaks into a coughing fit. He pulls an albuterol inhaler from his right jacket pocket, takes a puff, and says, "Sorry, I have somewhat severe asthma... **NO SHIT**... and I also have a bit of a disorder; kind of like a multiple personality disorder. **BUT BACK TO THE FUCKIN' POINT**... for this trial, all you have to do is answer one simple question."

Adam is immediately skeptical. "What's the catch?" he asks.

"The catch?" asks Recto-Verso in rebuttal. "Oh, nothing really. Just go stand in that corner behind that podium over there and you'll be asked the question."

"You LGBT's just love your questions, huh?" Adam thinks to himself as he slowly walks over to the podium.

He keeps an eye on the tall and handsome Trialmaster; weary of possible trickery. The author arrives at the podium and decides to stand in front of it rather than stand behind, as the Trialmaster had instructed.

"I SAID BEHIND THE PODIUM MUTHAFUCKA!" Recto-Verso yells across the room.

Reluctantly, Adam steps behind the podium and as soon as he does, shackles shoot out from little obscured trapdoors from underneath the podium. The shackles lock themselves around the author's ankles faster than an attack from a black mamba.

"Sonofabitch," Adam says aloud. "I knew this was gonna be some o' bullshit."

Recto-Verso giggles and says, "Now don't you worry about that – it's just so you don't try and escape."

"Oh yes," Adam thinks to himself. "*That's* plenty reassuring."

The Trialmaster coughs and takes another puff of his inhaler before continuing, "And now... **LET THE DAMN GAME BEGIN!"**

Immediately after Recto-Verso says this, Adam is enveloped in a dark haze and the room starts slowly spinning, as if a state of sudden vertigo had befallen the author. Bright points of white light like stars in the night sky begin flashing all around the author as the vertigo progresses and everything starts spinning faster. Disembodied voices from all around Adam start asking various questions and he can't even open his jaw to respond. There are so many voices that many of them overlap each other and most of what they're asking is indiscernible. Adam hears just a few miscellaneous questions above the rest: "Black or yellow?" "Grass or rock?" "Paper or digital?" "Top or bottom?" "Pen or pencil?" "Cat or dog?" The voices were all so loud as to disrupt Adam's very thought processes. He felt as if he were being torn in twain, and that those two halves were being assimilated into one central consciousness.

One booming voice suddenly says over the rest, "**NOW YOU SEE, FOOL**," it's Recto-Verso, "*this* is my trial! This is the ultimate question! But can you pick it apart from the rest of the unimportant questions? Pick the wrong one... **AND BE STUCK IN THIS WHIRLWIND OF WAILING WEAKLINGS FOR ALL OF ETERNITY!**"

The Trailmaster cackles maniacally, then his laugh fades away as the voices make themselves heard once more and the author feels his sanity start to slip.

Now, people from the author's past begin to appear out of the haze, asking some of the questions he hears: His 6th grade teacher, Ms. Matchbox, appears asking, "Penis or vagina?" The police officer who used to patrol the halls of his high school appears asking, "BMX or skateboarding?" His father's next-door-neighbor appears asking, "Four-door car or standard-cab truck?" At this moment, everything seems to be lost. Adam begins to forget who he is or why he's come. He begins to submit to this miserable plane of existence.

But then, Judge Composé appears asking, "Free or guilty?"

Adam's resolve returns to him instantaneously, as he finds the strength to close his eyes, plug his ears like he used to when he was a small child, and focus on nothing else except his own breathing. He finds his heartbeat and listens only to that rhythmic sound. The vertigo stops and Adam finds himself surrounded by white – though he can feel that his eyelids are still shut. The white plane stretches out for hundreds of miles, and large flocks of white sheep are grazing peacefully all around.

Dres from the mighty emcee duo Black Sheep appears standing before Adam and speaks his most well-known line: "You can get with this, or you can get with that."

Afterwards, Adam finds himself back inside the black-haze-covered library, eyes now open and ears unplugged, and he can hear the inquiring disembodied voices once again. He does not fret, however, as he now knows what to say.

"I'ma choose *this* because *this* is where it's at!" the author screams as loud as he can.

All of a sudden, the voices stop, the lights stop flashing, and the haze quickly dissipates. The shackles at Adam's ankles remove themselves and return to the trapdoors from whence they came. All Recto-Verso can do for a moment is stare at Adam, slack jawed.

"But how?" the Trialmaster asks. "Nobody has ever passed that test..."

"Well," Adam responds, "there's a first time for everything I suppose."

The library doors swing open and before he can leave, Adam is once again asked by Recto-Verso how he beat the seemingly impossible trial: "Before you go, tell me... **HOW THE FUCK**... did you find the Black Sheep?"

The author grins and replies, somewhat pompously, "Shit man, I write books for a living and at any given time I might have like 30 different ideas for how just one scene should go... Author's superpower is divining which one of those 30 is any good."

With that, Adam leaves the library; unaware of what he had just done. Recto-Verso thought he recognized Adam's last line from a book he read once – he just had to remember what book it was.

The torches lead further down the hall to the west-end stairwell. Standing at the foot of the stairs, the torches behind Adam all go out and blinding rays of rainbow light glare down from the top of the stairwell. A synth can be heard from somewhere on the second floor, playing some sort of bastardization of Bach's Fugue in G minor. The author slowly makes his way up the two flights of stairs, his eyes closed and his hand shielding his face from the awesome multi-color light shining from above. As Adam ascends the stairwell, the light grows even more intense and he can barely move against it; as if the light were some sort of mighty force which pushed him back like wind in a hurricane.

"Goddamn Jack!" the author says in frustration. "This light is a motherfucker! It better not be no extra bullshit getting this Sacred Text of Happiness up here!"

Once Adam steps through the open doorway at the top of the stairwell, the blinding light disappears as if the author had come through a big rainbow veil, and the synth player stops playing their version of Bach's Fugue. Adam now finds himself at the dead-end hallway where a mere ten feet before him stands the former den of the Calahoochi – what is now the throne room of the Queen of the LGBT's. The sight of the former den, though changed dramatically by the LGBT's, sent shivers down the author's spine.

"Fuck man," Adam murmurs to himself. "This is where that fucking snaggle-puss bitch-ass saggy-tit fuck used to torment me and certain other students. I really don't wanna go in there – I can still smell the rancid, rotten-fish-like stench of the Calahoochi – but I have to go in there so I can get this damned Text."

Adam hardly takes a single step before someone shouts, "Wait!"

Down the hall to the author's left comes running a little man, only about 5 feet tall, wearing a black tunic and white stockings with black leather turn shoes.

Once he reaches Adam the little man says, "Wow, you're tall! I mean, I could kind of tell from down the hall but up close; oh wow! But uh, anyway, my name is Prince Sebastian, no relation, and I serve the Queen as the Royal Music Programmer and I'm also acting as the Royal Greeter while Sarah, the usual Royal Greeter, is accompanying Ambassador Gaylord on a goodwill mission to Canada. We're considering moving there so we no longer have to hide in this smelly old school building under the reign of the Emperor – whose name shall not ever be spoken within these walls. So, I'll be introducing you to our queen as?"

"Adam Ordell," answers the author.

"Well, Adam Ordell," Prince Sebastian says, "I must ask before granting you an audience with the Queen: Why have you come here?"

"I am here to get the Sacred Text of Happiness," the author promptly answers.

Prince Sebastian smiles with relief and remarks, "I figured as much, since you did come from the West Stairwell of

Enlightenment, but I had to ask... Ah, how nice it is to finally have someone come here in search of happiness, rather than come in despair – seeking problems!

"Now, before we enter the throne room, I must tell you of only one stipulation that you are likely unaware of: Whatever you do, you must not dare call the Queen Tristan! Her true and formal title is La Sirène. Some of us refer to her casually by another name, but you may only call upon her by the name La Sirène. Do you understand? This is very important."

Adam nods in agreeance and the temporary greeter says, "Alright then; follow me into the throne room please!"

The author follows as Prince Sebastian opens the door of the throne room and enters. Inside the throne room, Adam is taken aback by its astounding size. From what Adam remembered, the Calahoochi's den had only been a little larger than the average high school classroom; maybe it was 1,200 square feet. But the massive space he found himself in now, which served as La Sirène throne room, had to be at least 20 times that, with a glass ceiling at least 50 feet high.

The huge room had a lush floor of thriving, emerald-green grass. A magnificent stream of crystal-clear water ran from wall to wall, horizontally through the very center of the room with a plethora of different fish swimming through it. There were a few trees growing throughout the throne room, 3 of them maple sycamore trees, 4 of them white oak trees, and one was a grand, flowering scarlet hawthorn tree which stood 10 feet from La Sirène throne – on the other side of the stream from Adam. Beautiful bluebirds, red robins, a rainbow array of songbirds, yellow-shouldered blackbirds, and other bird species Adam had never seen before roamed underneath the high ceiling of the throne room, singing songs and playing together in peace and harmony in what they thought was the open sky. The walls of the throne room were made of white marble, with rainbow-colored pillars lining them, each spaced 28 feet apart. La Sirène herself sat a few yards beyond the other side of the stream running through the throne room, on her exquisite purple velvet throne with gold accents. A red carpet lined with guardsmen, women, and everything in between and beyond led from the door to La Sirène.

As Adam followed the red carpet behind Prince Sebastian, he noticed the few people besides the guards scattered throughout the throne room. There were couples and small groups sitting on red-and-white-checkered blankets with picnic baskets. There were a few people running and frolicking through the meadow-like throne room, one or two people sitting underneath each of the 8 trees, either reading, napping or talking amongst themselves, and others taking walks along the beautiful stream; looking at the fish with peaceful gazes. Adam felt out of place bringing the recent chaos of his life into this place of peace and tranquility. Prince Sebastian and Adam both stopped once they reached the stream.

"Now I hope you aren't afraid of a little water," Prince Sebastian says, looking at Adam.

The Royal Greeter then steps into the water, which is chest-deep for him, and wades through the calm stream to the other side. Adam hesitates, peering at the water, seeing that it wasn't crystal clear as it had appeared from afar, but in fact had a slight pink hue to it. The stream looked unnatural with this pink hue, and the way it shimmered in the light like the surface had been sprinkled with glitter.

Suddenly, a pretty man with wavy black locks in a wolf cut, lush eyelashes and wearing sparkly-pink lipstick pops his head out of the water.

Adam can see what appears to be a large, black fishtail where the beautifully-effeminate man's legs should be.

The author asks about the tail as politely as possible: "Um, not to be rude and I'm definitely not trying to be judgmental but, uh, are you a mermaid?"

The man giggles softly with his hand over his mouth and responds, "Of course not, silly! There's only one mermaid here and that's our queen, Trish. Don't you speak French? But none of that is important right now. How about you just get out of those restrictive clothes and join me in the water?"

Adam attempts to reply "No" but for some inexplicable reason finds it impossible to do so. The fish-tailed man begins to look less like a man, and more like the most beautiful woman Adam had ever seen. Her eyes shone like diamonds, her smiling lips invited anyone to steal a kiss. Her bare, flat and toned pectoral muscles became perfectly-poised and perky female breasts. Her waist thinned while her hips grew wider and nude legs appeared where the black fishtail once was under the water. Beforc Adam knew what he was doing, he could feel his hands reaching for the hem of his shirt. The author tried to stop, but found he had no control over his own body.

"Ah what the hell is this?" Adam thinks to himself. "I thought I was already through all three of the trials; ain't nobody mentioned a fourth!"

As he thinks this, he removes his shirt; of course, not of his own volition. Then he begins to take his shoes off. Adam's mind races – scraping for a way to regain control over his body. Alas, the author can think of nothing and is left feeling helpless as his right shoe falls to the floor.

"Oh, why didn't I just get in the damn water when Prince Sebastian did?"

With that thought came a solution in Adam's mind. He figured it must have been his apprehension about the water, based on its looks, that had caused the shape-shifting creature to appear. The author would have to put away all his inhibitions in order to take the plunge into the stream – with all his clothes on – and reach the other side unscathed.

Adam accepts the water as nothing more than another small step on his Epic Quest and as soon as he does, he regains control over his body. The author proceeds to put his shoes and shirt back on, and finally steps into the once again crystal-clear water. As he does this, the gorgeous woman turns back into the gorgeous man with the fishtail and swims away with an almost inaudible scoff. Adam wades through the knee-deep water and emerges on the other side dry. He walks ahead of the gawking Prince Sebastian, and is told to stop by one of the guards once he's only five feet before the throne.

At this close distance, Adam is now able to see La Sirène clearly. The author thinks that she's not very tall for a queen, maybe 5 feet and seven inches tall, though her throne is elevated high enough off the ground so that her eye level is slightly above Adam's. She has a very slender build, though not skeletal and unattractive like that of an anorexic magazine model. Her skin is pale, yet iridescent as if she reflects all colors of the rainbow. Her hair is curly and golden-blonde and hangs just past her shoulders, with a strange fringe that looks something like choppy curtains. Her face is heart-shaped with a Greek nose, pouty lips, and big, round, slightly hooded brown eyes. She wore blue eyeshadow which extended to just the bottom edge of her naturally long, flat eyebrows.

Dangling from her ears were huge, gold hoop earrings the circumference of baseballs. She wore a magnificent white overcoat, unbuttoned, with a light-brown fur collar which extended down to the lapels. Underneath the coat, all La Sirène wore to cover her a-size breasts was a loose, sting-type bikini top which appeared to be made of cream-colored yarn. Perhaps to match her coat, she wore a grandiose white mermaid skirt with a very light sky-blue lace peplum with a floral pattern as well as lace at the hem with a matching pattern and color.

La Sirène flails her right arm into the air dramatically, the metallic-white nail polish on her long and pointed nails reflecting the light of the sun above like tiny mirrors.

"Prince Sebastian," calls La Sirène. Her voice is soft yet regal, with slight French intonations; though she also sounds British. "Who do you bring into my domain on this beautiful, sunny August day?"

"Adam Ordell, my liege," answers Prince Sebastian.

"Hmm, Adam Ordell..." La Sirène repcats, "Your name invokes the feeling of a term which has two meanings... *De toute façon !* You do not wear distress on your face, as many who come here anymore do, so you must have come for our Sacred Text of Happiness. Is this correct?"

Adam responds, "Yes."

With a bored look, La Sirène asks, "Then I know you have endured the Three Trials and have proved yourself in the face of each one... but tell me... Why should I bestow such an item upon you?"

Adam thinks to himself, "I already done showed you why motherfucker," but keeps this thought to himself as he takes a deep breath, and answers the LGBT Queen: "To say why would be to tell you what your own reasoning is and is not. Instead, let me state my case before you, Your Highness, La Sirène, and then you may find your own reasons based on what I have to say."

The Queen smiles slightly and says, "Very well then, Mr. Ordell, please state your case."

"Just two days ago, I was arrested and convicted of a crime I did not commit. This, in part, is due to the pigment of my skin. But it is mostly due to the fact that I have been vexed by a junkie voodoo wizard. I cannot beat the junkie alone and require 5 Sacred Items so I may clear my name; your Sacred Text of Happiness is one of them."

There's a moment of silence, then La Sirène says, "Clearing one's name is truly a noble quest... A moment of exposition for your weary ear: I am Queen of all the LGBT. That includes all the people under this umbrella name, letters listed or not. Yet I am merely one fish in a sea of many.

"The letter which represents the label society has put on me, that I embrace, is the letter T. There are many like me, and yet the T's are very few compared to the number of total humans on this planet.

"My people are but the latest in a long line of minorities to have been placed on this political hotseat. The 1234's claim that my people have committed the most heinous of crimes.

"The 1234's are an elite group of billionaires whom rule over the people with an iron fist shrouded in democracy. As not to leave too much up to interpretation: I mean that the

1234's say that my people have stolen the minds of the youth for use in our 'sick little games', when it is their generational, systematic oppression which holds the minds of the youth captive. So I understand your situation and sympathize with it so. Therefore I shall–"

The Queen is interrupted by Recto-Verso, who bursts into the throne room yelling, "Wait! That man is not who he appears to be!"

The bystanders of the throne room, who seemed so indifferent to Adam's presence until now, all gasp dramatically.

"Recto-Verso; why have you come here making such a claim?" inquires La Sirène.

The Trialmaster dashes across the throne room and once he's at the foot of his queen's throne, Recto-Verso pulls his smart phone from his pocket and shows La Sirène a screenshot of Adam's last-released book, *Literature to Go*. The screenshot was taken from a website dedicated to finding the real names of authors who use pen names, and thus directly underneath the book was a text box which read, "Written by Ardell Johnson – real name: Adam Ordell".

La Sirène, looking astonished by the news, procceds to say, "You're telling me the author of that, the forbidden 21st century book, so-called *Literature to Go*, is none other than the man I find in my throne room today: Adam Ordell?" The entire throne room once again gasps.

"Though I liked the majority of *Literature to Go*, Mr. Ordell, I cannot possibly give you our Sacred Text of Happiness now, knowing you are thou who wrote that awful poem within that forbidden book."

The throne room then fills with sounds of anger and resentment. Someone says very loudly, "I say we ban him from this place forever."

This statement triggers a common sentiment among the rest of the people in the throne room, and soon, everyone is congregating around their queen; prepared to remove this outsider they now hate from their hidden society forever – by force if they need to.

Adam, fearing the failure of his quirky quest, yells as loud as he can, "Wait a motherfucking minute!" The uproar abruptly stops, and the throne room falls silent.

The author clears his throat and continues, "I know that my poem is harsh, and perhaps now was not the time for me to write such a piece. I apologize for that, but I do not believe in taking words back – when you say something and mean it there is no turning away – thus I do not take back what I said. Instead, I offer further explanation:

"It seems to me that nowadays, people let the small statements get to them in ways that are far exaggerated. People seem to worry more about who's making fun of who, rather than ask themselves who is taking their rights away. Common people tend to fight other common people over disagreements, rather than fight the powers which shackle them to their true misery.

"So don't hate me for what I've said; hate instead the institution which has caused you to retreat to this abandoned school building. Because I am with you and I sympathize with your cause. But you must realize that what I said is true: You cannot call yourselves a movement if you stop every time an insignificant flea calls you a bad name! You cannot seek inglorious battles with keyboard warriors and those who have done nothing of worth with their lives!

You must instead stand strong; stand tall and oppose those in power who say you are not fit for their version of society – those same people who say you should not have the rights which allow you to be yourselves!"

The throne room once again falls silent. All that can be heard is the gentle flow of the little stream and the rustling of feathers and branches in a few of the trees as birds return to their nests to feed their young and rest their weary wings.

Then, two or three people from the small crowd begin to clap. A few more join them, and before long the entire throne room erupts in applause – even by Recto-Verso, who has a tear in one eye and a glint of fiery determination in the other.

La Sirène claps her hands twice to signal her people to grow silent, which they do, before she says to Adam, "Very well, Adam Ordell, I think I speak for the entire throne room when I say that I accept your explanation of that poem. And with that explanation I must admit that perhaps at times, especially on the internet, my people are too quick to heed the word of worthless hooligans. Therefore I will indeed bestow upon you our Sacred Text of Happiness."

As she says this, the LGBT Queen snaps her fingers, and Prince Sebastian runs behind his queen's throne, retrieving from some unseen nook the Sacred Text of Happiness. It is a tiny scroll, small enough to hold in the palm of one's hand, made of golden parchment, wrapped tightly around a crystal rolling stick and kept together with a tiny piece of rainbow-stripe-pattern ribbon, neatly tied into a bow.

The Royal Music Programmer hands Adam the scroll, and La Sirène says to the author, "However, I still do not like the wording in the last stanza of your poem. It is too harsh, even for a point to be made. Thus, I require you to do just one thing for me and my people once your quest to clear thy name is through."

Adam thinks to himself, "Oh come the fuck on! What the fuck else I gotta do now? 'Cause nigga I'm 'bout to dip with this fucking scroll if I gotta go through one more goddamn quizzical trial."

Adam simply nods to mask his frustration and the LGBT Queen says, "Speak in your next book of the struggle of my people which I have confided in you."

"Oh, that's it?" the author asks, relieved to hear that La Sirène request is a simple one. "Shit, I already got you covered, girl. As a rule, typically, I never tell nobody about my books before they're out, but I already copyrighted it, so let me tell you about one of the characters I made up – who's based off yall struggle."

Adam hoped that his bluff about having already copyrighted his upcoming book wouldn't become apparent if La Sirène talked to Larray, but he was willing to take the risk to put the LGBT Queen at ease.

So Adam explains in detail the character he based off the LGBT's struggle, as well as the sub plot surrounding them. By the time he's through telling the Queen about it, the crowd around the throne had grown in size with people from all around the LGBT hideout – who'd somehow heard the author of *Literature to Go* had been granted an audience with their queen. Everyone seemed to enjoy Adam's telling of the character, and many of them were whispering joyful comments about the character and their story among themselves.

"Wonderful," says La Sirène. "I look forward to reading the book once it's released – we'll all be looking out for it. Now, Noble Adam Ordell, go on to complete the quest set out before you so you may clear thy name! And know that no matter what, you are always free to return to this place and you will be received with open arms."

Adam thanks the LGBT Queen and finally leaves the throne room. He walks down the West Stairwell of Enlightenment and finds the entire hideout is now well-lit by the newly installed LED lights in the ceiling. There are also now a few members of the LGBT's walking around the halls, appearing to have specific destinations in mind.

At the front doors of the hideout, Kai the Guard once again appears and simply says, "Move now with haste, Adam Ordell; time moves fast when you are having fun." Adam nods at Kai's cryptic statement as he exits through the doors.

"Hm, it's still daytime outside," Adam says to himself as he squints in the late-summer sunshine. He proceeds to the little yellow Aveo, unlocks the doors, and gets into the driver's seat. The inside of the car is sweltering hot.

"Let's see if the AC works in this bitch," the author says to himself as he starts up the car.

He locates the button to turn the air conditioning on, presses it, and almost immediately after doing so he begins to hear an eardrum-popping screech. Adam thinks that he recognizes the sound, but tries to deny it as he pops the hood and exits the car to look under it for any loose bracketry that could cause such a noise. But, to his disappointment, the slightly mechanically-inclined author finds there is nothing loose under the hood, and when he put his ear close to the AC compressor, he finds it to be the source of the screech.

So Adam shuts the hood, returns to the driver's seat of the car, turns the air conditioning off, and rolls down the windows. He once again retrieves the list Lord Junkie had given him from his pocket and looks to see what he must procure now.

"Well let's see now," the author says to himself, "it seems the next thing on the list is the Black Power Gauntlet from the Secret Society of Black People over on the East Side of town..."

Adam flips the paper over, sees the reproduction Bill of Rights, then says, "Man, what the hell! How I'ma find some shit that's secret without no damn map or something? All it says is that the shit is on the East Side – fuck am I really supposed to do with that information?"

The author thinks for a moment, then says, "Ah, fuck it. I'll just drive 'round there; see if I can see anything. If not, then I'll return to that damnable palace and get a location from that damn junkie."

With no destination known to him – other than being pointed toward the East Side of town – Adam buckles his seat belt and drives away from the LGBT hideout – now on the hunt for the Black Power Gauntlet.

Chapter 5:

A Conference with The Count and The Priestess

Adam yawns as he drives down the road toward the East Side. "Damn," he says aloud. "I'm tired as a motherfucker now. But how? I mean, it felt like I was in there for a whole day, but seeing as the sun's only just now on the west side of the sky, I must've only been in there for a couple of hours. I shouldn't be tired from just that."

D the fairy godfather then appears, floating above the passenger's seat and asks, "Shit man, you ain't paid attention to that guard up in there?"

Beginning to get used his fairy godfather's sudden appearances, yet still slightly startled, the author asks in rebuttal, "What you mean? Kai? She ain't said nothing except for how I was supposed to get my hands on this Sacred Text of Happiness."

"I *mean* motherfucker," begins the fairy godfather, "that it's actually been a whole day – hell, a little over a day – since you entered in that motherfucker! Remember the guard said something like, 'Time moves faster when you're having fun' or some shit?"

Adam checks his watch, which has a built-in calendar, and sees that it's been about 28 hours since he first arrived at the LGBT's hideout.

"Damn!" Adam exclaims.

"Oh yeah," D says. "And the cops gon' be really watchin' out for you now – since you been missin' from that holdin' cell a whole two days now. Welp, good luck nigga! Sassafras!"

And as his fairy godfather disappears in a cloud of angel dust, the author notices a police cruiser pull out from a side street, and get directly behind the Aveo. Adam then looks down at the speedometer and sees he's going 45 miles per hour – 10 miles over the speed limit of the road he's on currently.

The police cruiser's lights begin flashing and Adam says aloud, "Of course! If D hadn't said anything, then not a single cop would've appeared... Motherfucker!"

The author promptly pulls over the car; his mind racing for a way out of this assured, impending arrest. He rolls the window down, shuts the car off, and puts his hands at 10 and 2 on the steering wheel. The police officer pulls over behind Adam, lights still flashing, exits his cruiser and walks up to the driver-side door of the Aveo.

The officer asks for Adam's license and registration, and the author instinctively reaches into his right cargo pocket slowly, while saying clearly and loudly, "I am now reaching for my wallet to retrieve my driver's license, in compliance with the officer's instructions." He finds that his wallet is not in his pocket, and remembers the court still has it.

"Not that it would've done me any good anyway," the author thinks to himself.

"Oh shoot," Adam says to the police officer. "I must have left my wallet at home; gosh darn it! But I can still get you that registration..."

Adam reaches into the glove compartment of the Aveo, finding it to be empty – without even an owner's manual.

"Oh boy," the author says nervously, "this is sure awkward. Officer, it appears my girlfriend did not leave the registration in the car. Because, you see, this is actually my girlfriend's car. Mine is in the shop right now–"

The officer cuts him off: "Well I can look up the car by the plate number. Just tell me your name and year of birth and I can look up your license too."

The first name that comes to Adam's mind is Bobby Watson. Bobby, because it's a phony name Adam was partial to using, and Watson, because the Johnny Guitar Watson song *What the Hell is This?* was stuck in his head.

Upon hearing the name Adam had thought he made up, the police officer asks, "Wait, you mean you're *the* Bobby Watson? Like, the critically acclaimed artist, photographer and cinematographer who started his career working as the unknown graphic designer for Tungsten Book Publishing?"

Adam replies "Yes" and the officer says, "Oh, wow! Well, sir, it is an honor to meet you. I've been a big fan of your art and photography ever since you were doing the book covers for Tungsten. And your short films? Truly spectacular!"

The police officer goes on raving for a little while longer before finally saying, "Oh hey, uh, don't worry about telling me your date of birth or anything, and I'm not going to run the plate number either. I'll just let you off with a warning –

just be a little more careful, okay? You were going a little fast."

Adam nods and responds, "Well thank you officer; will do." The officer proceeds to get the so-called Bobby Watson's signature on his pistol grip before letting the master-of-disguise author go on about his business. He resumes his drive and not long after the encounter with the police, the author arrives at the East Side of River End.

Adam has only to wonder aloud, "Now just where the hell is this 'Secret Society of Black People'?" before he conveniently stumbles upon a gate entrance to a large area surrounded by a grand brick wall. On the other side of the gate is the image of a civilian war-torn neighborhood. A bronze sign is attached to the gate, which reads, "Beyond this gate lies the Secret Society of Black People".

"Well, that was simple enough," Adam says to himself as he parks the car and proceeds to walk up to the 3-feet-wide gate.

A black man wearing a leather jacket, black khakis, short black boots, circular-frame sunglasses and a black beret with a rifle strapped to his back appears at the gate and asks Adam, "Young, yellow-skinned brother, what's yo' business here?"

Adam clears his throat and answers, "The Man done caught me up in a case; sayin' I fit the description 'cause of a vex that old junkie ass offa Douglass put on me. The only way for me to lift the vex and thus clear my name is to gather 5 Sacred Items on some damn quest – the Black Power Gauntlet is one of them."

The guard looks at Adam, studying this outsider for a moment while stroking his hairless chin before saying,

"Alright brother. Your story sounds legit and I see you got the Brother Fro, so I'll open the gate for you."

The guard says into a walkie talkie he pulls from his back pocket, "Disarm the alarm and open the gate," and the gate begins to open.

As the gate opens, Adam follows the guard inside the Secret Society and the image of the dismal, disarrayed ghetto disappears like a mirage in the desert. The gate opens itself fully and the true appearance of the Secret Society of Black People becomes clear: A high-class civilization with beautiful homes and upkept, high-brow businesses.

Businesses such as bookstores, computer programming shops that offer lessons, music stores without metal bars across bullet-proof windowpanes, black-owned tax firms that helped file taxes rather than get a hold of back tax payments, and restaurants that serve good food without all the sodium and high cholesterol that Adam was used to seeing. In the distance were lush, green meadows of natural North-American flora and fauna.

"Wow," Adam remarks in astonishment. "This is like some kinda Black Panther dream shit right here."

The guard grins and replies, "Yeah it is." Then, a grimace comes over his face and he says, "But not like what you're thinking."

Adam, immediately recognizing what the guard thought he had meant, stammers, "Ah shit man, I didn't mean it like that. I ain't tryin' to downplay yall as no comic book movie. And I can appreciate the hell out of the movement; reminds me of what the real Black Panthers had envisioned for our people back in the '60s and '70s."

A smile returns to the guard's face as he responds, "Thanks for the sentiment, brother. Now, since you're looking for the Black Power Gauntlet, you're first gonna wanna go talk to the oracle – everyone calls him The Count. He stays in his castle at the end of Dilla Avenue."

The guard points to a very tall hill with a castle atop it in the far distance. "To get there you'll want to take a hog from the hog pen; I'll take you there now." The guard then says into the walkie talkie, "Arm and alarm; shut the gate," and proceeds to lead Adam to the hog pen.

The author can't help but stare at the incredible sights he sees while walking through the Secret Society of Black People: He sees older black men playing with their grandkids, black women CEO's driving brand-new cars down the street with satisfied smiles on their faces, black teenagers spending time together in comradery, and other happenings only ever told of in Black American fairytales.

The streets all appear to be freshly paved, without craters or cracks which destroy the suspension parts of the cars which drive on them. The sidewalks are wide and regularly-maintained – no weeds growing out the seams and no tree roots misplacing the concrete. Adam takes a deep breath and finds the air to be clean and free of industrial odors or the stench of burnt drugs. There are no dogs barking and no broken subwoofers shaking the ground. Adam passes a mother and father pushing twins in two strollers; all four of them smile warmly and the parents greet the amazed author with friendly helloes.

Adam stares at all these beautiful sights around him, then looks at the rifle on the guard's back and asks, "This society yall got seems pretty peaceful to me, so why you brothers still carryin' guns?"

The guard hesitates, then answers with a level of seriousness in his voice, "This is just a very small pocket of the country. Niggas across America – and I call them that because that's just how they act: like niggas – still aren't with the program.

"It isn't all their fault, with systemic racism and high poverty rates and lacking education funds and all. But so many of our people got bitter, angry, and they just can't stand to see one of their own kind make it in this fucked-up world. So they sometimes come here to disrupt."

The guard reflects with a far-off look and a tear in his eye before continuing, "See, sometimes it isn't the pigs or the government or even the salt and swine we eat – sometimes it's ourselves.

"I once heard a brother on a record say that 'jealousy is the number-one killer amongst black folks'. Every year it seems he was more and more right."

The guard and the author continue their walk in silence for a few moments, before Adam says resolutely, "But we can't just accept that as a fact of life. Niggas aren't just niggas; they're lost and misguided black *people*. They're our brothers and sisters. I can't face a fellow black man in the street, pants sagged and a gun in his waistband and not still feel a certain level of comradery towards him."

The guard looks at Adam and a melancholic smile comes across his face.

"You sound like me when I was younger," says the guard. "So naïve, so honor bound. I like you, brother, so take it from me that some people are just what you said: lost. And there ain't a damn thing you can do to save them."

Adam replies, "But I've got to try; it is my duty as an author – something they never wanted our people to be able to be in the first place."

"Can't argue with that," the guard responds before the two finish their walk in silence – an unspoken understanding between the two of them now.

They reach the hog pen: a 20,000 square feet slab of asphalt, displaying an immense and diverse collection of hogs of all shapes and sizes. There were red, blue, black, green, purple, orange, yellow, pink, brown, gold, silver, gray, tan, and even white hogs. There were gigantic, ancient hogs from the times of bell-bottom pants and disco, smaller-size young hogs with futuristic technology, and everything in between. Many had chrome rims, some had gold, and a select few were completely black from the windshield to the exhaust tips.

As Adam gawks at the awesome pen full of beautiful hogs, the guard says sharply, "Pick your steed! It will take you through this land with great reliability."

The author looks carefully through the hog pen, discerning every little detail, making his selection precise and exact. After 15 minutes of examination, Adam makes his selection. He chooses a pearl-white, D'Elegance hog with gold trim, factory chrome rims with Vogue Tyres, off-white leather interior, and dark-tinted windows.

"Nice choice," the guard remarks. "Good mix of the old-school feel and modern-day advancements in technology and engine horsepower. Dilla Avenue is just beyond the hog pen." The guard points to a road just up the street from the hog pen.

"Just take it north to The Count's Castle. Good luck with your quest, brother."

The guard goes to return to his post at the front gate, and Adam gets inside the hog. The golden keys are already partially inserted into the ignition, so the author starts the car with a smile, adjusts the seat to conform to his form in perfect comfort, buckles his seat belt and heads for The Count's Castle atop the tall hill in the distance.

Dilla Avenue is a long and windy road with wide turns and sharp turns alike. There are potholes the width of a coffee mug and then there's crater-like potholes the size of punch bowls. Despite the terrain, the pearl-white hog drives smooth as an old comfortable couch rolling down a freshly-paved, flat highway. The hog maintains its silky-smooth cruise even when following Dilla Avenue up the hill that The Count's Castle is built on.

As the author climbs the hill in luxurious comfort, The Count's Castle comes into clear focus. Unlike the faux palace claimed from a dog-eared factory by Lord Junkie, The Count's Castle is a magnificent, Victorian-style work of exquisite architecture, constructed of polished limestone with touches of gleaming obsidian used in façade. The castle has a grandiose front lawn with a long, road-like driveway paved with bronze behind a 10-feet-tall, wrought-iron fence without a gate.

"That's one motherfucker of a castle," Adam says aloud.

The author finishes his drive up the hill and parks the car outside the fence, not wanting to drive on the bronze driveway out of fear of leaving tire marks on its spotless surface.

Approaching the brass-framed with red-stained glass French front doors, Adam is stopped by a man who jumps out from behind the very well-kept shrub to the right of the entrance.

The man now stands between the doors and Adam with his arms folded across his chest. This obstacle of a man is average height, stocky, with sepia-brown skin, yet another graying goatee and sideburns, almost-black eyes and black, nappy hair spilling out the sides of a bright-red baseball cap on his head which reads "I Got You Black".

He looks Adam up and down with one eyebrow raised and pursed lips in a frown as he says, "May name is Jack Allen and I'm the guardian of The Count's Castle. Now let me ask you: Whatchu know about hip hop?"

Adam, taken by surprise a little by the sudden appearance of the man, admittedly replies, "Not much."

Jack Allen shakes his head, arms still folded and lips still pursed, as he says, "Nah nah nah nah; that don't tell me nothin'. I mean, what is it that you *do* know about hip hop?"

Adam thinks carefully for a moment, then answers, "I know that Bushwick Bill from the Geto Boys tried to kill himself in '91, shortly before the release of that year's album *We Can't Be Stopped*, and ended up losing his right eye. I know that A Tribe Called Quest's sample of Lou Reed's *Wild Side* was never cleared so Reed got all the royalties from the original version of *Can I Kick It*. I know that Ice T famously invented gangsta rap, which was then called reality rap by NWA a little later on. I know that style of rap portrayed life in the ghetto streets of America as it really was and is – without censorship. And I know that real hip hop isn't on the billboard charts or on the radio, and mainly consists of underground emcees like Infinite EVOL."

Jack Allen scoffs and retorts, "But do you know Mr. Magic? You mighta heard Kool DJ Red Alert from Tribe, but what about Marley Marl? How about Chuck Chillout?"

The author remains speechless as the guardian of the castle laughs and continues, "Shit, I bet if I let you name some more rappers all you'd have to come up with is Tupac and Biggie! But check it out: If you're here to see The Count then you goin' to have to win in a rap battle against me. By the looks and sounds of you though… I doubt you could even spit the first verse of Rapper's Delight."

"Man, fuck it," Adam finally replies. "You gon' go and talk all that shit – less just see if you can put your money where your mouth is."

The author said this with faux confidence – for in reality he felt very unsure about this challenge.

"I can write an ill line in a book, sure," Adam thinks to himself. "But I can't just up and come up with shit on the fly."

Jack Allen cackles and with much bravado he says, "Shit, my money gets to stay in my pocket because even if this were a bet, I'd win without a doubt or a struggle."

Then, a very fit black man with a mid-height flat top and wearing a blue track suit with a comically-large gold chain and white sneakers appears. He has an awkward smile on his face.

Jack points at the man and says, "This is the world's greatest human beat machine. (He also just so happens to be the very first human beat machine.) His name is Fresh Factory Fred. He will provide the rhythm for our battle."

Fresh Factory Fred makes some noises with his mouth which so closely resemble the sounds of snare drums that it would have been impossible for anyone to tell the sounds came from a human, had they simply heard them and not seen Fred.

A small crowd of onlookers appears and Jack Allen says, "Now we'll flip this coin," he holds a silver dollar up at eye level, "to determine who goes first. Heads or tales?" Adam picks tails and Jack flips it: The coin lands heads-up.

With a toothy grin on his face Jack says, "Guess I'll go first."

Fresh Factory Fred begins beat boxing and Jack Allen starts his freestyle rap:
"Yo, yo
You's a wack motherfucker
Can't get no bitches
Workin' like a chump
Out there diggin' ditches
Stupid-ass nigga steppin' up to me
I bust rhymes like gats
Turn you into history
Bitch please
You can't even step to these
Wanna see The Count?
Well 1, 2, 3 and you're out!"

The crowd cheers for a moment, while Adam makes a final decision on what he's going to say, having been coming up with a rap while Jack Allen was saying his verse. The crowd quiets down, Fred begins once again beat boxing and Adam starts his first verse:
"Getting' smooth on the mic
Rippin' hoes like you tonight
I'm original, and you only bite
Flexin' top-deal skills for reals
With a flow that destroys
While all yours does is kills
Might as well get on the Poise
With rhymes weaker than Mc Donald's toys."

The crowd cheers, though with less excitement than they had when cheering for Jack Allen, before Fred begins beat boxing again and Jack starts his second verse:

"Slant-rhymin' like a motherfucker
Ain't it a shame
Ackin' hard and rappin'
Without an ounce of game
Callin' my lines weak
When yours are way too tame
Soundin' stuttery and meek
Not at all buttery, just like a dame
Can't even claim any fame to your name
Just a nobody nigga
Steppin' to cats that's much bigger
Like acetylene I'll flame
Your non-rappin' ass
Then go teach a class
On how to school uncool fools like you."

The crowd erupts in applause and Adam thinks to himself, "Goddman! I can't out do that slick shit! Man, what the fuck am I gonna do?"

Then, the evening sun moves to just the right angle in the sky, as to reflect blindingly off the chrome rims of the pearl-white hog at the end of the driveway. The lights hits the author's right eye and it makes him remember a poem he wrote years ago that may help him now.

"That shit might be too silly to work, but fuck it. I ain't got nothin' else to use in this fight so I might as well try."

The applause quiets down and Jack Allen asks rhetorically, "Had enough yet?"

"Never, punk," replies Adam. Fresh Factory Fred starts beat boxing again, and Adam puts up a hand to stop him and says, "I need some bass in the motherfucker. So unless you can do that, then I ain't even gonna need no beat from you."

Fred shrugs and, to Adam's astonishment, begins beat boxing and making sounds identical to the bassline in The Miracles' song, *Do it Baby* at the same time. Adam shows a satisfied smile and begins his final verse:
"I'm flyin' through the sky
Soarin' fast and high
I'm not your ordinary guy
So why try and deny
That I'm the Super Writer
Just like the Rhyme Fighter
Not a cocksuckin' biter
Do you girl, I think I mighta
Gotta supergroovalistic flow
Writin' fast not slow
Not your everyday joe schmoe
Shootin' a laser from each eye
And a look to make all the ladies cry
More
Turn a nun into a whore
While your bullshit make a nigga snore."

The crowd erupts in a mixture of applause and howling laughter. People are reaching out toward Adam and saying things like, "Dap me up brother," and "You killed it yo." Jack Allen tries to quiet them down, but they continue their joyous applause of the author's comical rap until Fresh Factory Fred makes a loud boom noise like the sound of a microphone being thrown at the floor.

Everyone once again grows silent and Jack Allen says to Adam, "I concede to you, brother. You've outclassed me at my own game; I can respect that.

"Now before I let you in the castle though, I gotta ask: What's your name so I can know who was emcee enough to defeat ol' Jack Allen; king of the MPC and the rhymin' ABC's?"

Adam tells the rapping guardian his name and Jack responds, "Well, Adam, next time you come around here you better be expectin' another battle – and you gon' lose next time too!"

Adam laughs and says, "Sure man, whatever. But I ain't losin' to nobody in nothing."

The crowd dissipates and Fresh Factory Fred disappears as Jack Allen opens the enormous front doors of The Count's Castle. A very unique and objectively better instrumental arrangement of *He Touched Me* can be heard being played on a Hammond Organ from somewhere within the castle.

"He's mostly a hermit," Jack Allen says. "Kinda like a vampire – that's why he's The Count. Just enter the foyer and you'll know what to do from there."

Adam nods Jack Allen a goodbye before finally entering the castle. The interior of the castle is dark, lit only by torches and a big crystal chandelier hanging from the high ceiling of the foyer. The foyer itself is small, leading only to a hallway straight ahead. All the walls are adorned in a black façade of obsidian, similar to the outside of the castle, with scenes carved into it which depict musicians playing their hearts out on big stages and in small clubs.

As the doors close behind Adam and he begins walking toward the single hallway, a voice from deeper within the castle says above the sound of the Hammond Organ, "Head straight through the hall before you, then pass directly through the courtyard and beyond the doors on the other side is where you will find me."

Adam shouts in response, "Alright," and does as The Count's disembodied voice has instructed.

Once he makes his way through the dimly-lit, obsidian-façade hallway, the author finds himself in the grand and serene outdoor space which The Count calls his courtyard.

In the beautiful courtyard, the unique arrangement of *He Touched Me* can no longer be heard and instead Adam hears the title track of the album *Everybody Loves the Sunshine*. Flowers and green grass thrive throughout the well-maintained courtyard, and a large pond with crystal-clear water is situated in the center.

As Adam walks through the courtyard, he can't help but stoop down next to the pond and say hello to the turtles sun basking on a log at the edge of the pond.

"Wassup little guys?" the author asks. "Just enjoying some time in this beautiful sunshine?"

One of the peaceful turtles looks up at Adam and responds, "Yes, the sun is quite exquisite today if I do say so myself. Why don't you come and join us, then?"

The author is taken aback slightly – not because the turtle can talk – but because the little shell-wearing reptile has an English accent.

"Shit," Adam replies, "wish I could. But I got this damn 'Epic Quest' to do. But hey, tell you what: I plan on coming back here later on anyway – so I can once again school that fool out front – so I'll come kick it with yall then."

"Indubitably," agrees the turtle.

Adam continues across the courtyard, and passes through the doors on the other side from where he had entered. Beyond those doors is a throne room adorned in black marble pillars, a golden façade lining the walls with similar depictions as the rest of the castle, a floor made of hardwood in an intricate diamond pattern, and The Count himself – at the very end of the room – sitting behind his grand

Hammon Organ. In the wall in front of The Count's organ is a stained-glass window about 10 feet wide, and about as tall as the ceiling: 18 feet.

The author walks up to the throne, which faces toward the stained-glass window with the Hammond Organ between the window and throne, and kneels 5 feet before the throne, saying to The Count, "Count, I know not who you are, yet I feel from you the aura of one who commands respect. My name is—"

The Count suddenly stops playing his grand organ and shouts, "Rise, Adam Ordell! I have already said your prayer for you."

Adam rises to his feet, and The Count gets out of his throne and turns around to face the author. The Count is about 6 feet tall, with medium-brown skin, a parted pencil moustache, and the facial features of a West Indian descendent. His shiny black hair is shoulder-length and professionally-straightened; not at all a Hollywood perm.

He's wearing an exquisite, Victorian-style black cloak over a distinguished, vampiric black suit. His gray suede loafers were almost comically long and pointed, but Adam thought they complimented the rest of his outfit quite nicely. Though the interior of the throne room was quite dim – lit only by the dying sunlight entering the room through the stained-glass window – The Count wore dark-gray tinted Ray Bans which obscured his eyes. He also wore a black gambler top hat with a wide brim.

Adam looks wide-eyed at the mysterious prophet and thinks to himself, "Goddamn! He's really some kinda Cloak and Dapper!"

The Count smiles wide and says, "You say that you don't know who I am, so let me clear that up first:

"As you already know, I am the one they know worldwide as The Count. I was once Gigolo C, and those who really know me call me MC Smoke. I'm the underground king who's only just recently been crowned.

"I've been making music for most of my life; what you just heard was my own arrangement of *He Touched Me*. I usually only play my own stuff, but occasionally I like to do covers and rearrangements.

"I discovered my ability to see into the future – which grants me the position of oracle – because of the music I've released into the public. My creative work has always been years ahead of everything else on the market; with a level of musical sophistication that takes a discerning ear to fully appreciate.

"Nowadays, I mainly spend time in my castle, composing new sounds and demonstrating to my discerning audience the benefits of constant forward motion in this: the true game of creativity. I do take leave of my castle every so often to explore the society which I feel blessed to have come into. I also attend sporting events occasionally and I foretell events to happen – such as your arrival this evening.

"I had a vision of your coming here late last night and I already know why you think you are here: to get the Black Power Gauntlet so you may clear your name. But I also know why you're truly here."

Adam, confused by The Count's words, says, "But I really *am* here for the Black Power Gauntlet, so I can clear my name."

"You did not hear what I said," The Count responds. "I said you *think* you're here for the Black Power Gauntlet, but that is only a minuscule reason for your coming. Your true purpose is one I cannot tell you, but will only say this:

"A time will come, Adam Ordell, when you must choose between two equal paths. I myself prefer to stay neutral in this life. I mind my own business and it has gotten me far. I've traveled the world and I've done things you could only imagine. I've worked alongside the greats and in the process, I have become one of them. That is not to say someone couldn't do things differently, however, I am just telling you how *I've* lived *my* life."

"That is very respectable," Adam says. "I too have taken the position of minding my own business in life and even though I hardly know you, I find myself looking up to your way of living. There is nothing wrong with maintaining a neutral position because not every fight is meant to be fought by every person. I can see how what you've told me aligns with my 'Epic Quest' without you having to say so.

"However, though I respect your way of living and have done the same for years now, I find myself being pulled into a battle which I must fight with my pencil and my paper. Once my 'Epic Quest' is through, and my name is clear, I know that I must fight this battle. Will I win or will I lose? I cannot say and I do not want the answer to be spoiled by you, with all due respect."

The Count chuckles a little and tells the author, "I may have predicted your coming and have seen some of your path, but I did not know you would catch on that quickly. You're a perceptive man, Adam, and I respect that.

"Now, as for the item which you seek, travel from here to the capitol building, The Black House, where you will meet the president of this Secret Society of Black People. The Gauntlet lies there.

"I would give you directions on how to get to The Black House from here, but you will benefit from not immediately having this information."

Adam thanks The Count for his guidance, and leaves the castle, not destitute but resolute on getting to The Black House.

As the author drives the pearl-white hog down the tall hill which The Count's Castle is situated atop, the sun begins its descent below the horizon.

"Man, it's about to be dark," Adam says to himself, "but I can't rest now – it done already been 2 goddamn days since I got started on this 'Epic Quest'. I can't afford to just be wastin' all kinds of time when I still got a book to finish."

Once at the foot of the hill, Adam drives back down Dilla Avenue and starts traversing the many streets of the black utopia; searching for its capitol building.

After a few minutes of driving around, the author sees a young man in a snazzy suit walking down the sidewalk and so he pulls the hog close to the curb, rolls down the window and says to him, "Excuse me, brother."

The dapper young man looks in Adam's direction and the author continues, "I'm a little new around here. Do you know where I can find The Black House?"

"For sure," the man responds. "Just keep straight for 3 more intersections, then take a left onto DuBois Boulevard, keep going until you reach Heron Court on your right, and The Black House is right at the end of that street. It's a big black building that kind of looks like the Great Mosque of Dijene, but it's made of Nero Marquina Marble instead of mud bricks, and it has no religious significance."

Adam thanked the young man for the directions, then asked him before heading to the capitol building, "And if you don't mind me asking, brother, where you going dressed in that sharp-ass suit?"

The man smiles and responds, "Oh, I'm just on my way home from work; I'm a fixed income analyst. I live three miles from the firm, but I like to walk to and from work – it's better for mind, body, and soul."

The author nods respect and wishes the high-level banker a good evening as he drives off toward The Black House.

"Damn man," the impressed author thinks aloud, "I only ever met one young brother in finance on the outside – and he was nowhere near the level that brother back there is at! Makes a motherfucker wanna just stay here forever – but I got stuff to do on the outside so I know I can't quite yet... Perhaps one day though."

The young, fixed income analyst watches Adam speed the pearl-white hog toward The Black House, thinking to himself, "You know, maybe I shouldn't have told him to go that way, because now he'll run right into the Five Percenters... Oh well! I'm sure everything will be fine."

Driving down DuBois Boulevard, Adam suddenly slams on the brakes of the hog as a black man dressed in a long, black leather trench coat jumps out in front of him.

The man's skin is black as coal, and he wears a hood over his bald head, with a long black beard, huge silver rings around his wrists, black steel-toe boots, and black cargo pants that can hardly be seen, being mostly obscured by his trench coat.

"Stop right there, God," the man says. "I don't believe you have knowledge of self."

Then, a crowd of black men of varying complexions, some clean-shaven and some with beards akin to the first man's, a few bald and most with either Caesar cuts or afros, all wearing black hooded trench coats and cargo pants, emerge from the shadows of the buildings on each side of the road. They all surround the hog and Adam puts it in park and cuts the engine off.

The original man with the long beard, bald head, and silver bracelets approaches the driver-side window and Adam rolls it down as he says, "Peace, God. My name is Draymond X and I'm one of the Five Percent – along here with my fellow Gods – whom teach the Eighty Five Percent what we know: what the ten percent do not want the Eighty Five Percent to know. So tell me, God, are you willing to learn what we know: to leave the Eighty Five Percent and join us in our righteous journey?"

The author looks at this black man, who speaks like a preacher yet wears the clothing of a vigilante, and thinks to himself, "Now just who the fuck is these niggas? Wearing these black trench coats and steel-toe boots and shit; lookin' like they gon' go stop a clown from robbing a bank right damn now."

Adam answers Draymond's proposal by saying, "Thanks... God, but I'm already on a bit of a journey myself–"

Draymond cuts Adam off and says, "And that journey has led you to us, God. Let us civilize you with the true black man's religion."

At this, Adam can't help but scoff – to the Five Percenter preacher's displeasure.

"Why do you mock me?" Draymond asks. "Is it because I don't preach about some white man sitting in the clouds, watching as his worshippers all suffer? Come on, God, you've gotta know in your heart that ain't right."

The author quickly replies, "No no, that isn't it. It's just the idea that I *need* religion in order to be civilized – I think that's ridiculous."

Draymond X and the rest of the crowd of Five Percenters gasp as Adam continues: "I mean, look, I think religion is good for some people, you know, to get them out of slumps in their life or whatever the case may be. And perhaps some people are just too weak-minded to not have some little book which tells them what to do; I get it. But I already know what to do with my life, and that ain't to spend it going to sermons and listening to podcasts talking about how much I should kneel every night and thank some motherfucker I ain't know who ain't done shit for me."

A sudden look of relief washes over Draymond's face as he says, "See, God, you're already recognizing the ten percent white man's religion as a bunch of nonsense that you don't need. But that's not what The Nations are about! We teach the black man that *he is* God – not some mystery man in the clouds. We believe in spreading knowledge to the black man across America – not for some ticket to heaven when we die – but for the creation of our own heaven right here on Earth."

"Well shit," Adam thinks to himself. "That doesn't sound too bad at all! Hell, I still don't need or want what he's selling, but I can respect the hell out of it! Instead of preaching fear and hatred, these brothers are out here preaching positivity and strength: telling black men they're Gods. I fuck with that, I really do, but I just can't buy into no religion. Though now I think I know how to get these brothers to let me go on about my day."

Adam smiles and says to Draymond, "Draymond, God, I can pick up what you're laying down: I get it now. Yall out here telling the black man that he's God; that he has the power to triumph over these systematically-placed adversities and live life the way their bibles say you only get to when you croak. But see, I'm already an author. My sole purpose in life is to put down on paper what knowledge I possess. Sometimes that knowledge is crazy comedic, sometimes it's straight serious, and sometimes it's one disguised as the other. But it's all knowledge, and I want to be able to spread it my own way – without religion."

Draymond is taken aback by the author's new and unique perspective. He strokes his beard, a look between astonishment and deep thinking on his face, trying to decide what to make of Adam's way of thinking.

Finally he says, "God, with your words you demonstrate your own civilization. Now I see, your journey hasn't led you to us, but our journey has led us to you.

"You have given us new perspective on the black man's situation in America. The solution is not religion itself, rather, pure knowledge and the strength it gives. We will keep you in mind in the future when we meet black men who cannot adapt to our ways of life. Thank you for this."

"You're welcome," Adam responds. "But I want you to keep this in mind as well: We are not just black men, but black men and women – we are a people. So don't just tell black men they are Gods, but black women that they are Goddesses too. We can't do this thing if we neglect our women and act as if they aren't equal to us in every way."

Draymond doesn't respond to Adam's suggestion with words, but instead resumes stroking his beard thoughtfully, as the other Five Percenters in front of the pearl-white hog move out of the way so the author can resume his drive to The Black House.

By the time Adam reaches the capitol building of the Secret Society of Black People, the sun has just gone completely under the western horizon and the waxing moon is bright in the sky. Streetlights cast luminescence onto The Black House, though only enough to see that it is indeed a large building built similar to the Great Mosque of Dijine and constructed of black marble.

There's a large parking lot to the right of the capitol building, only half-filled with hogs and other nice vehicles, where Adam decides to park the pearl-white hog. He gets out and approaches the large twin doors of The Black House.

There are two guards standing outside the capitol building doors – both dressed identical to the guard Adam had met at the front gate of the Secret Society of Black People. The guard standing to the left of the doors had a reddish-brown complexion, with no beret covering his long cornrows, a square face, clean shaven and wearing oval-shaped, black-framed glasses. The guard to the right looks to be of Melanesian origin, with naturally-blonde, curly hair in a loose afro cut, spilling out the sides of his black beret and a round face with a short, full beard. Both men were gigantic: standing around 7 feet tall with muscular builds like Mike Tyson in his prime.

Upon approaching the guards, Adam says as he tilts his head up to look them both in their faces, "Wow. It isn't everyday I have to look up to look someone in the face."

The guards and Adam share a short laugh, before the one on the left with the cornrows asks, "Have you come to see the leader?"

Adam replies "Yes" and both guards ask in unison, "What is your name and why do you request an audience?"

"My name is Adam Ordell," the author responds. "And I'm here on an 'Epic Quest' to get the Black Power Gauntlet and clear my name."

The guard on the right opens the door he stands beside and says, "You may enter then – The Count has called about your arrival."

Similar to the inside of The Count's Castle, The Black House opens up to a long corridor leading to a pair of doors at the end. Except instead of the corridor leading to only one other set of doors, the main corridor Adam finds himself in branches off into many small corridors and hallways leading to various other rooms. The hall itself is brightly lit by recessed LED lights in the high ceiling; unlike the archaic torches Adam had found to be the standard choice of lighting throughout almost everywhere else on his Epic Quest so far. There were pillars made of ivory-white marble and walls of black obsidian, with golden façades every so often, depicting ancient scenes of African Royalty legends and a purple rug lined with gold which leads to the main twin doors at the end of the long corridor.

The sound of the most beautiful piano playing Adam has ever heard echoes throughout the capitol building, and it sounds like it's coming from the twin doors at the end of the main corridor.

The observant author deduces that – following the pattern of his quest so far – the music should lead him to the leader of the Secret Society of Black People. So he walks to the twin doors at the end of the long corridor, and on the other side he finds a majestic black woman, her back towards Adam, playing the piano.

Adam finds the playing to be even better up close, as a tear streams down from his eye and he finds himself saying aloud, "Better than Bach."

The woman stops playing, spins around in her seat and rises until she's levitating 3 feet off the floor.

She has skin the color of dark chocolate, distinct African features, and perfect teeth. Her hair is obscured and wrapped within an African headdress befitting an ancient Egyptian queen. She wears big, profound green gemstone dangle earrings, and the most elegant black mermaid-style empire dress with a golden floral print across the waist and neckline. Looking at her, Adam knew he had never seen a beautiful woman until he'd seen this woman.

"Hello, Adam Ordell," the woman announces regally. "I am who they call The High Priestess of Soul – I am the leader of the Secret Society of Black People."

Adam looks at The High Priestess of Soul with a confused expression across his face and she proceeds to drop the regality in her voice, momentarily adopting what must have been her natural southern drawl as she asks, "Shit, who'd you think it'd be? Malcolm X or some shit?"

The author responds, "Angela Davis, actually."

"P'fah," The High Priestess scoffs, "you shoulda known it'd be me goddamnit! But anyway, ahem."

The High Priestess clears her throat and continues talking with her assumed regality: "I already know that you are here for the Black Power Gauntlet, since The Count told me, and he told me also that your intentions are true. But still, I need to ask a favor of you before I can give you the Black Power Gauntlet."

"Oh here we fucking go again," Adam thinks to himself before saying, "Name your price."

The High Priestess of Soul then makes a Polaroid picture appear out of thin air and hands it to the not visibly annoyed author. Adam looks at the Polaroid, and sees a somewhat portly black man with a circular goatee and a shag haircut without a fade, mostly obscured by a red baseball cap with an obscene image on the front.

"The husk of a man you see before you has long betrayed our people," The High Priestess says, "but now insists on destroying us. I need you to bring him here. I want to get him the help he needs. Here in this lavish society, we have the technology; given to us by our ancestors. I can rebuild him. He's said to be rallying over in the rural suburbs just east of town, over in Rustbin tonight.

"Do this, Adam, and the Black Power Gauntlet will be yours. If you leave now you should be able to catch him in the middle of his rally."

Adam agrees to go retrieve the lost man (secretly dreading the task) and before he leaves The High Priestess forewarns him: "But take caution! He isn't going to want to go and he won't come so easily – you're likely going to have to use force. And beware of the influence of the Carrot: Those rednecks out there get quite high off that moonshine and meth that they'll do just about anything to defend their redneck jesus and anyone who stands for him."

Adam nods, goes outside to the pearl-white hog, gets in, buckles his seat belt, and drives to the gate of the Secret Society. He parks it to the side of the gate, and the guard assures him it will be there upon his return. The author leaves the paradise-like Secret Society of Black People – in which he had found at least momentary comfort – and returns to the ass-backwards world in which he was once perfectly accustomed. He gets into the little yellow Aveo, buckles his seat belt, and booms it toward Rustbin.

Once Adam is on Lagoon Trail, he knows without an Atlas, MapQuest, or GPS that he's in Rustbin.

"The smell of cow shit and miles of corn fields and bean fields, with a barn every 50 acres," Adam says aloud. "Yep, this is the middle of butt-fucking nowhere: Rural outskirts of Rustbin. Midwestern-standard town."

The author drives down the dark and desolate backroad until he happens upon a spot of light emanating from the center of a cornfield up ahead.

He parks the car on the side of the road, gets out and proceeds on foot in between the rows of corn until he reaches the center of the field. There, Adam hides behind the stalks of corn and sees a crowd of about 30 people – 7 in white robes – gathered around a makeshift stage made of old, rotting wooden pallets. The light Adam had seen from the road was coming from 6 blazing torches surrounding the gathered crowd of hateful people. The author also notices a crew cab, army-green truck behind the stage with a lift kit on it that raises the fenders 6 feet off the ground. On stage is the man from the Polaroid picture. He's making a grandiose speech of absurdities to the gathered people:

"You know why Ronny A. Christ is so great? Because he's like America's own hitler! And hitler was a great guy! He believed in principles that this country needs. He hated everyone that wasn't white, right, and full of spite! Just like our beloved Ronny! Long live the Emperor! Long live Ronald T. Fump!"

The crowd cheers at the lost man's speech.

"Finally!" someone in the crowd who wears a confederate-flag-print tank top shouts, "A coon making some goddamn sense!"

Adam can only clench his jaw and crack his knuckles as he watches this rally of willful ignorance rage on.

"I just wanna kick this motherfucker in the nuts repeatedly," Adam thinks to himself. "But I gotta just do what I gotta do and take his Oreo Cookie ass back the Secret Society. But how the fuck am I gonna do that?"

Then, D the fairy godfather appears and says, "Don't you worry about that! I already got you covered."

The fairy godfather makes a rope and gag appear floating in the air before Adam, who promptly grabs the tools and thanks D for providing the equipment.

"No problem," the fairy godfather replies. "Just make sure you wait for his ass to break away from all them hilljacks – don't wanna have to fuck with them. Sassafras!" D disappears in a cloud of angel dust and Adam waits patiently for an opening to grab the lost man.

Eventually, after 20 minutes of self-deprecating hate speech from the lost man, the brainwashed buffoon tells his adoring fans that he's taking a short bathroom break.

The lost man begins walking away from the homely hand-built stage – conveniently directly towards where Adam is standing. The author tucks himself a little deeper into the corn, where the lost man cannot see him as he enters the rows for his break, and as the unsuspecting lost man walks in front of the obscured author, Adam lunges out and grabs the mind-swiped maniac.

The two fall to the ground and the lost man starts to scream out for his people, "Ni–" but Adam quickly stuffs the gag in his mouth. He then ties up the lost man, and quickly carries his helpless mass out to the Aveo.

Adam stuffs the lost man into the tiny trunk of pathetic clown car, thinking he's gotten away with the kidnapping of the lost man, but as he's finally shutting the trunk lid, a posse of his followers emerges from the corn field and one of them shouts at Adam, "Hey nigger boy, do you know where you are?"

The author looks the overall-wearing man in the eyes and says, "Hey now, don't call me no nigger! I'm just passing through – had to change a flat tire."

The man with the posse responds, "Now boy don't go getting' smart with me! Me and the fellers just lookin' for–"

Before the man can finish his statement, sounds of pounding come from the trunk of the Aveo.

"What the hell you got in yer trunk there, boy?" the overall-wearing man asks.

Adam thinks for a micro moment, then stammers, "I gotta deer in there! Must not be dead, or has a muscle spasm going on or something like that. I was just hunting a few miles from here."

The man then says, "It ain't deer season, boy. What you really got in there?"

The posse begins to approach Adam slowly, and the lost man – who must have somehow maneuvered the gag out of his mouth – yells from inside the trunk, "Help! This nigger's got me tied up in here!"

The author says aloud, "Oh shit," before scurrying into the Aveo, buckling his seat belt, and screeching the tires as the posse of the lost man's fans give chase on foot; the one in the front screaming, "Come back with our pet coon nigger!"

Adam laughs hysterically and says to himself, "Aha! I done got away with some more shit ain't nobody else would be able to get themselves out of! It oughtta just be smooth cruisin' from here!"

Just then, Adam looks in the rearview mirror and sees the army-green truck he had seen in the cornfield coming up fast behind him; men spilling out the sides with shotguns shouting, "Yeehaw! Let's go lynch us a nigger today!"

The men start shooting at Adam and he says aloud, "Shit! These motherfuckers are gonna kill my black ass if I can't get rid of 'em!"

The distance between the rear end of the Aveo and the diamond plate steel bumper of the jacked-up truck is shortening by the second. The bullets from the shotguns are peppering the poor little Aveo and Adam worries that soon enough one of them will pepper him too. He comes up on a field of soybeans and gets an idea:

"Hell it's awfully dark outside," Adam says to himself, "maybe I can get those stupid methed-out motherfuckers to run that street-legal monster truck into something that'll stop 'em dead in their tracks."

The author cuts the wheel right, dog tailing the Aveo into the soybean field. The hateful men in the truck follow Adam, and as he's straightening the car back out, one of them gets a clear shot of the rear quarter panel – just shy of hitting the trunk. The shotgun blast goes directly through the gas tank, and the little yellow car begins leaving a trail of fuel as it speeds through the field.

"Motherfucking no-good redneck!" Adam yells as he watches the gas gauge begin to steadily head to the left.

Fortunately for the author, however, a large drainage ditch is just ahead of him – which he knows he can trick the fascist fools behind him into getting stuck in.

The daredevil author continues speeding toward the ditch, only cutting right once more when the front bumper is hanging off the edge. The Aveo spins around 270 degrees, the passenger-side wheels just barely gripping the edge of the ditch, while the men in the army-green truck attempt to jump the drainage ditch.

Unfortunately for them, the front end of the truck is too heavy to come up off the ground and so it dips into the ditch and the whole truck is stood up with its rear end in the sky – stuck with the men scrambling to exit the vehicle and chase Adam on foot as he's driving away with his middle finger stuck out the window of the little yellow Aveo yelling, "So long, crackers!" Adam gets the car back onto the road, and sees that the gas gauge is almost pointing at E.

"Shit man," Adam says. "How the fuck am I gonna get back over to the East Side before this bitch runs all the way outta gas?"

D the fairy godfather once again appears – this time holding a roll of duct tape – and says, "Don't worry nigga; I'ma take care of this this Roadkill style!"

D poofs to the underside of the car, applies duct tape all over the gas tank, then reappears hovering above the driver's seat and says, "Alright, your gas tank is all good to make it back to the East Side. But you gon' hafta get a different set of wheels after that – unless you wanna start walking every which place. Sassafras!" Adam thanks his fairy godfather as he disappears in a puff of angel dust.

The author arrives at the front gate of the Secret Society of Black People, and retrieves the lost man from the trunk of the Aveo. The guard promptly unlocks the gate, and helps Adam load the screaming and kicking lost man into the trunk of the pearl-white hog. Adam then gets into the hog, buckles his seat belt, and drives it back to The Black House.

He pulls into the capitol building parking lot and proceeds to approach the guards at the front doors of the building, saying, "I got ol' Real-Life Ruckus in the trunk of the hog. But I'ma need some help getting him outta there – I got his arms tied up but the motherfucker has one hell of a kick – like some toddler being dragged away from the playground."

The guard on the right, the one with the blonde hair, responds, "The High Priestess has informed us all you had to do was deliver the lost man to us; which you did. We'll retrieve him from the trunk. You may go inside and the leader will give you the Black Power Gauntlet."

The guards open both grand doors of the Black House and walk over to the pearl-white hog. Adam pops the trunk with the key fob for them, and the guard with the corn rows effortlessly lifts the lost man up over his left shoulder.

The lost man is rambling on like someone from an insane asylum: "Mama! Where are you? My fans! My fans! Kim, no, what are you doing with that needle? Needle! Needle! Okay kay kay!" Adam shudders at the sound of the lost man's babblings as he enters The Black House.

Once again in the throne room, The High Priestess of Soul asks Adam, "So, you have been successful in capturing the lost man?"

The author responds that he has, and The High Priestess says, "Then I thank you eternally for bringing that traitor back so we may nurse him back to spiritual and mental health."

The grandfather clock in the corner of the throne room strikes 12:00 midnight, and The High Priestess of Soul tells Adam he can stay in The Black House for the night:

"It is late now, Adam Ordell. I know from The Count that your Epic Quest will be long and arduous, so I invite and encourage you to stay here in The Black House tonight and rest. I will give you the Black Power Gauntlet in the morning."

Adam wants to refuse the act of hospitality – feeling the need to complete his quest with haste – but knows that he cannot refuse the offer and disrespect the black leader. So Adam agrees to stay for the night, and The High Priestess shows the author to a spare room.

Once at the doorway of the spare room, The High Priestess says, "Beyond the door in the far-right corner is a bathroom. You may bathe – there is a robe in the bathroom closet and one of my maids will have your clothes washed by morning."

Adam thanks The High Priestess profusely and after she leaves the author alone, he takes a good look around the room. The walls are made of a light-gray marble, with black marble baseboards and adorned with several beautiful paintings. The flooring is plush, gray carpet which feels like a comforter underneath the author's shoes. The room is also quite large, looking to be about 242 square feet. The queen XL bed is covered with wine-red sheets, soft as silk, and a matching velvet blanket and down pillows with silk covers. Next to the bed is a nightstand made of African Blackwood, with a golden lamp atop it with a red lampshade.

The author looks at all this and says to himself, "Well damn! If this is just a guest room, then The High Priestess' bedroom must be so goddamn luxurious that any mere mortal would spontaneously combust at the sight of it!" Then Adam looks toward the bathroom and says to himself, "But now what I'm really after is a good shower!"

He proceeds to enter the bathroom, close the door, turn the shower on, disrobe and enter.

As he bathes Adam exclaims quietly, "Man! I'm glad to be finally showering for the first time since I started this damnable 'Epic Quest'."

His thoughts trail off as he proceeds to think aloud, "You know, I'll never understand why there's so many damn shower scenes in film. I mean, I guess if you want to explicitly mention a character's hygiene habits or if a shower scene just so happens to follow the narrative perfectly that makes sense. But nobody *needs* to see the actress' bare boobs and/or ass to get a sense of her hygiene habits, and for so many movies, the scene has absolutely nothing to do with the narrative – especially in action movies.

"And shit, you almost never see a shower scene with just a guy. Or if you do, then all you see is his face and maybe his chest – which is all you ever need to see from anyone in the shower. Hell, I can just see all the disgusted faces of straight men across America if in his next movie, Keanu Reeves strips completely bare-ass naked in front of the camera and shows all that he's got. But I'd never put a shower scene in any of my books – unless I was trying to prove a point."

The author finishes his shower, towels off, puts on the provided robe and finds an elderly maid just outside the bathroom door to hand his clothes to.

"You, uh, didn't hear me talking to myself in there did you?" Adam asks the maid.

She grins and replies, "Oh honey, I mighta heard just a teensy bit. And I would *love* to see a real-life shower scene with just you, baby!"

The maid laughs as she walks away with Adam's clothes and the author gets a strange feeling about what she had said and what she had heard.

Adam proceeds to throw himself onto the large, comfy bed and he falls asleep within mere moments of hitting the sheets – without even tucking himself underneath the blanket. That night Adam had a strange dream which he later got the feeling was prophetic.

Intermission:
Dream of Caution

I was being persecuted by the government. I knew they were tailing me hard as I drove my old Chevy truck through the city. Eventually, they caught me. They took me away to a concentration camp where my sentence was being levied – like some sort of unjust trial in which I had no input. I saw a flash of Ronald Fump in the shadows and felt a deep hatred boil within me.

After only a few minutes of deliberation – which felt like hours – they decided on deporting me. I knew for what I had done (speaking my mind) they could have locked me up and threw away the key. Or worse yet: they could have executed me. So I was relieved when they decided on deportation. In fact, I almost felt as if I had won the lottery – I had planned on leaving America some day anyway.

Then I saw people getting shots in their arms – which I was told by an official was the alternative I could have chosen to deportation. They didn't say it, but I knew that shot was meant to brainwash us prisoners into submission.

So I refused the shot, and a female pilot came to get me. I slipped her some money to allow me to take some luggage on the plane. We get into the little white, single-propeller biplane and I realize that I don't have my laptop with me. I thought that maybe there was a laptop at my final destination. So I ask the pilot about it and she says there will be no laptop awaiting me where I'm headed. I slipped her another 20 which I miraculously passed off as a 50 and she let me go grab my laptop.

I leave the plane and start walking down some corridor at the end of which, my laptop should be. I am stopped halfway between where I entered and the end of the corridor, however, by Ronald Fump. He stood there, arms folded, in the center of the corridor; cackling like a hyena.

A minute later, he stops laughing and says to me in his raspy, businessman-gone-bad voice, "Why don't you just give up already, Adam Ordell? It's futile to fight us; it's pointless trying to change the tide. You know you can't just change the course of history – that has been repeating itself since the very beginning of humanity – right? You can't possibly expect to defeat me with your little words, can you? It's one nation, not one man, Adam, and this nation has bowed down and pledged their allegiance to me and my new form of government. You have no allies, no connections – you've already been defeated. So now, maybe you think that leaving America will do you some good? Escaping your problems to live in a 'less problematic country'? Hahahaha! Good luck! You can leave this country, but this country will never leave you – the stain of the USA will always remain."

I found myself back in the biplane next, laptop in tow, and I started to worry that this plan wasn't going to work and that at any minute now they're going to arrest me again and change my sentence to life in America.

Chapter 6:

Old-Fashioned, Country-Style Prison Camp

Adam awoke from his nightmarish dream in a cold sweat.

"What in the fuck was that?" the author asks himself. He then looks around the room, still half asleep, making sure of his surroundings and reminding himself that he is currently safe inside The Black House.

Once fully awake, Adam hops out of bed and finds his clothes neatly folded on the nightstand. He proceeds to get dressed, and before he's completely dressed – still buckling his belt – without a shirt on – the maid from last night bursts into the room.

"Oh, uh, oops; sorry," the author stammers as he hastily finishes buckling his belt.

The elderly maid, with a look between disappointment and excitement on her face, responds, "Oh it's alright honey – I done seen plenty more than that before! I jus' came to take that robe offya before you go."

"Oh, of course," Adam says and quickly grabs the robe off the bed and hands it to the maid. The maid hurries off and Adam finishes getting dressed.

The author then proceeds to return to the throne room of The Black house, where The High Priestess of Soul sits behind her piano, playing a very blue song and waiting for Adam.

"You slept quite late," The High Priestess states. "I had to almost beat my maid away from your door, you know. Had you slept any later I may not have been able to prevent her from entering your room."

The author looks down at his watch and sees the time reads 11:16am. "I apologize," responds Adam. "I'm not an early riser."

"That is alright," The High Priestess says. "According to The Count's prophetic vision you will need every minute of that sleep for what comes next for you.

"But anyway: Adam Ordell, for bringing us the traitorous lost man, I will now bestow upon you the Black Power Gauntlet that you have come here for."

The High Priestess raises a mighty fist high into the air and a black steel gauntlet materializes on her hand. The dorsal side of the gauntlet is engraved with the words "FIGHT THE POWER" in all capital, crimson-red letters.

The High Priestess continues, "With this Gauntlet, Adam Ordell, you will become an enemy of the American public. They do not like it when a young man is black and proud in this nation; they'd rather you be overly humble or else be a caricature of a real black person. You can never place this Gauntlet anywhere other than its final destination – meaning you must wear it for the remainder of your quest. Is this acceptable to you?"

"Yes," replies Adam with a nod of his head.

The Black Power Gauntlet then instantaneously disappears and reappears on Adam's right hand. The Gauntlet begins changing shape slightly, forming with writhing movements to conform to the exact shape of the author's hand.

"It's conforming to the every feature of my right hand in comfort!" Adam exclaims in amazement.

The High Priestess of Soul then says, "This way it should not interfere with your writing – if you do indeed get the chance to write before your Epic Quest is through."

Confused, Adam asks, "How did you know I'm an author?"

The High Priestess replies with a slight, soft chuckles, "Because you talk with your hands; as if you're trying to write the words you mean to speak. It's the mark of a true literary artist."

The author thoughtfully reflects on the High Preistess' words for a moment, before accepting their meaning. He then thanks her for the Gauntlet and her hospitality, and asks for an additional favor as well: "I thank you profusely for both this gauntlet and your hospitality in letting me stay the night in your luxurious capitol building. But before I go, I must ask one more favor of you: The vehicle I have used to travel from destination to destination up to this point has been mortally wounded by the rednecks I encountered when rescuing the lost man. In addition, I have grown quite accustomed to the pearl-white hog which I have driven through this magnificent hidden society. Its luxury is one I have never known before. My request is to use the pearl-white hog for the remainder of my journey."

The High Priestess shrugs her shoulders and answers – once again adopting the southern-drawl of her natural speaking voice, "Sure, you can have that ol' thing to keep; even after your Epic Quest is through. Hell, the way you was soundin' for a minute I almost thought you was gonna ask to use *my* car."

"Your car?" the author asks. "If you don't mind me asking, which one is that?"

The High Priestess answers, "Oh, you haven't heard? I drive a silver, 1958 Mercedes-Benz 220SE Cabriolet W-128 with red leather interior.

"But that isn't important. As I said, you may have the pearl-white D'Elegance hog as yet another gift of appreciation towards you for bringing the lost man here. Just drive it to the front gate, and it will open up wide enough so you may drive through.

"Also before you go there is one more thing I will tell you about the Black Power Gauntlet: Its power is subtle and exacting. This is to say it will not activate until it is absolutely needed."

Adam thanks The High Priestess once again and exits The Black House. He proceeds to get in the pearl-white hog, buckle his seat belt, and drive it up to the front gate of the Secret Society of Black People. Just as the black leader had said, the gate miraculously opens up wide enough for the hog to drive through.

The author gets a block down the road, and it occurs to him that he needs to once again look at Lord Junkie's list to see where it is he needs to go next. Adam pulls over and retrieves the list from his pocket.

Peering at the piece of hypocritical paper for a moment, the author says to himself, "Alright then, it looks like I'm headed to the South Side to get the Ultimate Green Card. That shouldn't be too much of a hassle – my Latino brethren over there love me so I don't see having a problem, anyway."

But as Adam is about to pull away from the curb to head toward the South Side, he notices a group of people creeping up on a Messla car parked crooked on the side of the road. Each person in the group is holding either a gasoline tank or a blunt object (such as a brick, large rock, or two-by-four). The author knows exactly what's about to happen, and instead of minding his own business – as he usually would – he swiftly pulls the hog to the curb. He puts the hog in park and exits the vehicle.

"Hold on now fellas," Adam begins. The group stops in their tracks and looks toward the author. "It doesn't have to be like this."

The apparent leader of the group, a pale man with a green bandana obscuring the lower half his face, steps up to Adam and retorts, "This is the only way it can be! You know who owns the company which makes this car! And by driving it, the motherfucker who owns it is supporting his bullshit!"

The apparent leader turns back toward the Messla to continue his path of destruction and Adam yells after him, "I understand your deep-seated ire! But the driver of this car ain't done shit wrong! Check the license plate!"

The leader of the group creeps up to the license plate and finds a renewal sticker placed crookedly over 3 other renewal stickers.

"See," Adam continues, "that car was bought years before all this new-age bullshit!"

The group gasps and their leader replies with a grimace, "OK fine; *this* car wasn't bought recently – and I guess cars are expensive enough these days to warrant not buying another one to replace this piece of electric shit. But what about Messlas bought within the past few months? What about dealership cars?"

"What about dealership cars?" Adam asks in rebuttal. "When you burn a dealership car, you're only putting insurance money in Husk's pocket. And as for people who bought a Messla in the last couple of months: Some of them only bought one because they wanted an electric car, some have maybe been saving up for one since they came out and finally got the chance, and a few think they're supporting the 'good guys'. We can't just punish the blind for their lack of sight – we have to fight the institution which causes their blindness!"

Everyone falls silent for a moment, then the leader begins clapping. The rest of the group starts putting down their weapons and joins their leader in applauding Adam's speech.

"I never thought about it like that," says the enlightened leader. "All this time I thought we were fighting the Man, but we've really only been fighting *fellow man*. Thank you for showing us the error of our ways." Adam and the man shake hands as Adam replies, "You're welcome."

But before the author can return to the pearl-white hog, the previously misguided revolutionary stops him and says, "And hey man, you seem really conscious. Maybe you could lead us in the direction of true revolution?"

Adam responds to the leader's proposal by saying, "Sorry man, but I'm not really the front lines type of fighter. I prefer influencing things from the sidelines."

Disappointed, the leader says, "Well alright then. But we'll always remember your words man, and we'll find a new way to fight against evil." The small group cheers at their leader's promise and Adam finally gets back into the hog, buckles his seat belt, and continues his drive toward the South Side.

As he drives, Adam wonders aloud, "Why the hell did I just do that? I mean, I guess I did a good thing and all, but that ain't have shit to do with this 'Epic Quest' and it sure enough wasn't none of my business what the hell they were about to do to that Messla."

Just then, D the fairy godfather appears and answers, "Shit, you goddamn right that wasn't none of your business what them crackers was about to do to that car! And I wouldn't have intervened in that shit my goddamn self. But really, you stopped them niggas from doing that shit because traveling through the Secret Society of Black People done changed you a little."

Adam asks in response, "What you mean it 'changed' me?"

At this question D scoffs, then replies, "Well, maybe changed isn't necessarily the correct term. See, that place is spiritually healing for a black man, and being there brought out the little part in you that feels the need to help your fellow man – your compassion has been restored. It's all good though, you still the same ol' motherfucker you always was. Don't worry about it nigga; sassafras!" And with that, D once again disappears in a puff of angel dust and Adam reflects on his words for the remainder of his drive to the South Side.

When he begins seeing businesses with signs he can't read and the smell of good and spicey food is in the air, Adam knows he has reached the South Side.

The author has a melancholic smile on his face as he drives past the friendly faces of children running through the streets; laughing past storefronts with metal bars in the windows and condemned houses with boards and signs from the city in their windows – all the while throwing water balloons at each other and flying toy airplanes through the air above their heads. An elderly man drives his little budget car down the street with the sound of old Mexican music from the 1960s barely creeping outside the car.

But as the author cruises the pearl-white hog down the street, the part of town affectionately referred to as "Little Mexico" begins to look less like an impoverished neighborhood full of golden-hearted, friendly-faced people and more like a ghost town. The sound of happy children and salsa music fades away, leaving only silence. Houses with doors wide open – some looking as if they'd been beaten down with a battering ram, others looking left open by the occupants – are all around Adam. Children's toys and little abandoned bicycles litter the streets as if the kids playing with them had all-of-a-sudden disappeared. That old stoop the author recognized as the one where the elderly lady sat all day in the summertime, sometimes reading to her grandkids and other times knitting, was now lifeless. A mother sat on the curb where tire marks began, crying into her palms and screaming, *"¡Mi familia! ¡Se llevaron a mi familia!"*

Adam sheds a tear and says aloud to himself, "God fucking dammit man! This is bullshit! How the hell they just gonna let this happen to these people out here! It's just like I been knowing since I was a ten-year-old fucking kid man – they treat all of us who got tan skins the same. They treat us all like fucking animals. Black people, Latin people, Native Americans, brothers and sisters from the Middle East, even Asian people – these evil fucks do us all the same. And now they especially fucking with the backbone of this country:

the nicest and hardest-working people America has ever seen!"

The author gets a little further down the road, and begins to once again smell the delicious scent of Latin cooking. He looks to his right and just up ahead he sees a Mexican restaurant with a name he can't pronounce. Adam's stomach then rumbles and he realizes that he hasn't eaten since he started on his Epic Quest.

"Shit," Adam says to himself, "I'm hungry as a motherfucker. I'm gonna have to stop at that little restaurant and get myself a bite to eat." The author parks the hog in the tiny parking lot – which is empty aside from three other cars parked in it.

He steps into the little restaurant and cantina and begins taking in the welcoming atmosphere. The short wooden bar top with the four tall chairs being used as stools along the wall to the immediate right of the entrance and the neon-lit whiteboard hanging above it with "Mexican Beer: $5" written on it. The counter situated in the adjacent corner where you order your food has the entire miniature-looking kitchen fully exposed behind it. The top half of the walls are painted yellow, while the bottom half is painted orange; and along each wall are decorations celebrating the proud culture of the owners and their patrons. Adam smiles at all of this as well as the little ice cream cooler a few feet before the counter with a Spanish brand name and some cute-looking character on it.

The author walks up to the counter and a very pretty, young Latina girl greets him there and asks him with a smile, "Order?"

Adam looks at the menu a moment, then answers, "I would like the number 3 and a cherry Pepsi."

The girl at the counter hits a few keys on the cash register and repeats, "Number 3 and a cherry Pepsi?" Adam nods his head and she tells him the total is ten dollars and seventy cents.

Adam reaches into his pocket, remembering as he does that he still does not have his wallet. Yet somehow, he miraculously produces a ten-dollar bill and a one-dollar bill from his pocket.

"Must be the doing of The High Priestess of Soul," the author figures in his head as he hands the cash to the girl behind the counter. The girl gives Adam his change and tells him he can wait at a table, and his food will be brought to him shortly.

But before the author goes to sit at a table, he asks the girl, "Also, if you could tell me where to find it; I'm looking for the Ultimate Green Card."

The girl looks shocked, and answers in a low voice, "That man over there," as she points to a man sitting alone at a two-seat table in the corner next to a window.

Adam thanks the girl and goes over to the man, asking him, "Hey, uh, I was told to speak with you about the Ultimate Green Card?"

The man says without looking up at the author, "Ain't you an American citizen, homie?"

Adam responds, "Yeah, and so are all of you. But you know that isn't what this is all about. The government is trying to put me under – probably for being too black and too strong – and I gotta gather some 5 Sacred Items on this bullshit 'Epic Quest' to beat a case."

The man looks up at Adam, notices the Black Power Gauntlet on his right hand, and says, "Alright, sit down across from me."

The author sits down and studies the face of the man across from him. He has a rugged and handsome, short-bearded face with distinct lines and wrinkles telling stories from a long life of struggle, frowns, strength, smiles, and laughs. His black hair is cut short and in no particular style, appearing to be regularly covered by a cap. The sclera of his dark-green eyes are pink with sleepless nights, with bags underneath his eyes as well.

The man wears a well-worn, blue Carhartt tee shirt, khaki-colored, fire-resistant Carhartt works pants with a few holes torn in them, and tan leather boots. The man's rippling muscles give the clothes he wears shape.

Before Adam can say anything, the man says, "My name is Luis. What is yours?"

"Adam," the author responds.

"Nice to meet you, Adam," Luis responds. "So you say you need the Ultimate Green Card from my people?"

Adam nods and a Luis says with a grim facial expression, "Then I need to ask of you a serious favor."

Just then, the girl brings both Adam and Luis their food, and Luis suggests that Adam eats before he tells him what he needs him to do. "I do not want to ask a man to do anything for me on an empty stomach. Please, eat." The author accepts and begins to rapidly devour the tamales, beans, and rice before him. He takes hold of the 20-ounce cherry Pepsi and downs half the bottle in one swig.

Within 3 minutes, Adam has cleared his entire plate and Luis chuckles and remarks with wide eyes, "Woah! I've never seen someone eat like *that* before!"

The author chuckles too and says back, "Yeah I've always eaten real fast since I was a kid. I also hadn't eaten anything for days so I was pretty hungry."

"Then it's a good thing you stopped here," Luis responds. "What better for a starving stomach than the best tamales in River End?"

Luis proceeds to finish eating his chimichanga, then explains to Adam what he needs the author to do: "Adam, I'm sure it is no secret to you what has been happening to my people across America.

"We've been under scrutiny by the government for things the majority of us have nothing to do with. We had enough faith and love in our hearts for America that we've abandoned our various countries of origin and pledged our allegiance to the American flag.

"We come here, we work hard doing all the jobs that natural-born citizens either don't want to do or are too lazy to learn to do for themselves, we abide by the most minor of laws; all that American dream shit. And what do we get for it? Lies and accusations spread by the very government we had enough faith in that we learned every little detail about how it works just so we could work under it.

"There are always going to be a few bad apples, sure, but they are such a small percentage of us that they almost don't exist – especially when compared to those born here with bright complexions who have committed such crimes as the very ones we're charged with.

"And now is worse than ever. They've been snatching our people off the streets and scattering them across the country to concentration camps. Those masked men who capture my people act like they're the army of god, but they're more like the devil's army."

Tears begins streaming down Luis' face as he says with a frog in his throat, "Adam, they have kidnapped my nephew, Nico, just the other night. He's a law student who's studying down in Massachusetts, with the intent of eventually becoming Chief Justice. They kidnapped him down there and have taken him back up here to a camp out west of town in Dogwood County – probably tempting him with lying offers to be reunited with his family if he gives up his great plans for his life. I only know of his location because of the tracking app my sister has on his phone."

Adam thinks to himself, "Oh sonofabitch – now I gotta go out to the country on the *other* side of town. At least the folks of Dogwood are mostly good people – unlike some of the redneck motherfuckers I encountered over there in Rustbin."

Luis continues, "I ask you, please, Adam, save Nico from the clutches of evil. I sense you have the spirit of justice within you, and I can see that you have already acquired the Black Power Gauntlet. I have heard of the strength that it carries."

Adam promptly agrees to save Luis' nephew; not only to get the Ultimate Green Card, but also feeling a certain comradery with the Latin community in America: "I agree to save your nephew, Luis."

The devastated uncle hands Adam a smartphone and says, "Here is my phone, my sister put the tracking app on it so you can see his location on it. There should be a picture of Nico in my photo gallery so you know who to look for when you get there. For this favor my family will be eternally grateful. Much luck to you, Adam, much luck."

Adam smirks a little and says confidently, "It won't take any luck for me to save your nephew, Luis. I give you my word that I will not return here without Nico." Adam's confidence in saying this comes from his being fully aware of the dangers which lie ahead: He knows that either he will be reuniting Nico with his family or he'll end up dead trying.

The author hops into the hog and looks at the smartphone while parked. The tracking app shows Nico's location to be near the construction site where a big company had been building a new factory.

"How ironic," Adam says to himself as he turns the phone off and puts it into the center console. "Got a concentration camp right where construction for some shady-ass so-called 'factory' that nobody knows anything about is going on. That doesn't sound familiar or anything." Adam then buckles his seat belt and speeds toward Dogwood County.

The author arrives in the rural and typically friendly county of Dogwood in a matter of 20 minutes, pulling over as the image of the construction site comes into view. The hog parked on the side of the road, he once again looks at the tracking app to find Nico.

"So it looks like I'm close; only about 7 more miles away," Adam says aloud. "Looks like I need to keep going straight, then hang left onto Poppy Road for a while then go right down some road called Mourningwood... Man, they really got the poor kid out in the boonies."

Shortly after Adam turns onto Poppy Road, he finds himself behind a huge green tractor taking up both of the narrow lanes of the road. The tractor is moving at a turtle pace when compared to the speed limit of 50 miles per hour: the tractor is only going 20 miles per hour. The author continues patiently driving behind the tractor for about two blocks before he becomes irritated.

"Damn," he says aloud. "I get that he's gotta get to where he's going somehow but goddamn! This shit is gonna take forever!"

Adam drifts the hog slightly to the left, then to the right; looking for a way to get around the slow-moving tractor. The right shoulder seems to have just enough room for the author to squeeze the hog around the tractor. So Adam decides to thump the gas pedal and pass the tractor on the right; skillfully maneuvering the 4,000-pound hog to keep it as close to the tractor and as far away from the ditch on the immediate right of the shoulder as possible.

As Adam passes the tractor, the farmer driving it shakes a fist at the author and screams at the top of his lungs, "You damn somnabitch! I'll fuckin' remember you dammit! Mark my words, I'll remember you!" Adam laughs hysterically as he drives off and the sound of the farmer's voice fades away into the wind.

Shortly after passing the tractor, the author finds Mourningwood Street: a narrow dirt road. He turns onto the street and continues straight until he comes upon a strange-looking area apart from the rest of the construction site. He parks the hog and studies the area.

The area is to his left, about 20 yards off the road, across a field of lima beans. It is surrounded by a ten-feet-tall chain-link fence. The front entrance side of the barrier is a 12-feet-tall brick wall about 70 feet across, which blocks the front from view. Barbed wire runs across the top of the front wall and the entire fence. Two soldiers stand guarding the front entrance. Both are dressed in slate-gray military trench coats with matching balloon trousers, knee-high black leather boots that are polished like mirrors, red armbands on their left arms with the initials "R.F." colored brown inside a white circle, and bandanas over the lower half of their faces. Both soldiers are also holding Uzis.

Adam looks again at the tracking app, and sees that within the fenced area is Luis' nephew, Nico.

"Figured this would be the concentration camp when I saw it," Adam says aloud. "Now, just how in the fuck am I supposed to get in there? Ain't no way I'ma be able to climb over that wall or the fence part, and I damn sure can't get through those soldiers."

As he asks this, the author remembers the Black Power Gauntlet on his right hand. He holds it up and looks at it, saying to himself, "Well shit, now is a time when the power of this here Gauntlet is needed; let's try it out!" Adam steps out of the hog, and calmly walks across the field toward the entrance of the concentration camp.

As he approaches, the two guards point their weapons at Adam and one shouts, "Hold on right there boy! Just where in tarnation do you think yer going?"

The author continues approaching, saying to the guards, "I don't think you really want to fuck with me, cracker! With this Gauntlet, I got enough power to fuck both you up nice and proper!"

D the fairy godfather appears in front of Adam and stops him, shouting, "Wait boy, wait!"

The author stops a few yards from the front entrance of the concentration camp and asks with a puzzled look on his face, "What'd you stop me for? I'm about to kick these crackers' ass!"

D asks Adam to go back to the hog so they can talk, and the author begrudgingly obliges, pompously yelling over his shoulder as he does, "Don't worry motherfuckers – I'ma be back for both yall asses real soon!"

Once D and Adam are inside the pearl-white hog, the fairy godfather yells, "You stupid motherfucker! Are you trying to get yourself killed?"

Adam retorts, "What, killed by those two? D, are you forgetting I got the Black Power Gauntlet? Can't nobody fuck over me with this Gauntlet; I'm like a one-man army."

D shakes his head and says, "Nah nigga you don't get it! That thing didn't activate yet! It's only gonna activate when it's really needed!"

"How do you know it's not activated?" asks Adam.

"I know 'cause I done seen it in action before!" D answers. "The words on the back glow real bright and shit when it's activated."

The author looks down at the Gauntlet again, and sees that the letters are not glowing. "Oh," he says.

"Yeah," D says. "Believe me, I done seen that shit fuck up a whole motherfuckin' nation before. I know its power, but it don't like to work unless it feel like it. So you gon' have to find another way in that motherfucker; sassafras!"

The fairy godfather disappears in a puff of angel dust, and Adam says aloud, "Well then what the fuck is a nigga supposed to do?" Just then, Adam hears the familiar bone-rattling sound of a horn from a semi truck.

The author looks out the window of the hog, and sees a metallic-purple 18-wheeler with gold, 280-spoke, 45-inch rims. It's towing a 70-feet-long, enclosed trailer that reads in big, bold black letters across both sides, "Mo' Sexy than a Pregnant Toad". A man wearing a cheap-looking spandex costume, color-coordinated with the truck, is standing outside the cab, with some kind of strange smile on his masked face.

Adam smiles wide, steps out of the hog and says while approaching the man, "Well if it isn't my best friend: that no-good trucker, Stinkbug! How you been man?"

Stinkbug laughs heartily and says, "You know me – I been smokin' weed and feeling alright! I might even go to a bar tonight and get a little more tight!

"But anyway, I heard from the skreets that you got a pearl-white hog and when I seen this one here pulled over I just knew'd it'd be you."

Stinkbug and Adam laugh and embrace and talk for a little while, Adam filling his friend in on what had been happening in his life lately.

"Well goddamn!" Stinkbug exclaims. "The motherfuckers finally tryin' to get ya, huh? Yeah, motherfuckers tried to do me in before plenty of times. But you can't do me in without catchin' me goddamnit! So, why you out here now?"

Adam replies with a grimace, "Oh, you know, now I gotta rescue some motherfucker's nephew from inside of that concentration camp, but I ain't got no way of gettin' inside."

Stinkbug cackles and says with much bravado, "I can get you in there! All the motherfuckin' shit I've mastered: Like how I blew the evil space knight's dick into pieces with just one blast of my ray gun! Like how I rammed Godzilla in the ass and made him call me daddy! I drove over the grand dragon of the klu klux clan and I fucked chicks across all the swingin' states in America! I can get you in there with ease goddamnit 'cause there ain't nobody badder than me! I done kicked plenty of crackers' ass before and these cold motherfuckers ain't no different! I could just drive my truck through that motherfuckin' place!"

Adam begins to advise his big-mouthed friend against doing something so reckless, but Stinkbug says before Adam has a chance to speak, "But I don't need to do all of that shit! I can trick those two dumb motherfuckers into letting us in with some shit I learned down in Louisiana."

The author interrupts Stinkbug and says, "Now I'ma stop you right there. You learned some shit down in Louisiana? Like, voodoo or some shit?"

"Motherfuck yeah!" exclaims Stinkbug. "What the hell else is there to do in Louisiana? Get some gumbo-smelling pussy?"

"Nigga!" exclaims Adam. "Now, I just told you 'bout how I got a voodoo on my ass and I'm on this damn 'Epic Quest' jus' to lift it. So why in the hell wouldn't you just lift this shit up offa me so I can be done with it?" (It occurs to Adam as he says this that he still made a promise to Luis, and would have to save Nico regardless.)

Stinkbug replies with a heavy voice, "Nah, that's not possible. I ain't know enough to lift no curse – I only learned a little brain voodoo, that's all."

"Damn," says Adam. "Well then, how we gon' trick these motherfuckers into letting us in?"

Stinkbug replies with a cough, "Man, this shit boutta be slick! I'ma make them crackers think we's two of them." Adam puts his trust in his best friend, as the two walk up to the entrance of the concentration camp.

Before the soldiers can even say anything, Stinkbug chants, "Weak minds, weak minds. Concave behinds and big butts too. We some honkies, the same as you!"

The soldiers' eyes become wide and vacant, and they say in unison, "Yall are honkies like us. Come on in then." They proceed to open the gate for Adam and Stinkbug to enter.

Adam looks at Stinkbug and says, "Man, ain't that some shit? Now *I* need to go down south when this shit is over with and learn me some voodoo also. Can you make them do other shit too?"

"Way ahead of you, good buddy," Stinkbug replies before he chants, "Let's sixty-nine, let's sixty-nine. The man next to me looks fine; I'm gonna lick his dick and put my fist up his behind!"

Adam looks at Stinkbug in disgust, but his revolt quickly turns into laughter as he sees the soldiers take off all their clothes and go frolicking – each holding onto the other's hand – off into a nearby corn field.

"Haha that shit was great!" Adam says while high-fiving his friend. "You had me there for a second; thought you mighta been on some fruity shit yourself! But making those two crackers go off and do themselves – that shit's hilarious!"

"And I had a reason too," Stinkbug says as he picks up one of the soldier's uniforms off the ground and hands it to Adam. "Now you can get through the rest of that place undetected. I can't mind fuck all of them crackers at once! The most I can take is three at a time!"

The two best friends laugh for a full minute before Adam suggests, "Hey, Stinkbug. How about you put on that other uniform and come on with me into this motherfucker? Hell, it'd be nice to have you on the rest of this 'Epic Quest'."

Stinkbug declines the offer, saying, "Nah, I can't leave my rig for too much longer. I gotta make a delivery all the way in Georgia and this load I got ain't gonna contain itself for too much longer. But I'll see you next time I'm around the butt-fuck middle of nowhere!" Stinkbug laughs as he dances back to his 18-wheeler.

Adam then quickly hides the uniform left lying on the ground, changes into the soldier's uniform Stinkbug had handed him – remarking as he does, "Damn convenient that guard just so happens to wear the exact same size clothes as me." He then puts his own clothes in the trunk of the pearl-white hog, and finally enters the concentration camp.

Inside the concentration camp, Adam feels sick to his stomach as he looks around. Soldiers in the same garb as the ones who were guarding the entrance marched groups of prisoners of varying national origin – none of them European – away to various sectors of the camp, such as garment-making stations, re-education zones titled "Americanization Stations", and small shacks with no windows, visible plumbing, or electricity. The author sees a soldier sexually assaulting a young woman by the edge of the fence at the far side of the camp and all he can do is grit his teeth with rage.

Adam is approached by a soldier wearing a red hat who asks the author, "What are you, some kinda sissy? Where's your gun? And since when did they start letting yeller coons like you join IKEBB?"

The author replies while clenching his fists, "Well, they ain't give me no gun yet. And about me being in the IKEBB... they couldn't find anyone else to do the job because of the liberals. Also, I keep forgetting: What does IKEBB stand for again?"

The soldier's entire attitude changes as he hears the word "liberals", and he says while patting Adam on the back in comradery, "Oh, of course! Goddamn liberals – go cry me a river, why don'tchya?

"IKEBB stands for Idiots Killing Everyone Brown Brigade. Not sure who came up with the 'Idiot' part. Well, fellow IKEBB member, just head over to the church and grab a gun. Should be a few lined up in the pews."

The soldier points to an old brown barn with a cross hanging upside down by a nail above the doors.

"Dagnabbit," the soldier remarks. "I just had Jim Bob put that cross back right! Don't know why it keeps on falling down like that." The soldier then walks away in the direction of one of the windowless shacks where they keep the prisoners.

Adam then walks over to the makeshift church and enters. He is appalled by what he sees inside: The interior looks like a standard small-town chapel, except where there would usually be depictions and statues of some religious figures, there were banners with Ronald Fump's face circled in gold, painted statues of Ronald Fump's face placed on white-robe-wearing bodies, murals of white men whipping black people – the black people shackled in chains – while they harvest crops, large-print cloth banners with a single hateful doctrine which reads, "Leviticus 18:22 – Read it Fags", an Uzi placed every 2 feet on every single church pew, and a golden cross at the back of the altar with the orange-skinned Fump nailed to it.

The author walks through the church – a look of absolute disgust on his face – and finds himself at the foot of the altar. He walks to the back of the altar and spits in the face of the IKEBB idol.

"Fuck you motherfucker," Adam says angrily. Then the author begins to stare at the golden cross and after a minute he grins and asks mockingly, "Can I speak to jesus?"

Adam snickers and turns around to walk away, when he hears what sounds like the opening guitar riff to the ACDC song, *Thunderstruck*. He pauses, and suddenly the entire church feels as if it is shooting into the sky at a rapid pace –

much like wat happened to the lunchroom in the LGBT's hideout – which sends Adam crashing to the floor.

"Not... this... shit... again," Adam manages to say as the makeshift church rises into the sky.

The repurposed barn stops abruptly when the disembodied voice of Brian Johnson says, "you've been." A blinding light like lightning flashes on the altar before Adam as the chorus booms, then the music stops.

The author slowly rises to his feet, and sees the image of a tall black man in robes with a red cape around his shoulders and a crown of red roses around his dread head.

The man gives Adam a crooked-tooth smile and asks, "Yo nigga, wus good?"

"Jesus is real?" Adam asks in shock.

"Hell nah I ain't no jesus!" the man exclaims, offended, in response. "You know that shit my nigga! Nah, I'm motherfuckin' Super Jesus! But I ain't no theme park in the sky type of nigga ya heard?

"I used to pimp back in Golgotha, and one of the girls I had in my stable was a white Roman. Well, that bitch's daddy found out his little girl was whoring for a big, black nigga, and so he came his ass all the fucking way to Golgotha just to hang me on a fucking cross and make an example outta my ass!

"But somehow, the white man done got the shit all fucked up and think I'm some nigga in the clouds' son or some shit. Really though, I'm just a skraight motherfuckin' mack who been pimpin' across the universe ever since I was killed and brought back to life – but tha's a story for another time."

Adam is still shocked at the appearance of the apparent pimping deity as he says, "Well goddamn! With a backstory like that, it's no wonder somebody wrote a whole book about your ass!"

Super Jesus laughs a deep, cackling yet joyous laugh before saying, "True dat! But check this shit out: I'm really here though 'cause I know you needs some help right now. These motherfuckers is crazy to the mizax and you gon' need this pimpin' I got fo' ya to grab your boy, Nico, and get the hell up outta here.

"I'ma make it so that hog of yours'll be able to fly you back to where you need to go. But it's only gonna be able to fly till you get Nico back to his uncle, Luis. Drivin' flyin' Cadillacs is really my thang and I likes to keep it that way. But anyway, yeah, go grab your boy and take him to the hog – everything beyond that's covered by me already. Awright?"

Adam nods and replies, "Alright," as the image of Super Jesus fades away and the church returns to the ground. The author looks at the guns on the pews but doesn't take one as he takes out the smartphone and checks the tracking app to see if it will reveal which building Nico is in exactly. The app points the author to the immediate right of the church, so he exits and sees to his left one of the windowless shacks. This particular shack has a sign above it which reads, "New Liberations/General Prisoners".

So the author walks up to the guarded entrance, and the soldier there asks him, "What's yer business over here boy?"

Adam quickly responds, "Boss told me to get a head count in there – we're getting' ready to send 'em on back."

The guard purses his lips as he stares at Adam's poker face scrutinizingly for a moment, then says, "Alright, but make it quick! I got somebody comin' to buy one of the girls soon – so make sure yer count is minus one." The soldier unlocks and opens the door, Adam walks in with his jaw clenched, and then the door shuts behind him.

Inside there are three very young Latina women and one young Latino man, who's sitting on the floor with them – attempting to comfort the three crying women.

Adam calls, "Nico?" and the young man promptly stands up and with a serious look he says, "Get my name out your fucking mouth you nazi!"

The author responds, "I am not one of them, I'm a friend sent here to rescue you."

Nico retorts, "Then why do you wear the same clothes as the devil's army?"

Adam explains himself: "I stole this uniform from one of the guards out front! Your uncle Luis sent me here to save you!"

Nico repeats softly, "*Tio Luis*?" He thinks for a moment, then says, "Okay, but if you are saving me then you have to save these girls as well – two of them are 20 and one has only just turned 18 last month. They have families, parents who fear for their lives and have no way of contacting them." Adam agrees to save the women, and proceeds to help them off the floor.

Adam, Nico, and the three women leave the shack, and are met outside by the soldier who was standing guard in front of the shack, who is now conversating with the man who wanted to buy one of the girls. Unfortunately for Adam, the man intending to commit the heinous purchase was the farmer who the author had cut in front of while driving down the road earlier.

The farmer had been saying, "Yeah I wants the youngest one ya got," before Adam walked through the door.

Upon seeing the man who had cut in front of his tractor, the farmer screams, "You somnabitch! You're the coon done almost ran my tractor off the road!"

Adam quickly lies, "Sorry, but you must have the wrong person. I've been here all day."

"Nah boy," the farmer furiously responds. "I knows a face when I sees one – them tinted windows ya got on yer car ain't that damn dark!"

Then, suddenly, another soldier runs over, carrying by the hair on their heads the two front-entrance guard soldiers (both of whom are still nude). Both of them have some sort of white substance slowly dripping from the corners of their agape mouths.

"These two goddamn faggots were found fuckin' and suckin' each other in a corn field over yander!" the soldier screams as he throws the two hypnotized soldiers onto the ground.

One of the hypnotized soldiers looks up at Adam and points and says, "Hey, it's one of us honkies!"

The two non-hypnotized soldiers and the farmer begin to look horrified, as the farmer says with a shriek, "Oh shit! I heard about this kinda thing before! These two musta been hypnotized by a voodoo! And it musta been that coon what done did it – that's how he got that uniform!"

The soldier who had previously been guarding the holding shack points his gun at Adam and asks in a terrified voice, "J- just who the hell are you?"

In that singular moment of desperation, the author gets an idea as he shouts, "I am a voodoo master from down in New Orleans! I can make you shit out your guts or even turn your mind into mush! I turned these two men gay and I can do the same to all of you too!"

Adam holds up his hand, pinching his thumb and middle finger together as if he were about to snap, the men shriek out of fear and he continues, "And I will if you do not allow me and my compatriots here to leave this place in peace!" The soldiers and farmer promptly agree to let Adam, Nico, and the three women leave.

But after the five had made it outside the concentration camp, right as they were all loading into the pearl-white hog, the voodoo suddenly wears off of the two guard soldiers.

They both quickly tell the farmer and the other two soldiers that Adam isn't the one who had brainwashed them, and all five of the IKEBB members get into a nearby white van with the IKEBB logo on the side and speed toward Adam as he gets into the driver seat of the hog, buckles his seat belt and speeds away down the road; yelling out the window at IKEBB van, "You'll never catch me now, suckers!"

The van, however, is far faster than Adam had anticipated and before the author can get a quarter mile down the road, it's a car length behind him.

"Shit," Nico says in a panicked voice. "How we gonna lose them?"

Adam answers Nico with a smirk: "We're gonna fly away. I just gotta find out what it is I gotta do to *make this* fly." Nico looks at the author like he's crazy and begins praying in Spanish.

Adam ignores Nico's wailing prayers and the terrified cries of the young women in the back seat as he thinks to himself, "Now, Super Jesus said this thing is supposed to fly now, but his black ass didn't say shit about how to make that happen. Now who else do I know that tells somebody how to do something but forgets to mention one crucial detail?"

The author searches the steering column and the dash with his eyes, until he notices something different just above the steering column, on the shifter display. There is now a little letter "F" to the right of the first gear "1".

"Oh," Adam says aloud. "I must be blinder than Stevie Wonder." He proceeds to grab the shifter and push it to the little letter "F".

The hog begins to take flight just as the IKEBB van got within 2 inches of the rear bumper.

The women stop crying and Nico exclaims, "Oh man! You were being for real about flying away!"

"Damn straight," Adam responds as the hog cruises through the sky, over the seemingly endless fields of corn and lima beans of Dogwood County, and back to River End.

Adam and party arrive hovering above at the Mexican restaurant's parking lot, a mere moment after having taken flight.

"Well let's see here," Adam says with a poker face. "Now maybe I just gotta shift it into park to land it…"

The author shifts the pearl-white hog into park, and it begins slowly floating down downward, before suddenly crashing to the ground when it's still a foot in the air.

Adam apologizes to Nico and the three women, who accept his apology as they quickly exit the hog – scared the vehicle might self destruct next.

The five walk into the Mexican restaurant, and before anyone can say a word Luis runs up to his nephew and embraces him – tears of joy and relief running down his face – for a long moment. Luis begins asking Nico questions in Spanish, which Nico answers promptly, and Adam decides to go outside and let them have their moment. The three young women follow Adam out the door.

The author starts walking toward his pearl-white hog, but is stopped by the 18-year-old girl he had saved, who says to him, "I thank you for saving me and my friends' lives. We were all minding our own business late one night – headed for Alexandria's mom's house after a concert we'd gone to – when those devil pigs jumped out of some bushes, grabbed and gagged us, and threw us into their van. We are not even from this state – we all live in Tennessee.

"All three of us were born in the United States – not that it should really matter – but they claimed that we were illegal immigrants.

"They keep saying that all of us who have tan skin and are of Latin descent are the biggest problem with this country. But that is just a way of using us as scapegoats. It is my hope that one day, the American people see this and rise up against this tyrannical rule."

The author nods his head in agreeance as Nico walks out of the restaurant and tells Adam, "My uncle wishes to speak with you."

Adam goes back inside the restaurant and is instantly seized by Luis' embrace; and the teary-eyed uncle says, "I thank you eternally! You have done more for me than earn just this card."

Luis hands Adam the Ultimate Green Card and the author hands back Luis' smartphone. Luis then continues, "Please, tell me something else I can do for you to repay this favor."

Adam requests that Luis finds safe transportation back to Tennessee for the three women he saved from the concentration camp.

"I would do it myself," Adam adds, "but I have an 'Epic Quest' to finish."

Luis agrees to return the girls to their families, then says, "But still, I feel I am indebted to you. Here, take my phone number and call me anytime you need something."

Luis finds a pen and grabs a napkin out of the holder on a nearby table, writes down his cellphone number and hands it to Adam.

The author thanks Luis, who responds, "No, thank you," and then Adam bids everyone farewell as he exits the restaurant.

The three young women are still waiting outside, and Adam tells them to go into the restaurant and a man named Luis will get them back home to their families. The girls thank Adam once again before he gets back in the pearl-white hog.

Inside the hog, the author pulls out Lord Junkie's list and checks it for the next item he needs to get.

"Let's see…" Adam says to himself as he reads the list.

After reading what and where he needs to go next, an angry expression comes across his face as he asks, "Man, what the fuck? The next fucking thing is all the way over back by that ol' junkie-ass's castle! It's some damn Lost Bottle of Old English underneath some damn ruins on Example Street! And, man, I hope these damn ruins ain't too close to the motherfuckin' police station! I know they gon' have word out on what my black ass looks like by now!"

The author sits in the hog and calms down a little, before finally saying to himself, "But whatever, let's just go on over there and do this thing."

Adam buckles his seat belt, starts the hog, and begins driving back north toward Example Street so he can find the Lost Bottle of Old English.

Chapter 7:

Old Winos Can't Learn New Tricks/A Plot Revealed

Driving back down Example Street – in search of some unknown ruins, where the Lost Bottle of Old English should be – Adam looks at the Black Power Gauntlet on his right hand and says to himself, "You know, I've had this thing on my hand all day now and I ain't even really thought about it except once. Maybe all black people already have the Black Power Gauntlet then – maybe we just choose not to show it or forget it's even there."

As the author approaches the intersection of Example and Noxpin – the corner of which the police station and the River End County Jail is situated – he glances down at the digital gas gauge. Instead of showing him how many gallons the hog has in its tank, the gauge simply reads "E" and the digital estimated milage gauge shows "LOW".

"Oh shit," Adam says aloud, "I didn't realize I'd run the hog this low! I'ma have to get some gas as soon as I see a station!"

The author brings the hog to a stop as the light at the intersection of Example and Noxpin turns red, looks to his immediate right and sees the county jail, then looks to his diagonal left and sees a recently-built gas station.

"Great," Adam grumbles. "Let's just hope those pig motherfuckers ain't paying too much attention to that gas station."

The displeased author pulls the pearl-white hog into the gas station parking lot and up to one of the pumps. But as soon as he gets out of the hog, he realizes he still has no money.

Before Adam can say anything to himself about the situation, a middle-aged black woman calls to him from the sidewalk near the entrance of the gas station convenience store:

"Young man," the woman calls.

Adam turns to face the woman, and she motions with her hand for him to walk over to her. Never afraid to talk to a stranger, and figuring whatever the woman needed couldn't possibly be any more demanding than his Epic Quest, the author promptly approaches her.

The woman has skin as dark as black coffee, natural dreadlocks down to the ground, a smile as warm as the August sun she sits under, and eyes the color of dead pine needles. She wears a yellow and orange dress, styled like that of a great African Priestess.

She asks Adam, "You are on a quest, are you not?"

Adam nods and the woman says, "Then reach out your hands so I may feel the nature within you and determine if your quest is just or not."

Adam is reluctant to reach his hands out, thinking now that the woman might be up to something, but she insists and so he does as she instructed. The woman closes her eyes for a moment, then takes her hands away as she opens them.

"So you are the prophesized one," she says.

"So a few people have said," Adam replies with a touch of sarcasm in his voice.

"Ah yes," the woman continues, "you were destined for this path and yet you are the one who carves it. You have met La Sirène, whom gave you the Sacred Text of Happiness as well as insight into the recent plight of the People of the Rainbow – especially that of the transgender people. Then you met The High Priestess of Soul, whom reminded you of your people and gave you the Gauntlet which you wear on your right hand. And just before you came here, you witnessed firsthand the atrocities happening to brown-skinned immigrants across America, and earned the Ultimate Green Card.

"Now you are in search of the Lost Bottle of Old English – a seemingly pointless item in the grand scheme of things. And it appears you require money in order to complete this latest task... I know this, so take this 50-dollar bill and use it to refill the fuel tank of that gaudy vehicle."

The woman hands Adam a 50-dollar bill, Adam thanks her profusely, and before the author can step away she warns, "But be wary, Adam Ordell. The crucial choice at the fork in your path is soon approaching and your selection could determine the fate of this land and quite possibly the world. Do not take this lightly." Adam accepts the woman's warning as he steps into the convenience store to pay for gas.

He gives the attendant the 50-dollar bill and tells her to put it on pump 3. Adam proceeds to go outside and pump the gas, saying aloud to himself as he does, "Now, just where in the hell are these so-called 'ruins'?"

The author absent-mindedly looks to his right, and sees to the immediate right of the gas station parking lot large piles of rubble where a building likely used to be. A big, debilitated neon sign with pieces broken off still stands atop a 26-foot pole and it reads, "FUN RUINS".

The dumbfounded author facepalms and says to himself, "Ah, now I see. I really am a more blind than Stevie Wonder."

Once the hog is full of fuel, the author parks it in the gas station parking lot and walks over to the ruins where the Lost Bottle of Old English should be. Adam begins picking over debris around the ruins, the woman's words still playing in his head.

"Shit, just what have I got myself into now?" the author asks aloud. "I started this out thinking it was just some ridiculous 'Epic Quest' – but it seems like every damn thing I do, some motherfucker's telling me I got some kinda serious responsibility on my hands; and I don't like to take shit seriously!

"It's just like I told The Count the other day: I feel like I'm being pulled into some kinda battle that I gotta fight with my pencil and paper."

The author pauses, grinning to himself, reassured by his own words, then says, "And that's exactly what I'm gonna do when I'm finally done with this damn 'Epic Quest'."

As Adam absent-mindedly picks up another brick from the rubble, the ground beneath him begins to shake. The shaking lasts for a full minute, and when it's over a wino with a long, scraggly and kinky black beard appears standing before him. The wino is wearing a tan, suede leather jacket, ruffled khaki-colored cargo pants about 4 inches too long, and black military boots.

He takes a big swig from the bottle of Wild Irish Rose in his right hand before slurring, "Halt yee traveler! Have you come in search of the Lost Bottle of Black Crow?"

Adam raises and eyebrow and asks, "You mean the Lost Bottle of Old English?"

"That's what I said nigga!" the wino exclaims.

He takes another swig of the Irish Rose and continues, "I don't know why you young mothafuckas always gotta try and ack better than a nigga… You lookin' for the Lost Bottle of OE or what?"

The author opens his mouth to respond "Yes" but is immediately interrupted by the wino: "Don't try talkin' over me boy – I know what you're here for… In order to obtain the Lost Bottle of Old English, you must first answer just one riddle."

There's a long moment of silence. Birds fly overhead in the evening sky, cars wiz by the ruins – some of the drivers slowing down and peering confusedly at the tall, lean black man standing in a pile of rubble with a wino.

Eventually, Adam asks, "And that riddle is?"

"The riddle is nigga will you ever shuddup!" the wino responds with a hiccup.

There's another long moment of silence, and just as Adam is about to inquire about the riddle once more, the wino slurs, "But the riddle is this: What ain't no person, no weapon, drug, or food and still kills the most black people every year? And before answering the riddle; be warned! You only get to roll the dice on this question once – you seldom get to roll them twice."

"So, sometimes you *can* answer twice?" Adam asks.

"Don't contradict me boy!" the wino screams drunkenly. "You have to answer correctly the first time or you have to take my place here guarding the bottle."

He takes another swig of the swill in his right hand and continues, "Shit, how you think I ended up here? Only plus side is you get this bottomless bottle of Rose to keep you nourished for... the... all of eternity."

Adam ponders the riddle in his head; thinking hard about what the answer could be. It doesn't take long before the author recalls the words of the front-entrance guard of the Secret Society of Black People:

"I once heard a brother on a record say that *'jealousy is the number-one killer amongst black folks'*."

A confident smile comes across the author's face and he answers the wino's riddle: "Jealousy kills the most black people every year."

At first, nothing happens. Then, the ground once again begins to shake as the rubble between Adam and the wino parts, and a liquor bottle starts slowly rising from the parted rubble until it's floating at eye level with Adam. The author slowly reaches out his hand and grabs the bottle.

He examines the bottle for a moment, then says, "Man, this is just a regular-ass bottle of Old English!"

The wino chuckles and retorts, "Oh no, young padawan! It is said that is the very bottle of 8 Ball which froze Eazy E's balls over three decades ago!"

Adam looks scrutinizingly at the bottle, then responds, "Whatever nigga," before walking back over to the gas station.

The author enters the pearl-white hog, stuffs the Lost Bottle of Old English underneath the passenger seat, pulls Lord Junkie's list back out of his pocket and says to himself,

"Well shit, that was easy! Now all I gotta do is get the last thing on this list, which is..."

He pauses to read the list, then continues, "The Forbidden Flavor Funyuns from Hood's Grocer. Man, that's not even a block down Noxpin from here!" Adam buckles his seat belt, starts the hog and pulls it out of the gas station parking lot.

"Let's just hope getting these damn Funyuns is as easy as it was getting this bottle of FDA-approved poison," the author says to himself as he approaches the storefront.

Once he arrives, Adam parallel parks the hog across the street from the storefront. He exits the car and begins to cross the street. But at only halfway across the street, a 14-feet-tall tyrannosaurus rex with pink scales covering its massive body and big, bug eyes falls from out of the sky – creating a large crater of broken-up concrete underneath its giant feet where it lands. Adam immediately recognizes what the creature is.

"By god," the author remarks out of astonishment as he points dramatically at the creature. "It's Crackasaurus!"

Crackasaurus lets out a strange, eardrum-piercing, howl-like roar which sounds somewhat like a rooster's call as it proceeds to bust a funky move and stick the middle of the three claws on its right hand out at Adam. The author is thrown back – as if hit by a powerful gust of hurricane wind.

"Dear motherfuck!" Adam shouts. "That's only Crackasaurus' stance; it's only preparing to fight! But its power level is so high that its mere stance is enough to knock me back, flat on my ass! This means that whatever its first attack is could be enough to rip me to shreds!"

Crackasaurus looks to the sky and opens its mouth wide. A bright ball of white light begins to form between its jaws. Adam cleverly waits for the beast to launch its attack, before dodging at the last possible moment before it can hit its target. After its initial attack, Crackasaurus appears momentarily stunned.

Adam takes this moment as an opportunity to attack the beast, thinking as he rushes at the beast, "Well fuck it, I'm gonna have to fight this battle with my fists; though this damn Gauntlet still ain't activate itself."

He jumps up and punches Crackasaurus in its jaw in a corkscrew motion, while the beast's head is still hanging low. The fearsome pink monstrosity stumbles slightly, then lets out another eardrum-piercing roar.

The author tries again to strike Crackasaurus, but the creature is no longer stunned and so it swiftly turns around and smacks its attacker with its tail. Adam is flung far back, all the way back across the street into the unused plot of land which has become an unkept field of overgrown grass and wildflowers.

Lying in the grass – dazed and with the air knocked out of his lungs – Adam wonders within his mind, "What the hell am I gonna do now? There ain't no way I can beat that thing!"

A few minutes pass, and Adam is once again able to breathe. He slowly rises to his feet, and as he dusts himself off, D the fairy godfather appears to answer the author's question:

"Whatchu gonna do is return to Lord Junkie's Palace and finally clear your name."

Adam, confused, asks in rebuttal, "Yeah? And how am I gonna do that without the fucking Funyuns I'm supposed to get outta this ghetto-ass, would-be 'grocery store'?"

D gets within an inch of Adam's face, smacks him with all his little pixie fairy strength (which feels to Adam like a mosquito bite) and responds, "Boy, ain't you smarter than that? Ain't I raised you better?"

"Nigga you didn't raise me," Adam says.

"That ain't the point!" D exclaims. "Now, let me point out some obvious shit to you real quick: See that crater where Crackasaurus' crack blast hit? And see how its got those little white rocks scattered around it?"

Adam looks and says, "Yeah, what about it?"

"That's crack rocks you fool!" the fairy godfather replies. "Remember what that old basehead was saying about being from the old school back in Chapter 3?"

Adam thinks back for a moment, then remembers what Lord Junkie had said about being from the old school:

"I'm from the old school young nigga. I remember sippin' *crack* out the bottle while cuddlin' in my momma's arms; *oh how I miss those days...*"

After remembering this line of the junkie king's dialogue, Adam asks, "So you're trying to say that if I give that ol' junkie punk some of that crack, he'll lift this voodoo offa me?"

D replies with an exaggerated nod and Adam excitedly exclaims, "Yes! Now I can finally clear my name and–"

The author then has a revelation. A look of extreme anger comes over his face and he asks, "Wait a motherfcukin' minute! Why the hell did I just go and waste time – time I could have been spending finishing my upcoming book mind you – on some damn 'Epic Quest' if I could've just gave the nigga some crack in the first place?"

"Oh, you know nigga," D starts saying, "I got kids and an ex-wife and shit to take care of! I can't just be poppin' up every time your black ass needs somebody to tell you some obvious shit! Besides, maybe I didn't think about it until just now myself. And just where else you gon' get crack from nowadays except for a literal dinosaur? You know all the kids these days only do meth and shit.

"Also, you better hurry up and get that crack to Lord Junkie; you know the cops gon' end up rollin' through here anytime now – this being A: the hood and B: so close to the police station. Sassafras!"

The fairy godfather disappears in a cloud of angel dust and Adam calms himself down, before dashing across the street, grabbing a crack rock from the crater, then making his way back to the pearl-white hog.

Before he's able to enter the hog, however, he hears someone shout with a snort, "There he is!"

"Oh goddamnit!" Adam exclaims. "That damn D – always gonna go jinx some shit into happening!"

Adam looks in the direction of the shout and sees a dozen police officers just up Noxpin, beating on a black man. They all stop beating the man at the one officer's call and look over at Adam.

The officer who had shouted before now yells, "That's that nigger done escaped the jail the other night! Get 'im boys!"

The police officers begin loading into their cars and Adam says aloud, "Shit shit shit! There's no way I can escape a couple of police cruisers in this hog!"

Fortunately for Adam, however, a young Latino man pulls up to the little ghetto grocery store in a black and red pin-striped, hot-rodded, 1985 Monte Carlo SS. The car sounds like it belongs at the drag strip, with side-pipe, stainless-steel exhaust and a big, chrome-plated blower sticking out the custom-made hood.

Adam sprints over to the man as he's stepping out of the car and says, "Hey man, the police down there are comin' after me–"

The Latino man holds up his hand and says, "Say no more, I already know who you are. You are Adam Ordell, no?"

The author nods and the Latino man continues, "I thought as much – Uncle Luis described you as a giant with an afro. My name is Pedro, and my brother is Nico, the one you saved from that devil's army. You saved my beloved baby brother, so you can have this car to use to escape the police – though it still is not enough to repay my family's debt to you."

Pedro hands Adam the keys to the Monte Carlo and Adam thanks him as he jumps in the barely street-legal racecar and fires it up.

"Oops, almost forgot to put on my seat belt," Adam says aloud as he quickly buckles up then peels out toward Lord Junkie's Palace.

The police brigade doesn't take long to catch up to Adam, and the cruiser in front almost collides with the rear bumper of the Monte Carlo as the author cuts a sharp left onto Example Street. The brigade stays within 2 cars' length of Adam as he turns right onto Peanut Drive.

"Fuck man!" Adam, the apparent racecar driver, exclaims. "I gotta put some distance between me and them rollers!"

Then, Adam notices two buttons zip-tied to the gear shifter: one blue and one red.

"Fuck it then," the author says as he presses the blue button.

The Monte Carlo gets a sudden jolt of speed – the speedometer needle pushed until it breaks – and the police squad becomes nothing but a spec of red and blue in the rearview mirror. Adam laughs triumphantly as he approaches West Douglass Boulevard, applying the breaks as he draws closer. The break pedal instantly goes to the floor.

"Uh oh," Adam says aloud as he pushes the emergency brake pedal – only to find it too is nonoperational.

The author begins to panic – the dog-eared factory known as Lord Junkie's Palace now coming quickly into sight. He slams the gearshift into reverse, but the car continues on forward at the same velocity, without change.

Now only 500 feet from Lord Junkie's Palace, Adam exclaims, "Damn man! Just how ghetto is this car?"

In anticipation of his inevitable death, the author begins to curse every single person he believes led him to this point, before looking down and once again seeing the little red button zip-tied to the gear shifter, as well as a little black switch just below the radio.

"Let's hope this button is for line lock – 'cause I'm really not ready to die you know!"

Adam flips the switch and pushes the red button. The tires begin screeching down the road, and just before the Monte Carlo slams into Lord Junkie's Palace, Adam cuts the steering wheel left as far as it can go. The car spins sideways and comes crashing through the front wall of the ghetto palace.

Sirens can be heard in the distance, so Adam stumbles out of the Monte Carlo and runs deeper into the palace to get to Lord Junkie. He makes his way to the dilapidated throne room where the junkie king sits atop his throne of rubble and garbage.

"Alright you junkie bitch," starts Adam, "I went all across the motherfuckin' city and I got the shit you asked for! Now lift this voodoo up offa me!"

Lord Junkie cackles and chortles, "Gives me the items first young nigga, then I lift that curse offa ya!"

A rotted, moldy old table appears before Adam and the author asks, "But of course, wouldn't you rather have what's behind the third door?" Adam smirks and pulls the crack rock from his pocket as Lord Junkie begins to drool.

"Is that... crack?" the junkie king asks.

Adam replies that it is and Lord Junkie begs, "Man, you gotta let me have it! Look man," he pulls a McCancer bag from somewhere behind him, "I got a double cheeseburger I'll trade you for it!"

The author just looks at Lord Junkie with an expression of disgust, as the junkie king continues his haggling: "Okay okay, then what about this?"

Lord Junkie produces an old car radio, which looks suspiciously like the one stolen from Adam's own truck a few months ago.

"This stereo is top of the line baby! It's worth like 500 dollars! I'll trade you this for that little, itty bitty crack rock."

Adam almost laughs at the now desperate junkie as he continues his plea: "Man, come on! I'll suck your dick!"

Lord Junkie then gets on his knees before Adam and the author yells, "Motherfucker you know what I want! Lift this damn voodoo off me and I'll give you the junk!"

"Oh, that old shit?" replies the basehead. "I had forgot all about that shit."

Suddenly, a cold chill sweeps through the room, and a raspy, con-man-like voice commands, "Lord Junkie! What the fuck are you doing?"

A fat man in a long, hooded black cloak comes out of the shadows of the throne room, holding a small pistol and pointing it in Adam's direction.

Lord Junkie begins to stammer "Oh, uh, I was jus–" but is interrupted by the mysterious cloaked man: "Don't even talk right now! You're fired!

"Now, Adam, place all three of the Sacred Items on the table and Lord Junkie will remove your curse accordingly."

"I've heard his voice somewhere before, but where?" Adam thinks to himself as he slowly puts the Sacred Text of Happiness and the Ultimate Green Card on the table before him. The Black Power Gauntlet remains on his hand, however, as it will not come off.

The cloaked man notices this and says, "Eh, whatever – that puny thing never stopped us from keeping you animals in the ghetto anyway. Probably because it doesn't even really work."

The items on the table then disappear, and the sound of sirens now blares just outside the palace walls, then stops and is replaced by the sound of pigs' feet reverberating throughout the palace walls.

"Lord Junkie!" the cloaked man calls once more. "Lift the curse now – we have no more use for him."

Lord Junkie then pulls the Uzi from his waistband, fires off a couple of rounds into the open air above his throne and proceeds to chant, "Little feets, oh little feets! Bright-blue piss and monkey meats!"

The sound of the police officers storming through the palace all-of-a-sudden disappears.

Adam recognizes the way in which the cloaked man called his people "animals", and so he yells, "Now just hold on a second, I know who you are! You're the goddamn president!

The evil and idiotic, Ronald T. Fump! What iniquities are you looking to enact with those items?"

The cloaked man laughs and throws off his cloak – revealing that he is indeed who Adam accused him of being: Emperor Fump.

His carrot-colored skin seems to flake away with the breeze which blows into the throne room from the massive hole in its ceiling. His platinum-dyed hair is stringy and thin like corn silk. His eyes are angry, showing feelings of incompetence, the compulsion to overcompensate, and the hunger for power.

He wears a slate-gray jacket similar to the trench coats worn by the IKEBB soldiers, only with a gaudy-looking brown leather belt worn on the outside of the coat, pulled tight around Fump's massive waist and some sort of black cross on his left breast pocket.

Fump lets out a long-winded, high-pitched laugh which sounds similar to a snake's hiss before he retorts, "So you figured out it was me, Fump, the king of America! And now you want to know what I'm going to do with these Sacred Items? Well, I guess I'll tell you about my plot since you are so harmless:

"For some time now, a revolution has been brewing about this area. I know this because of snitches in the street. I also know of a prophesy which works against me, stating that you would gather the three Minority Powers to oppose me."

Fump pulls out the Sacred Text of Happiness and the Ultimate Green Card from his jacket pocket. "See, these 'Sacred Items' are actually two of the Minority Power Items. I would have liked to have that Gauntlet too, to be safe, but it seems quite attached to your useless right arm. And the other two items you went to retrieve were all Lord Junkie's business – I'll have to have a talk with him after this." Fump glares in Lord Junkie's direction as the junkie king yelps.

"But anyways," the evil emperor continues, "as the Emperor of the New Empire of the United States of Oppression, I cannot afford a shift in public compliance. So I manipulated you, Adam Ordell, to gather all three of the Minority Power Items so that the revolution may be foiled!"

Emperor Fump cackles in his hissing laugh and Adam screams, "You won't get away with this, Fump! The people have the right to fight against you and your evil tyranny!"

Fump chortles, "The people have the right to fight *me*? Ha ha! The people have only those rights that *I* choose to give them!

"And besides, the people are and always will be too willfully blind, too lazy and too complacent to resist me! It was only those items which gave them hope! But now that I possess those items, they have no hope and no future!"

But then, all of a sudden, the Black Power Gauntlet begins to glow. Adam can feel a newfound strength coursing through him. His body feels light as air, his mind clear of thoughts of despair and defeat. The author feels stronger and more powerful than ever before – like some sort of superhero.

"Oh it's your ass now, Fump!" Adam triumphantly exclaims as he rushes at Fump faster than a 9-milimeter bullet.

Lord Junkie steps in his path before he can reach Fump, however, and says, "Oh no baby! You gonna hafta get through me first!"

"Gladly," Adam responds as he strikes Lord Junkie across his jaw before he can move out of the way. Meanwhile, Fump once again disappears into the shadows of the throne room.

Lord Junkie falls back, then in a blur of rapid movement, he dashes to the other side of the room from Adam, saying, "Ooo, I'm bleedin' now! But I bet you won't be able to lay another hand on me baby!"

Adam dashes after Lord Junkie, who evades him with effort. Adam chases Lord Junkie around the throne room, until the junkie king ascends with a great leap to the second floor of his palace.

"Damn you motherfucking junkie!" Adam screams as he chases after the junkie.

The second floor of the crumbling factory appears to have used to been an office space, with rotting cubical walls creating a labyrinth of mold and mildew-covered office chairs, desks, tables, filing cabinets, and other such office supplies.

Adam cannot see Lord Junkie but hears his wheezing, high-pitched cackling. So he runs around the office space, knocking down entire cubical walls with effortless swings of the mighty Black Power Gauntlet. Rats, roaches, squirrels, bats, birds, and racoons scatter about in the author's path as he searches for Lord Junkie. The author knows he's drawing close when he begins to smell the foul, rotten stench of the basehead.

Finally, he finds Lord Junkie sitting in an executive's easy chair behind a large, rotting oak desk. Adam takes the junkie by surprise as he drop kicks him directly in the chest. The author kicks him straight through the wall behind him, back through to where the massive hole in the second floor is.

The two fall back onto Lord Junkie's throne and Adam says, "I didn't have to lay another hand on you – junkie punk – a foot, rather."

The author begins to walk over to where he'd seen Fump last, but Lord Junkie steps in his path once again and says, "Nah baby, you can't just knock me through a wall and think that's it – I'm Lord Junkie! And junk is one helluva habit baby! Can't just kick me in the ass cold turkey – you can't just say no."

Adam jumps back from the basehead and thinks, "Now what the fuck? This ol' crackhead motherfucker just can't be beat if not even some caved-in ribs in his lungs can kill him! But I gotta get through him so I can defeat Fump! So there's gotta be a way..."

The author thinks for a moment, looking around the throne room for a way to defeat his opponent. He notices the four large brick pillars which hold up the ceiling – each the same distance away from each corner of the room.

"Those must be central pillars that's holding up this whole factory," Adam thinks to himself. "I'm sure with the power I got from this here Gauntlet I can knock 'em all down. If I can just find a way to get that junkie bitch to sit still for a minute, I can crush him and his master underneath this whole motherfuckin' building!"

He then remembers the crack rock he had placed back in his pocket. He retrieves the rock, looks at it, and grins.

"Don't you still want this here crack?" Adam asks.

Lord Junkie's eyes grow wide, saliva black as tar starts running from his open mouth as he says, "Oh wait a minute baby – I almost forgot all about that! I'll still suck your dick for it!"

"Nah, you ain't gotta do hardly a thing to get it now," Adam responds. "I'm admitting defeat to you and your junkie ways, and this here crack is a peace offering. All you gotta do is sit on that throne of yours, grab your pipe, and smoke this shit up."

Lord Junkie falls for Adam's ruse, of course, and immediately takes a seat atop his garbage throne. Adam tosses Lord Junkie the crack rock, which the junkie puts into his pipe and begins smoking. As Lord Junkie is getting high off the crack, he doesn't pay any attention to Adam, who is running in a big circle around the room, knocking out each support pillar as he passes by it.

Once the last pillar has been knocked down, a loud cracking sound like a small explosion can be heard as the palace begins to crumble. Adam runs out of the ghetto palace – Lord Junkie still smoking his pipe – and as he goes through the front doors he stops running and simply walks away as Lord Junkie's Palace crumbles, and the sun in the sky sets behind him.

After he's a few yards away from the now crumbled ghetto palace, Adam begins jumping for joy and punching the Black Power Gauntlet toward the sky.

"Yes!" Adam exclaims, thinking he has been victorious. "I finally done cleared my name, defeated that junkie sonofabitch, and I even took out Fump as a bonus! This is motherfuckin' great! My 'Epic Quest' is finally through!"

But as he's celebrating his apparent victory, D the fairy godfather appears once more and stops him, saying, "Nah man, that wasn't really Fump in there! That was just a damn hologram; the real Fump is laughing his ass off right now in Washington DC!"

Adam stops his joyous dancing and says, "Oh what the fuck? Can't this damnable 'Epic Quest' just be over with already?"

D answers Adam's question: "Your quest *is* done, boy! I was just telling you the facts about Fump! Didn't want you goin' around believin' some shit that ain't true."

Adam stands, looking into the distance for some time. He stares, not knowing what to do next. Has he completed his quest? Has he fulfilled his duty? Could this whole thing just be over? He didn't know. The author felt as if he had only won a battle – yet the war still raged on.

"But don't feel bad or worry about it," D says to Adam. "You did your part – you cleared your name. Now you can go back to being an author. You can finish that next dope-ass book you been working on and leave all the Epic Quest shit behind you."

Adam thinks about what his fairy godfather said, then asks, "But what about that prophesy? Ain't there something else I'm supposed to do besides just clear my name?"

"Psh, fuck that prophesy right in the ass," the fairy godfather responds. "There ain't nothing you gotta do now. Like I said, you can go back to being an author now."

Then, Adam remembers The Count's mention of a critical choice he gets to make. He smiles, knowing what path he's going to go down now.

"Yeah, I'ma go back to being an author alright," Adam says. "But I'ma also get my fucking revenge on that damnable Fump for setting me up on this 'Epic Quest' in the first place. And maybe in the process, I'll help a few people out too."

D the fairy godfather smiles, then a serious look comes over his face as he asks Adam, "Are you sure you wanna do this? I mean, hey, it's like I told you in the beginning: I'm your fairy godfather motherfucker! I'ma be here with you no matter what and honestly, I stand for what you fight for.

"But I'm just letting you know that humans are ungrateful. If you do this thing, they'll never appreciate it or thank you for it. Maybe if you're lucky, they'll come around a few decades after you're already dead and give your name some kindsa phony-ass award, but that's it. Hell, you might just come outta this thing people hating you for what you've done."

Adam replies, "I know. And to be honest, I'm thinking more about my revenge than the greater good of humanity right now anyway – I didn't just say that to be coy.

"But I also see how people struggle, how much pain this motherfucker has caused already and I can't take the shit no more. So I gotta fight this bitch to keep riding – and that's that."

D nods his approval and then says, "Alright then, I ain't mad at ya. Sassafras!"

Adam then says to himself, "Well, first goddamn thing I'ma do before I get to all that shit is go home, take a shower, and sleep in my own motherfuckin' bed!"

Then he looks at the huge rubble pile which used to be Lord Junkie's castle, with the crushed rear end of the Monte Carlo sticking out.

"Guess I'll be walking home though," he says.

But miraculously, the pearl-white hog appears before Adam's very eyes. The author gets in the driver's seat, and a sticky note is stuck onto the steering wheel, reading:

"Saved the Caddy for you; hate to see it go to waste my nigga.

-SJ"

Adam smiles as he takes the note off the steering wheel, puts it in the visor, then puts on his seat belt, starts up the hog, and finally drives back home with a satisfied and determined smile on his face.

Meanwhile in Washington DC:

Fump laughs his hissing laugh in a hysterical manner as he turns off the hologram projection machine.

"That fucking dummy," Fump chortles to himself. "To willingly give up the Minority Power Items just like that – how wonderful! Now I will have them destroyed at my next rally – live on TV – and then there will be nobody left to stop our plans!"

Fump sits back down behind his desk, looks at the framed portrait of *Kroshechnyy Von Chlen*, his secret gay lover, and begins to lightly caress the picture with his finger as he speaks to the picture passionately, "It's all for you, baby. And just to think, my sweet Petunia, this has been the biggest and boldest tomfuckery in the history of the United States, and it's all been a one-man job at that!"

Suddenly, a white-as-snow, insect-like, anthropomorphic creature enters the Oval Office. The creature's body is the size of a regular human male, standing about 5 feet and 10 inches tall, with four long, skeletal, insect-like legs with two knees per leg – one knee bending backwards and the other bending forward. Its torso is short in proportion to the rest of its body, with an excess of fat protruding obscenely at its belly and chest area. Its two arms are short and girthy, with only three elongated fingers, which appear to be without bones, as its hands. The creature's head is somewhat human-like, yet two times the size of a man's head and bulbous, with a far over-sized mouth which wraps around, almost to the back of its head. The eyes are large and situated on opposite side of the head – both solid green without visible pupils or iris. And instead of hair, the creature has only a pair of long antennae protruding from its forehead.

The creature wears no pants or shoes, with what appears to be a fully-erect, peanut-size male sex organ between its legs. It wears only a coat like Fump's, except with a red armband which has some vile-looking symbol in place of the initials "R.F.".

The repulsive creature approaches the gagging Fump and asks menacingly in its robotic voice, "You mean it was a *two-man* job, correct?"

Fump stammers, "Erm, yes! I-I meant to s-say a two-man job, Mr. Husk, sir!"

Mr. Husk attempts a smile as he begins caressing Fump's cheek and leans in close to the Emperor and whispers in his ear, "That's good to hear you sexy porpoise-shaped thing you."

He then starts licking Fump's ear with his long, sticky tongue and says, "You know, I designed the new Messla SUV after your body... Now... Give me some of that man pussy."

Red-cheeked with a half erection in his pants, Fump slams the portrait of *Kroshechnyy Von Chlen* down on his desk and begs, "But Mr. Husk, the election is long over! I got what I wanted and so did you! And me and *Kroshechnyy Von Chlen* are getting pretty serious; I can't just keep sneaking around behind his back anymore!"

Mr. Husk slams his three-fingered, hand-like appendage down on the desk and asks sharply, "Must I remind you of all the sacrifices I've undergone for you? Yes, the election is over you pathetic imbecile but the degradation of my business is not! Not to mention, Ronny, how it was your little European boy toy who recruited and convinced me to help you in the first place! So you *will* bend that ass over this desk, and I *will* stick my dick in it, and you *will* like it!"

Fump gives in, and the two have prison-like sex for the next two minutes. As usual, Fump doesn't feel anything until Mr. Husk is close to climax, at which time two-inch-long spikes eject from all sides of the creature's sex organ and tear Fump's insides out.

Once he's finished, Mr. Husk exits the room without another word, leaving Fump with his pants around his ankles, curled up into the fetal position at the foot of his desk – crying softly like one of his own past victims.

A few minutes pass, and Fump's cellphone begins ringing. He scrambles off the floor to see who it is, and the caller ID reads, "Petunia".

He promptly answers the phone, saying, "Hello, Petunia baby."

"Hello my sweet carrot cake princess," *Kroshechnyy Von Chlen* answers from the other side of the call. "I miss you so much! How are you faring lately?"

Fump opens his mouth to answer, but breaks out in a crying fit instead. "What is the matter?" *Kroshechnyy Von Chlen* asks sincerely. "Is it that fucking electric-brained monstrosity again?"

Fump cries harder and louder and his secret lover screams, "That son of a bitch! Did he put his hands on you again? I'll hang him with his own tongue for this! Don't worry, baby, once the Minority Power Items are destroyed and our plan can be fully enacted, I will have him turned inside-out – asshole first.

"And speaking of destroying those items, were you able to obtain them?"

Fump's sobbing subsides and he responds, "Yes, I'm going to destroy them at my next rally."

"Excellent," *Kroshechnyy Von Chlen* responds. "Make that rally tomorrow morning – I feel a disturbance quickly arising. I must go now, my sweet carrot cake – these war-prisoner families are not going to kill themselves. I love you dearly."

"Love you too, Putunia," Fump responds before his secret boyfriend hangs up the phone.

Chapter 8:

The Offenders

Adam awoke late the next morning feeling refreshed and full of confidence in his own abilities. He gets dressed, eats some toast made from slightly stale bread, then heads for the LGBT's hideout, once again seeking an audience with La Sirène.

As he drives the pearl-white hog down the road, his seat belt snug against him, Adam's fairy godfather appears once again, floating above the passenger's seat, and he asks, "So, I know you gonna go fight and get your revenge and all, but just how are you planning on doing it?"

Adam's eyes stay focused on the road as he answers, "I'm gonna do what that sonofabitch said that damnable prophesy said I'd do: gather the three Minority Powers."

"You already did that shit," D replies. "Unless you sayin' you gon' drive all the way to DC and take them shits back from Fump yourself."

The author glances at D, thinking his fairy godfather must be blind, and replies, "Hell naw I ain't goin' over there to take that useless paper and card back! I already got the Black Power Gauntlet and that's enough.

"No, I'ma gather the three groups of minorities because that's where the power is: *the people.* We'll join together to form a team unlike any other seen before to fight that carrot-looking motherfucker right in Washington DC. Since, you know, it's only like a 1-hour drive from River End."

D begins to laugh as he says, "Boy, that must be the most unrealistic plan I ever heard! You know different peoples can't work together! That kinda shit only works in movies and TV and fairytales!"

The fairy godfather thinks a minute about what he's just said, then says, "Actually, nevermind. Your plan will probably work."

"What made you change your mind that quick?" Adam asks.

"Ah it's nothing," D replies. "Just be careful out there and holler if you need something – but don't be depending on me neither! Sassafras!" With that, D the fairy godfather disappears in a puff of angel dust and Adam is left to drive the rest of the way to the LGBT's hideout in silence.

At the front doors of the hideout, Adam is met by a melancholy welcome.

"Oh, it's you again, already," says one of the Twins of Confusion with a sigh. "Glad to see your return, I guess. What're you here for this time?"

Adam raises a skeptical eyebrow and responds, "I need to ask La Sirène for her aid in something... But hey, uh, why are you two so down-in-the-dumps looking?"

The other identical twin answers, "Because, this morning Fump destroyed our Sacred Text of Happiness. And we're not only 'down in the dumps', we're all furious with you!"

The first twin to speak continues, "We trusted you with our Sacred Text of Happiness and you let it fall into the hands of that rat-bastard, Fump!"

Adam apologizes profusely, and the twins say in unison, "Oh, it isn't us you're going to apologize to; it's our queen who you're going to answer to – go right in. She's waiting for you in her throne room." The doors to the hideout open and Adam thanks the Twins of Confusion as he enters, but the two ignore him.

Inside the hideout, as Adam walks through the halls he senses the overwhelming feelings of betrayal coming from the LGBT members. The glares of the few members wandering the halls feel like little pebbles being thrown at the author. Adam knows that the members must feel that he is a traitor and they likely want to execute him. But the author also knows how it feels to project hatred for your true enemy onto someone else who is closer, easier to reach and so he doesn't feel too distraught about the LGBT's current feelings toward him.

Once inside the throne room, La Sirène bellows at Adam with much anger in her regal-sounding voice before the author can even defend himself or make his proposal:

"Adam Ordell, how could you do this to my people? I've told you of our woes, and you listened with what seemed like such concern! But now, I see you have sold us out in order to clear your name. I thought that you were on a noble quest, but clearly I was wrong!"

Adam tries to speak up and plead his case, but La Sirène does not let him:

"Silence!" she commands. "I do not wish to hear any more of your lies! If my people cannot have their happiness, then they shall have their revenge on at least one of those who have aided in their destruction.

"Living in the wrong body, being forced into living society's view of how you should live your life: it is like being imprisoned. Therefore, Adam Ordell," one of La Sirène subordinates spits on the ground beneath them as Adam's name is spoken, "I shall imprison you in the dungeons underneath this hideout for the rest of your life! Guards! Take this traitor away to the dungeons!"

Two of the biggest, burliest guards step out of the line along the red carpet before La Sirène throne, and apprehend Adam, each taking one of the author's shoulders.

"Oh fuck," Adam thinks as the guards begin to carry him away. "I don't want to do it, but I'ma have to use this Gauntlet to break outta this shit here."

The Black Power Gauntlet on Adam's right hand glows bright as he almost effortlessly breaks free from the two guards' hold, throwing them both to the floor. The other guards leave their posts and rush at Adam, all at once.

"Ah come on!" Adam shouts. "I don't wanna hurt none of you! Just let me explain myself!"

"We've had just about enough of your explanations," a female-looking guard says as she attempts to drop kick Adam, who evades the attack with ease.

The author runs around the massive, nature-engulfed throne room, dodging and ducking the many capture attempts made by the LGBT guards.

Eventually, after watching her guards run around her throne room for more than ten minutes trying to capture Adam, La Sirène finally commands, "Enough! Traitorous Adam, bring yourself hither posthaste!"

The author promptly steps in front of La Sirène throne and the LGBT Queen asks furiously, "You've come back here, after your betrayal against my people, and you resist your punishment? And you tell us to hear you out? What could you possibly have to say which would change my mind about your sentence?"

"Your Highness, La Sirène," Adam begins, "I truly do apologize for what's happened to your people. But I did not betray you! As I told you before, my name's sake was at stake. A voodoo junkie had placed a curse on me, and at his mercy, I had to gather 5 so-called 'Sacred Items' so that he would lift the voodoo.

"But he was working in cahoots with the evil, Emperor Fump and I did not know! So when I finally did return to his castle with the items in my possession, Fump used his powers of trickery and greed to overpower me and take from me those Sacred Items."

But before Adam can finish his explanation, Recto-Verso once again bursts into the throne room and shouts, "If he did indeed take all of the Sacred Items from you... **THEN WHY THE FUCK DO YOU STILL HAVE THAT GAUNTLET IN YOUR POSSESSION?**"

The entire throne room gasps dramatically, and Adam says before any verbal speculation can be made, "I still have the Black Power Gauntlet because it is stuck to my hand."

The author did not like being interrupted, yet again by Recto-Verso, and so he angrily retorts, "If you knew anything about this gauntlet, then you'd know that."

The two begin arguing from across the throne room, throwing accusations and furious insults at each other before La Sirène once again commands, "Silence! So, you did not sell out my people to the evil one, fine. But surely telling us that is not the only reason you have come back here? You must offer my people an alternative for our Scared Text of Happiness."

Desperation can be heard in the LGBT Queen's voice as she continues, "Please, noble Adam Ordell, please say you have come here to offer us our happiness once more. All over the world they are taking away my people's Sacred Texts and before long, we won't have anywhere left to flee.

"We'll have to hide away once more like those before us did. Many of us will end up like Tilly and nobody deserves to live or die that way. Please, please offer us our happiness back!"

The rest of the throne room begins crying and pleading with Adam, whose hands are trembling with anger.

A vein bulges on the right side of the author's forehead as he shouts, "Shut the hell up!"

The throne room immediately falls silent and Adam continues, "You're all acting like some goddamn little piece of paper has the power to allow you to be who you are – as if man-made laws can govern your happiness. Well, fuck all that shit! No law, no rule, no guideline can give you your happiness! Only you yourself can do that! To hell with the various powers at hand and all that hateful shit they insist on enacting! Just because you may no longer have that little piece of paper which tells you who you are does not mean that you are no longer that person. You are who you are and can't nobody take that away from you!

"You must do like those before you and fight for your freedoms! And that is why I'm truly here: to ask for your hand, La Sirène, in defeating once and for all the wicked Fump. He is the one who almost forever disgraced my good name and he is the one who sent me on that ridiculous fucking 'Epic Quest'.

"I plan on taking him head on in his evil lair, but I cannot penetrate his security alone. That is why I am gathering a team of three of the most abused, hated, and feared minorities across the United States to create a team which will vanquish Fump and foil his fiendish plot. So what do you say, your Highness; will you join me? Or will you let a goddamn piece of paper decide your fate?"

The throne room remains silent for a long moment after Adam is done with his speech. Almost everybody from the hideout has crowded into the throne room, having heard Adam's verbal outrage coming from their queen's dwelling. They all stand, slack-jawed and staring at the author. Even the fish-tailed man from the stream had emerged from his aquatic dwelling to hear what Adam had to say.

Finally, someone from within the crowd speaks up: "Um, well, I don't speak for the Queen, but I'll go to fight the evil one with you."

Another person says shortly after them: "Yeah, I'll go too."

Then another person chimes in: "Count me in! I'd like to put this high-heel pump up the evil one's orange ass myself."

Before long, everyone in the throne room is voicing their commitment to Adam's plan to fight against Fump. Even the other two Trialmasters, Lily Green and Larray, enter the throne room and join Adam's growing army.

After a while, everyone quiets down and Adam asks their queen, "Now, La Sirène, I want your answer: Are you with me, or would you rather stay here and hope for a strike of lightning?"

La Sirène smiles, a single tear, colored blue by eyeshadow, running down her cheek as she replies, "I'm with you, Adam

Ordell, and so are my people. When are you planning on attacking?"

"I doubt you'll be all the way ready," Adam responds. "But I want to do this thing tomorrow. I'm going to gather the other two minority groups today, and I want all of us to meet tonight. Do you have a number I can reach you at?" La Sirène promptly gives Adam her cellphone number and Adam thanks her, leaves the LGBT hideout, and heads for the Secret Society of Black People.

Adam arrives at the front gate of the Secret Society and it opens wide before he gets a chance to put the hog in park. So the author drives through the gate and quickly arrives at the Black House. He is promptly let in, and once again finds himself in the incredible throne room of The High Priestess of Soul, where the black leader is sitting at her piano, not playing it this time but sitting in anticipation of Adam's arrival.

"The Count prophesized your swift return," The High Priestess greets Adam. "Though he did not say why you have come here, I can assume already why it is you have come back so soon: You want revenge on that Lord Junkie and Fump for their betrayal."

"Yes," Adam replies. "But it is not so simple as revenge itself. I want to unite the three most wanted minority groups in America and use their power to defeat the evil and wicked Fump once and for all."

The High Priestess of Soul looks out a window to the left of her piano, an angry expression across her face, as she retorts, "No. I have much respect for you, Adam Ordell, but I cannot help you nor can I send my people for this fight."

"But why not?" the author asks, confused. "That fat fuck has been terrorizing this nation for too long now! He has to be taken down–"

"You don't get it you fool!" The High Priestess booms. "Fump is only a threat now because he has fucked with the rights of *white* people – those of the rainbow affiliation! Where were the white protestors when Rodney King was beaten half to death in the nineties? Where were they when our ancestors fought in the streets for basic civil rights throughout the decades? Where were any of them during all of America's existence? In the ghettos, the so-called 'hoods' across his shithole of a country? Nobody ever gave a fuck about *our* struggle, Adam, so why should we put our lives on the line for theirs?"

Adam remains silent, and so The High Priestess of Soul continues: "If Fump had continued his crusade of fascism only against those with brown skins – such as the great people of Mexico, as well as all the other brown-skinned immigrants of this country – then very few would oppose him.

"But of course, now that he has directed so much hatred toward those transgenders, many of whom are white, now everybody all-of-a-sudden cares to revolt against him! Everyone now sees what we have been able to see this entire time: that Ronald T. Fump is a dictator and the true enemy of the United States of America!

"So my answer is no, Adam, I will not participate in this battle – because it is not ours to fight. Let some white man with an acoustic guitar he barely knows how to play make a folk song and sing about it on television or some shit."

The High Priestess turns away from Adam and begins playing a familiar tune on her piano. She also begins to sing lyrics about young, black talent.

Adam cracks his knuckles, and yells at her, "Man, that's fucking bullshit!" The High Priestess only sings louder, and continues to play her piano.

So Adam takes a couple of deep breaths, thinks for a few minutes, then says calmly, yet loud and assertive, "Alright look, I know what you mean. I know how it is, nobody giving a fuck about a 'black issue' until it's everybody's problem. I went through that ol' bullshit in school. But we can't just sit and do nothing! Once Fump's done with the LGBT's and the brown-skinned immigrants, who do you think he's gonna fuck with next?"

The High Priestess stops her playing, and answers Adam, "Mr. Ordell, I'm not concerned with that little-dick grapefruit coming after my people. In this Secret Society, we are safe from his attacks. And we still have our item of power: The Black Power Gauntlet."

The High Priestess then turns to face Adam once again as she continues, "And since that Gauntlet lies with you, Adam, I ask that you make a choice: Either you stand with *them*, and fight a million battles for a million different groups who would never truly appreciate you for anything more than a black version of their white heroes.

"Or, you can fight with us, your own people – who have showed you nothing but kindness and respect, comradery and love – and fight for what our ancestors would have wanted: our true freedom. You can stay in this Secret Society forever, live here as a successful black author amongst black people! You have many allies here, Adam Ordell, and you can have many friends too. Your name can go down in history with some of the greatest black people raised outside of Africa. You know in your heart what is the correct choice to make."

The High Priestess sits in anticipation of Adam's answer, while the author thinks to himself: "Damn, she makes a damn-good point. I could live amongst my own people! I could finally be appreciated for my diverse writing skills, my humor and my social and political awareness by a people who essentially created the only culture the United States has ever known…

"But, then, what about everybody else? What about the LGBT's I just recruited? What of my Latin-American comrades in the outside world? All the people living in poverty because of the one percent, the stories I'd never get to share with the rest of America. I can't just abandon my own people, though. Even so, I want my literature to be read by those who appreciate it, without it just being a 'black thing'… But, maybe that isn't all that I want in life."

The author finally responds to The High Priestess' proposition: "High Priestess of Soul, I have just considered your two choices over the last few moments. One seemed more alluring than the other, I'll give you that. But to be frank: Both choices laid out before me are bullshit! I shouldn't have to choose between any two groups because I fight for all people!"

The High Priestess gasps, exclaiming, "Explain yourself!"

"Gladly," Adam responds. "Look, I love my black brothers and sisters. It's true that over my few years on this planet, I've found time and time again that black people treat me with more respect than many white people.

"However, I have met many white people who treat me with the same respect! I have white family, white comrades

– I've worked along side white people who have treated me as equals and I've met many white people with not a racist bone in their body.

"Sure, I've met white people who probably burn crosses at night. I've worked for white people who almost made me abandon them and their cause. Same thing with the LGBT people.

"I've met some of them who are entitled, who seem to turn their noses at any issue that does not pertain to them. I've met some who can't take a goddamn joke; even when it's a joke meant to boost their moral.

"But, I've also met many more LGBT people who are kind, considerate, and give a damn about more than themselves! And also, a trans never called me nigger.

"But more to the point: We cannot act like this fight is only fought for the sake of one or two groups! We all can see that Fump is not going to stop until only the rich, white, blue-eyed and blonde-haired remain. He'll let just enough poor people live in their ghettos so that the rich may feed.

"You have this Secret Society, sure, a little pocket of heaven. But wouldn't you rather your heaven be spread across all of America? You mention also how you have this Gauntlet I wear on my hand, but has it really gotten us very far in all these decades? We must join forces with the other minorities, put our differences aside, and fight the real enemy! Not only Fump – we will only focus on him for now – but we must revolt against the entire system which keeps anyone it doesn't like down!"

The High Priestess rises out of her piano throne until she is floating in midair, then says to the author, "Adam, you are truly wise. You must have gotten such wisdom from someone much older – perhaps you are the direct descendent of someone of a superior intellect who raised you to be the incredible man you are today.

"But anyway, I agree with everything you've just said. For a long time now, I've been cold, bitter, angry at the world. Like I said previously, nobody ever seemed to care about the struggle of black people and it had filled me with hatred for this country and its people. So I built this great society and took in as many of our people as I could.

"But now you show me a new perspective. That perhaps, all this time I have been playing right into the government's hands. I've been segregating myself and my people from the rest of the country. So now I know what I must do: I must join you, Adam Ordell, and together with the power of the LGBT's and the Latin people of America we will vanquish the Fump and stop his evil plans. When and where shall we go?"

Adam explains to The High Priestess his loose plans: "I want to bring a swift end to his tyranny, so we will go to Washington DC tomorrow and defeat him. But, I also want us all to congregate together – La Sirène, you, one other and myself tonight. Do you have a way I can reach you at a moment's notice?"

"Just press the button on the interior wrist of the Black Power Gauntlet," responds The High Priestess. "Then say into it whatever you need to tell me; it's like talking over a cellphone, except more instant."

Adam flips his right hand over, and sees now a little red button on the interior wrist.

"Has that always been there?" Adam asks aloud.

"Yes," The High Priestess responds. "It has indeed."

"Okay, and can I call anyone with it?" the author asks. "Or, like, is it only registered to you? Because if I could have just called all you motherfuckers in some sort of conference call via whatever magic or voodoo this is imbued with, then this all woulda been a helluva lot easier…"

"Never mind that," The High Priestess responds. "And you know damn well that gauntlet has no magic or voodoo; only Black Power. Now hurry and gather the rest of this army so we can discuss the plan and be prepared to defeat Fump tomorrow!"

Adam nods in agreeance as he exits the Black House and heads for the South Side, in hopes of recruiting what remains of the Latin-American population to aid in defeating Fump.

The author arrives at the same restaurant where he had met Nico's uncle, Luis. Conveniently for Adam, Nico is already inside, sitting at a table, enjoying some tamales.

Upon seeing Adam walk in the little restaurant, Nico smiles wide as he stands and says with open arms, "Adam! You have come back so soon! That means you must need something. Tell me, what is it you need? I'll be happy to accommodate you and repay you for saving my life any way I can before I go back to Massachusetts to finish my studies."

Adam and Nico embrace, then sit down at Nico's table as Adam explains what he needs from the young Latino revolutionary: "Nico, what I need from you will more than repay what I've done for you. I'm gathering a group of America's most hated minorities to defeat Fump.

"It turns out that junkie punk-ass bitch was working with that oversized clown fish this whole time. Sadly enough, the quest I was on was all being influenced by him, and now the Ultimate Green Card has been destroyed."

Adam pauses for a moment to allow Nico to react the way the other two minority leaders had, but instead the law student had this to say: "I am not upset by the destruction of that card, my friend. The laws of this country mean almost nothing while that vile man is in charge anyway.

"I assume, based on what you have just said, that you want me and my people to fight with you against Fump. If that is correct, then my answer is yes: I will gather as many of my people as I can and we will join you and whoever else in defeating that fiendish Fump."

Adam finds himself momentarily at a loss for words, having expected Nico to be just as reluctant, if not more so, to join the battle against the Emperor than La Sirène and The High Priestess of Soul.

"Well, I," Adam stammers, "alright then! I want all of the members of the team to meet tonight and we'll attack tomorrow. Hell, if it's fine with you I'll just call the other two and we can meet here actually."

"You'll have to ask the owner," says Nico. "I'll go get him."

Nico walks over to the counter, tells the cashier girl that he needs the owner to come out so he and a friend can ask a favor, and moments later the owner is sitting at the table with Adam and Nico.

The owner is a big man, about 6 feet tall and maybe 260 pounds, with a shiny bald head and a big bushy moustache. He appears to be in his mid fifties, with wrinkles across his jolly face and some gray and white hairs in his mostly black moustache.

"My name is Jose," the man introduces himself. "As Nico has told you, I am the owner of this restaurant. I hear you have something to ask of me?"

"Yes," Adam responds. "I want to have a meeting with the leader of the LGBT's, La Sirène, the leader of the Secret Society of Black People, The High Priestess of Soul, and Nico here. I am attempting to overthrow Fump, and I require all of their help to do so."

Jose nods and says, "Of course, anything to get that damned Fump caricature out of office for good. His devil's army was just about to steal my son and daughters last night, but I have a way of warding off evil spirits."

The restaurant owner returns to his office space at the back of the restaurant and Adam calls the other two minority leaders to meet him and Nico at the restaurant. He calls The High Priestess of Soul first, and she knows exactly what restaurant Adam is talking about when he says it is "the little green restaurant that comes right after the underpass, going east down Orchid Avenue". But when he calls La Sirène, she has a hard time understanding where she's supposed to meet the author:

"Okay, so like I said," the author says into his smartphone, frustrated, "it's a little green restaurant offa Orchid—"

"And like I said," La Sirène cuts in, "I don't know where that is. I haven't really ever been to that side of town."

"Big surprise," Nico retorts under his breath, able to just barely hear the LGBT Queen's words through the phone.

Adam covers the microphone end of the phone and asks, "Hey Nico, what is the name of this place? I can't read the sign."

"It's called *Las Adelitos Taqueria*," Nico responds.

"Okay," Adam says into the phone, "it's called La Odaleetoes Tackereea."

Nico snorts as he chokes back a laugh and La Sirène asks, "Wait, how do you spell that so I can put it into my phone's GPS?"

Adam asks Nico how to spell the name, and Nico says with a smirk, "Just give me the phone, I'll tell her myself to make things easier." The author hands Nico the phone and he spells out the restaurant's name for La Sirène.

About half an hour later, when the night sky is just falling upon the little town of River End, all three members of Adam's team are huddled together at the biggest table inside of *Adelitos Taqueria*.

Adam begins: "Alright, I have officially got the most bad-ass group of motherfuckers America has ever seen: the three of you and myself. You all already know why it is you're here. We're going to take an army to DC tomorrow and we're going to finally defeat Fump. Tonight we talk a bit of strategy."

"Well," The High Priestess speaks up, "Since we've spoken earlier, I spoke with the rest of the Secret Society, and everyone that is able bodied is willing to go to DC.

"I also spoke with The Count, and he used some old Tennessee connections of his to recruit a couple hundred from outside the Secret Society to join us. With so much Black Power united, we are sure to vanquish Fump and any army he has to throw at us."

La Sirène then scoffs and The High Priestess raises and eyebrow and asks, "Um, excuse me, but did you have something to say, queenie?"

The LGBT Queen retorts, "Yes, actually, I find your talk of 'Black Power' to be very exclusive to only you. I mean, what about what the rest of us have to bring to the table? We are all equals here!"

"How contemptuous of you," The High Priestess says with some anger in her voice. "Yes, we are all equals here. But sometimes I wonder if *some of us* realize that or not."

La Sirène glares at the black leader and asks, "What are you trying to say?"

"I'm not trying to say anything," The High Priestess retorts. "You're the one who seems to have a problem."

The LGBT Queen jumps out of her seat and shouts, "Oh you just think that black people are the only ones to have suffered in this country, don't you? My people have endured just as much strife as yours!"

The High Priestess then rises out of her seat as well, slamming her fists on the table as she bellows, "Your people know nothing of the strife black people have endured in America! You've been put on the fast track to true freedom by the white man himself! That's the only reason you're even here in the first place! You don't think there are gay, lesbian, bisexual, transgender or otherwise amongst my people? Black people don't have the *liberty* of self expression in this country!"

La Sirène snorts and chortles, "Oh, it's funny you mention your people, seeing as plenty of them seemed to have come to my people's place of refuge instead of seeking respite amongst your sanctuary! It's almost as if they were shut out by their fellow black people!"

"Fuck you!" The High Priestess yells. "Those who have found their peace only with the likes of you are Oreo Cookie motherfuckers – willing to act as white as you command so they'll fit into your little clique of elitist rainbow assholes!"

The two minority leaders begin walking around the table toward each other, prepared to fight, as Adam thinks to himself, "Oh shit, I'm gonna have to break this shit up before both of these bitches end up killing each other and ruin the whole fucking plan."

He steps in between the two leaders and exclaims, "Enough of this shit!" He looks at La Sirène and says to her, "Look, La Sirène, I understand where you're coming from –

I really do. But there is no comparing your strife to that of Black Americans.

"Because, at the end of the day, no matter how much it hurts, you have the ability to hide the fact that you are LGBT or whatever else. I'm not saying that you should ever have to – that is fucking stupid – but when you are black, you do not even have that ability. When your skin is tan in this damnable country, one look is all it takes for them to discount you."

Adam then looks at The High Priestess and says, "And High Priestess of Soul, I know that the LGBT's have acted selfishly in the past – I have felt their misplaced wrath before myself. But now is not the time to dwell on past transgressions. We have to move past what divides us so we can come together and destroy our one common enemy."

Nico, who had been sitting quietly and minding his own business until now, chimes in: "The evil government."

"Exactly," Adam says as both The High Priestess and La Sirène sit back down in their seats. "For too long now have we been played like a grand piano by our own government. It has always been run by the rich and powerful, who tell us lies about each other; segregating us like different breeds of cattle, so that we're divided and confused – too weak to fight against them.

"But I'm telling you right now that this shit has to stop! Because if we continue to stand alone – believing some things are only black issues while other are LGBT problems and some are just immigrants' business – then billionaires like Fump will always rule the world and our battle will be forever lost. We have to unite under one cause: the final overthrow of the vile rich who would have us believe that we are each other's own enemy!"

The High Priestess and La Sirène look at each other, and La Sirène speaks first: "I didn't mean a word of what I said. And I apologize for my people's insensitivity toward the black cause."

The High Priestess then says "I accept your apology and I apologize for believing that all LGBT people are nothing but elitists. I can see that all you want is what anyone wants on this boiling hell we call Earth: happiness."

The two get out of their seats and embrace in comradery. Nico stands as well, and all three of the leaders and Adam raise their drinks to their newfound collaboration. They all sit back down, and discuss strategy and devise a plan of attack for the next couple of hours. After everything is said and done, the four rise out of their seats and begin to part ways for the night.

But before anyone leaves, Nico asks Adam, "Hey, since we're all working together as a team now, what are we going to call ourselves? We can't just call ourselves The Minorities."

Adam thinks for a moment, then an ear-to-ear grin comes across his face as he answers, "The Offenders. We've all been affected or otherwise offended by something the government has done at one point or another – it's about time we give them a taste of their own medicine."

Everyone likes the name, and so Adam Ordell, La Sirène, The High Priestess of Soul, and Nico become the supergroup known as The Offenders.

As Adam drives down the desolate nighttime streets, his seat belt buckled, on his way back to his humble, top-story abode, he thinks to himself, "Man, now I done got myself into some serious shit. I assembled The Offenders, a supergroup of my own design, and tomorrow we'll be fighting against Fump and his evil army! Am I really ready for something like this?"

The author looks at the Black Power Gauntlet on his right hand – the gauntlet radiating with power and emitting a faint light in the darkness of the night.

He then smiles and says, "Yeah, I'm ready."

Adam continues on home, and there he takes a quick shower and goes straight to sleep in his bed – his only preparation for what he anticipated would be the biggest battle he had ever fought before. A fight in which he would have to utilize the physical powers of the Black Power Gauntlet, the overwhelming unified might of The Offenders, and his supreme intellect to defeat once and for all one of mankind's most dastardly and wicked of all evil villains: Emperor Fump.

Chapter 9:
The Failure of Fump's Fiendish Plot

The sun rose over the horizon, bathing the land in its magnificent rays of powerful light. A few hours later, at 10:30am, Adam rises from his bed. The author gets dressed and eats breakfast. He then goes to the bathroom to brush his teeth and fix his hair.

As he's picking out his afro, Adam peers into his own eyes in the mirror and says aloud, "Man, I can't fail here. I done been fucked all the way up by this bullshit system and if this shit I'm about to try don't work then I'll never have my revenge, and the people will never have their freedom.

"And besides all that, man, I *still* ain't finished my next book! This fucking klu klux billionaire sonofabitch has got to go down! Hell, at this point I'ma miss my fucking due date. I hope my publisher was just bluffing about dropping me if I'm late."

His hair finally fixed, Adam leaves his apartment and finds himself torn on whether he should drive his old and reliable Chevy truck, or his recently obtained, pearl-white hog to Washington DC. His indecision doesn't last long, however, as he says to himself, "Meh, fuck it. I love you truck, but I ain't never had a nice-ass car before so I might as well ride it out for the rest of this story."

Adam arrives just outside the fence of the backyard of the White House, just over an hour after leaving his apartment, at 12:22pm. La Sirène, her army of L's, G's, B's, T's, Q's, I's, P's, A's, 2S's and many more are already waiting with Nico and his huge army of Latin-American people.

"Glad to see yall are already here…" Adam says. "But, uh, where's The High Priestess of Soul and the rest of my black brothers and sisters?"

La Sirène whips her long, curly hair dramatically and responds impatiently, "Where are they, you ask? Where the hell have you been? I've been waiting here with my army for 2 whole hours, and Nico says he and his people arrived at 5:00am!"

"Oh, shit, my bad," Adam says. "Must be that CPT, you know."

The three Offenders and the two armies stand idly by, outside Fump's usurped lair, awaiting The High Priestess' arrival for another half hour. The High Priestess arrives at 5 minutes until 1:00pm, with a large army of black Americans following behind her.

"Oh, were we the last to arrive?" The High Priestess asks.

La Sirène and Nico only glare at her, and Adam looks at her sympathetically, saying, "I got here a little late too; about 30 minutes ago."

"I apologize," The High Priestess says, blushing, then her face grows angry as she continues, "I really meant to get here sooner but *certain* members of the community took their sweet-ass time getting ready!"

A man from the black army speaks up, saying, "Hey now! I done said already: You can take a nigga out the ghetto but you can't take the ghetto out a nigga!"

The High Priestess yells back at him, "Hey! I told you already, we are not niggas! And there is no ghetto inside you – being 'ghetto' is just an ignorant mindset!"

Adam can see the tension building between the two, and so he shouts, "Shut the hell up! Don't do this in front of the others! Ahem, I'm glad that all of yall could make it – conscious or ghetto or otherwise."

The author finds a conveniently placed, large boulder to stand on and so he climbs up on it before facing all three of the other Offenders and their armies and gives a speech:

"Alright everybody; we all know why we're here today. We're finally going to take what is ours, what the evil and wicked government of this country has held from us for far too long now: our freedom!

"Today it is Fump and tomorrow it is Fump Mach II if we continue to allow them to multiply. Decades ago, when it was Nixon, the people attempted to cut off what they thought was the head, but found that this creature which oppresses us is akin to the Hydra. That's why today, Offenders, we cut all the fucking heads off and burn the stumps!"

The Offenders and their armies cheer Adam as he continues: "Just to make sure we're all on the same page, I'm going to go over the plan one last time:

"La Sirène, you and your people are to join forces with The High Priestess of Soul and the Black Society to obtain the Bill of Rights from the National Archives, wherein Fump has buried it deep underground, within its dark and desolate, hidden catacombs.

"Nico... wait, how the hell did you come up with that many people?" Adam now notices how large of an army Nico has gathered, maybe 5,000 people in total.

The young Latino revolutionary responds, "My people began hiding as soon as the devil's army was formed; it is only the ones who could not take scuddling around like mice that have been captured so far."

"Oh," Adam replies, "well, that's good because you're going to need all the manpower you can get. You are to lead your people to the IKEBB head office to take down their power station – it turns out none of those frozen fucks is actually human. They're all evil robots controlled by Fump's computers. You take down their station, I take down their leader, and they should all malfunction and burn out.

"I, of course, will take on Fump myself inside of the White House. If I am to perish, however, and you are all still successful in your individual missions, then combine your forces to take him down yourselves."

Adam steps down from the boulder. Then, a wheelchair-bound man with a salt-and-pepper goatee and apparent schizophrenia appears before The Offenders.

"It's The Grandmaster!" Adam exclaims.

The Grandmaster laughs a little and replies, "Yes, the Leopard Superhero is here at last, with the lyrical ability to blast at foes of the past. Power flows nobody knows where it goes except when it's pointed out the window of a bucket, through a musket at the player of a trumpet.

"Adam, you have done well to have followed The Prophesy thus far. This is where the tapestry ends, however, with you having gathered these powerful beings, whom you call, 'The Offenders'. From here on, success nor assured destruction is guaranteed."

Adam looks at The Grandmaster quizzically and asks, "Wait, you said something about success or destruction not being guaranteed from here on out. Does that mean that so far, no matter what, I was gonna succeed in my 'Epic Quest'?"

"Uh, well," The Grandmaster responds. "Man, don't be worrying about all that! You only succeeded because you didn't know that you would, and because you are who you are: Adam Ordell, the prophesized one. Look, just do what you do and everything'll be alright."

The Grandmaster suddenly disappears and Adam remarks sarcastically, "Oh, so I see, all these niggas got Houdini teleportation powers except me. Fine, whatever."

Adam then asks, "Everybody ready to do this thing?"

Everyone – armies included – say yes simultaneously, and so Adam says, "Alright then. Offenders, let's make some orange juice outta this dictator!"

The other members of The Offenders and their armies go their separate ways from Adam, and the author stands before the fence, preparing himself in those final moments before his great battle. A foreboding feeling of terror and the anticipation of calamity begins to come over the author like an all-consuming tidal wave devouring a small coastal village. Despite this, he uses the almighty strength of the Black Power Gauntlet to grab the wrought-iron fence of the White House and tear a 2-feet section from the ground with ease.

He is immediately surrounded by guards – each clad in the same slate-gray attire as the rest of the IKEBB – who jump out of the trees and bushes armed with Uzis and grenade belts.

Before the first guard can strike or yell the tired old phrase: "Give up; you're surrounded!" Adam jumps 20 feet into the air, then dives down and sends the guards flying from the shockwave of his impact.

The author proceeds to run toward the rear entrance of the White House, where he is confronted by yet another member of the IKEBB. This one appears to be a ranking officer of some kind, with a black armband on his left arm with two mistletoe-looking leaves printed above three horizontal green lines. He had a square-shaped face with large ears, bloodshot, furious eyes, and graying hair slicked back poorly with pomade. His face seems frozen into a strange expression, looking something between a scowl and an arrogant glare.

The man cackles and says, "You cannot go any further, see, and if you try then I'll shoot. Hell, I can shoot you where you stand for what you've done. So surrender and I'll only take you to justice."

Adam, who recognizes the man and thinks his appearance is quite laughable, replies, "You wouldn't shoot me – you never had the guts."

This remark makes the guard angry, as he shouts back, "I would too shoot you! I was in the army once, you know! And I wrote a book! That makes me doubly qualified to shoot you!"

The guard then lists off all of what he feels are his "qualifications for killing", and as he does Adam thinks to himself, "Goddamn! This motherfucker must have one of the smallest dicks on Earth or something 'cause don't no cold-blooded killer need to list off all these goddamn qualifications and shit."

While the guard is still talking, Adam hits him with a right cross and knocks him to the ground, unconscious. The author kicks his body to the side and as he lays a hand on the back door handle, he hears a voice behind him yell, "Not another move nigger!"

Adam slowly turns around, and sees a big, red, white and blue, Ford F250 with even more soldiers spilling out the cab and bed. One of the soldiers situated atop the Ford's roof (presumably the one who'd commanded Adam to not move) is pointing a sniper rifle at Adam's head – a laser from the scope shining a red dot on the author's forehead.

"Get your high-yeller ass on the ground, spread your cheeks, and prepare for your biggest butt fucking!" the sniper yells.

Adam is stuck where he is, like a deer in headlights, as the truck speeds toward him. At the last second the supernatural instincts given to him by the Black Power Gauntlet kick in and the author jumps up and drop kicks through the front windshield of the F250. He proceeds to throw all of the guards inside the cab out, and takes control of the wheel of the truck.

"Alright you honkey somnabitches!" Adam exclaims. "Yall better hold on because this ride is about to get a little Duke Boys!"

The author then does multiple donuts around the back yard of the White House, effectively sending the remaining guards in the bed of the truck hurdling all over the yard. The sniper on the roof, however, miraculously manages to keep a firm grip on not only the roof of the F250, but his rifle as well.

"Have it your way then," Adam says.

Adam then points the truck toward the back door, and pushes the accelerator at full throttle. At the last possible second, he jumps out of the truck as it crashes through the White House rear entrance.

The superpowered author laughs to himself and with a big smile he exclaims, "Oh yeah!"

Adam finally enters the White House, wherein he is suddenly overcome by feelings of extreme fatigue and total exhaustion. An invisible crushing weight upon his entire being, as if the effect of Earth's gravitational pull were instantly multiplied tenfold, overcomes the author as he collapses on the floor.

A sinister laugh can be heard from the shadowy, unseen depths of the White House as Adam struggles to ask aloud, "What... in the hell... is this?"

A hillbilly in nothing but overalls emerges from the shadows, the sinister laugh now revealing itself to be coming from his mouth.

"Yer a goddamned fool boy!" the hillbilly chortles. "Them Black Powers yall got ain't no good here – there's a barrier 'round the place what protects it from yer kind. That's why that coon Obama couldn't do hardly a damn thing an' why his hairs turned all white. There's a reason they call this the *White* House after all."

A horde of eleven more hillbillies, each more hill than the last, emerge from the shadows – each of them pointing a sawed-off shotgun at Adam.

The apparent leader hillbilly then states, "Now, I done said 'nuff to you; it's 'bout time I be lettin' my kinsfolk from West Virginia have a word with yall."

"No, not West Virginians!" Adam exclaims. "They might be carrying ducks that are carrying koi fish with them!"

The leader hillbilly snickers some more as his brethren advance on the debilitated author. Adam feels at his absolute worst. He cannot so much as lift a finger under the oppressive weight of his enemy's vile forces.

"So," the defeated author thinks to himself in what he believes are his last perilous moments, "it looks like I'm finally at the end of my rope. It was a good fight while it lasted, I guess. Hope the others are faring well in their battles – hopefully they'll find a way to defeat Fump on their own. Everybody either dies or gets killed at one point – I just wish I could have defeated that punk motherfucker first."

As the world seemingly begins to fade to black, shouts arise from the darkness, and then the sound of a glass bottle shattering and a small explosion can be heard. Suddenly, the all-encompassing darkness around Adam disappears and the author finds that he can once again move his body with ease.

He rises from the ground and finds a group of young, vigilante-looking people rushing into the White House; throwing Molotov cocktails at the hillbillies and wildly swinging baseball bats and large tree branches about them. Adam almost immediately recognizes this group as those he had stopped from destroying a Messla much earlier on his journey when he sees their leader approaching.

"Sidelines my ass!" the leader exclaims when he reaches Adam. "You're leading a whole damn revolution over here! And we're here to help in any way we can. We've already deactivated the white power shield so that shouldn't be a problem anymore. What else you need us to do?"

"Just hold off any other guards from getting in my way," Adam instructs. "I'm headed for the Oval Office now to finish this shit once and for all."

The former Messla leader promises he and his people will do as the author has said, and Adam races down the hallway toward where he, for some inexplicable reason, knows the Oval Office is.

As Adam runs through the hall, the rage within him grows. He begins to think of all the people Fump has hurt – so many lives thrown off bridges because of his evil policies. He thinks of the LGBT's hiding underground – unable to surface because of Fump's scapegoat plot. He thinks of Latina mother crying in the street – her family gone and presumably lost forever. Adam thinks of the impoverished Americans without the means to survive; without food or a job – some disabled and unable to get the medical help they require.

The author thinks last of all the poor fools brainwashed by the untruths being fed to them by their trusted government as he kicks down the doors of the Oval Office. The first thing he sees is the image of Fump sitting behind the desk, pouty expression of hatred and bigotry across his unsightly face, one hand obscured underneath the desk and the other on top of the Confederacy Constitution as if it were the bible.

Adam storms in and flies into a rage as he screams, "Motherfucking little-dick trick; I've got you right where I want you now! You've slandered my country's name beyond repairable damage and you've hurt countless people with your policies and orders! You've raped and pillaged your whole goddamn life but now you gotta answer to Adam Ordell; and I ain't takin' that shit from you!"

Fump begins cackling in his regular hissing manner as he pulls a hidden lever from underneath the desk, which causes a metal cage, just large enough to fit a human, to drop out of the ceiling, inconveniently, directly over where Adam is standing.

The evil emperor hisses some more before saying, "You were a fool to come here, Adam Ordell. The people have chosen me for this position. They all knew what my views were; what plans I had for their economy. But they chose me anyway because–"

"Because they have been brainwashed!" Adam cuts in, his hands clenched around the bars of the cage.

Fump scoffs and retorts, "That is an irrelevant piece of information. What I was going to say is that the American people voted for me because they are stupid and lazy. It requires too much thought process and too much effort to fight for a 'decent candidate' for their leader, so instead they have all given up. And now, America is completely under my control!"

"Don't forget about me," remarks the robotic voice of Mr. Husk as it staggers out from some unknown and obscured corner of the room.

Adam is repulsed by the appearance of the sub-human hybrid so much that he projectile vomits at the sight of it. Mr. Husk approaches Fump and French kisses him, his stumpy arms held out and his six long, boneless fingers wrapped around Fump's head. The trapped author has to look away from the horrendous scene to keep himself from vomiting any more.

Mr. Husk attempts to laugh, but all that comes from his mouth is a loud, mechanical-sounding whir like a malfunctioning machine as he says, "Adam Ordell, you fucking fool! You idiotic peon! You completely useless clump of hydrogen, oxygen, and carbon! Do you have any idea what it is you're up against? This is a power which takes over entire planets for breakfast – the very same power which created me!"

Adam looks at Mr. Husk, still gagging at the sight of the obscene and pantless creature, and asks, "What power, you pasty, froggy fuck?"

Mr. Husk makes another whirring laugh as he replies, "I suppose I will enlighten you to my origins; seeing as you won't be alive for very much longer."

Mr. Husk kicks Fump out of his presidential easy chair before continuing his exposition: "You see, amateur writer, I am a biologically-engineered, android-organic hybrid created by mistake on a planet very far away from here.

"The scientists who created me were attempting to recreate three Earth creatures to experiment on. It was well within their power to come here and take them without anyone's notice, but they wanted to see the origins of life on Earth, and just how evolution's course on a molecular level went so wrong. Their original intention was to create a bullfrog, a praying mantis, and a human.

"But they were careless, egotistical, and they accidentally added Chemical X instead of adding water to the solution. This resulted in the three life forms to become one, and as a result, I was born.

"The scientists could have just destroyed me, but they thought it more humorous to add cybernetic enhancements; giving me hyper intelligence (when compared to the average human) super strength (when compared to the average Earth creature) and one more that I will not disclose to you.

"They then sent me to Earth to live out my life amongst humans. I quickly advanced in your primitive society, and before long, I had obtained wealth, the power that comes with it, desperate females, and fame.

"But I wanted more, and that's when *Kroshechnyy Von Chlen* came into contact with me. He proposed that I aid his useless lover, Fump, in becoming supreme leader of the United States of America.

"I refused at first. Not because of morals or feelings of loyalty to this country where I have lived out my entire exile, but because there was nothing I thought he could offer me. But *Kroshechnyy Von Chlen* was very insistent, and one day he told me to name my price. I told him I wanted more power: the ability to rule over financial matters within the American government itself. He said he would provide this, of course. Still, this did not seem sufficient to me. So I explained to him my origins, and demanded he create a way for me to return to my planet of origin so I may exact my revenge on my creators who have banished me so.

"I didn't think that a lowly human would be able to procure such a thing for me, yet he said it could be done, but he wanted me to get Fump into office first.

"So I bought this pathetic excuse for a man his position, and shortly after, *Kroshechnyy Von Chlen* delivered his end of the bargain – he gave my space program the boost it needed to make it all the way to my planet of origin.

"There, I killed the scientists who created me, their families, friends, and anyone who got in my way. Before long, I had to slaughter the entire planet's population of intelligent life – thankfully it was only 155 due to the very limited amount of dry land – the planet's surface was 99.95% uninhabitable sulfuric swampland.

"So now you see! *I* have been the one pulling the strings this entire time! It has always been I, the one you call Mr. Husk, who has been ruling over you from behind the shadows! And now you get to take that little piece of information to the grave!"

Mr. Husk had been oblivious to the fact that the Black Power Gauntlet was now glowing brighter than ever before, and Adam's eyes now shone a brilliant light of rage like diamonds. The author could feel the immense power of the Black Power Gauntlet, now at a maximum, coursing through his veins like electricity through a closed circuit.

Adam's mind was clouded by this anger, as he effortlessly rips the front of the cage away. He lunges at Mr. Husk, who suddenly demonstrates extreme agility, not unlike a spider monkey.

Mr. Husk evades Adam's attack and proceeds to taunt, "But then again, Fump is the one who insisted on all those hateful policies," before jumping up through the ceiling of the Oval Office, ascending all the way to the roof of the White House.

The author still cannot think straight, and so he heeds the words of the biological abomination as he points a menacing finger at Fump and says, as if possessed by an angry spirit, "Husk is but a catalyst – the harbinger of the damage and pain you have caused... You are my true enemy." He then rushes at Fump, pinning him against the wall by his fatty throat.

The enraged author punches Fump in the face 20 times in rapid succession, but Fump merely laughs and asks rhetorically, "Is that all you got? My daughter used to hit me harder when I used to touch her back when she was 15 years old."

Adam's fury grows even more, as he slams the Emperor to the ground, grabs him by the ankles and swings him like a sledgehammer through the desk. Still, Fump only laughs and makes sarcastic remarks. The author jumps up and pencil dives, landing on Fump's chest. The wicked ruler is still unhurt.

At this point, Adam can see nothing but red as he instinctually throws punch after punch at Fump's face, screaming, "How do you live?"

Adam's heart begins beating at a rapid pace, the power of the Black Power Gauntlet thrashing through his veins like lightning. He feels as if his blood vessels will soon burst from the pressure – yet he cannot stop himself from trying to completely annihilate Fump with his bare hands. This is because the usual rationality within Adam's mind is being held hostage by the fury and the hypocritical hatred that he has allowed himself to be overtaken with. All the author wants is to see Fump's blood running through the gutters of all the American ghettos.

Then, to the author's rescue comes D the fairy godfather, who appears and yells, "Boy! Have you lost your mind?" Adam involuntarily ignores his fairy godfather as he continues to beat on Fump as if he were a tribal drum.

"Goddamnit!" D exclaims. "You gon' die if you keep on like that! The High Priestess of Soul forgot to tell your ass, and I didn't think about it until just now, but that Gauntlet can inadvertently cause hatred within you to grow until it kills you! Something about becoming a monster in the process of fighting it or some shit. The point is, motherfucker, you gotta regain control of yourself 'cause that cracker ain't givin' in and you know this ain't the way anyhow!"

The author continues to disregard D's words, and as he's being beat, Fump snickers, "It looks like you're too late to save him little pixie! He's going to kill himself trying to kill me and there's nothing you can even do about it! And what a shame – I'm sure all 5 of his fans were looking forward to his next book. Guess he won't be able to finish writing that now."

Fump cackles some more, then stops as Adam abruptly stops beating him.

"Hey, what's the matter?" Fump taunts, slight unease in his voice. "Don't you still wanna see me dead?"

But Adam isn't listening to the evil emperor – he's considering what he had just said a moment ago: that Adam would never be able to finish his upcoming book. The author's mind begins to race as thoughts of his next release, the framework for a book he wants to write after it's done, and many more literary ideas flood into his mind.

D the fairy godfather can tell immediately that Adam is thinking of his book and so he encourages him: "Remember, you still have a book to finish fool! It's gonna be the craziest shit you done tried yet! You can't *not* put out something like that!"

Adam's heart rate steadily decreases until it's back to normal, and the Black Power Gauntlet goes back to emitting a soft light of Black Power, rather than the almost blinding glow of foolish hatred.

"Shit, you're right D!" the author remarks. "I still got a book to finish!"

He then looks down at Fump, who's looking like some kind of idiot sitting on the ground. "But I still gotta defeat this bitch right here. How the fuck am I supposed to do that?"

D answers, "That's some shit you should already know by now! Remember what Mr. Husk was saying about pulling the strings and shit? And also that shit about a third power he got from his cybernetic enhancements?"

Adam thinks for a moment, then says in realization, "Oh goddamnit! I shoulda known it was Mr. Husk who I needed to defeat even before he said that shit anyway! Everybody already knows that motherfucker's the one who bought Fump's seat in the White House."

"Shoulda coulda woulda nigga," says the fairy godfather. "Just get up on that roof and turn that overgrown bug into another world-famous dead bug! Sassafras!" D then disappears in a cloud of angel dust.

Slow to realize what's going on around him, Fump only now attempts to stop Adam from going up to the roof of the White House.

"Wait, stop; that's a presidential order!" Fump bellows while trying to grab Adam by the arm.

The author flings Fump across the Oval Office with a simple movement of his arm, saying to the pathetic president, "Don't worry, Fump, I'll be back for you," before jumping up through the ceiling and all the way up to the roof of the White House.

On top of the dome roof of the White House, Adam finds Mr. Husk crouching over the edge, scowling and hissing as he watches the united army of black people and LGBT's emerge from the National Archives, victorious, the Bill of Rights held high in the air by The High Priestess of Soul.

"They are so pathetically weak," the extraterrestrial monstrosity remarks. "They continue to fight in this land wherein everything has been stacked against them; how tragically comedic."

Adam shouts at Mr. Husk in rebuttal: "They fight because they are strong! My people will continue to fight until they either obtain their freedom or the human race dies out! These are things a robot-animal hybrid creature like you will never understand.

"But enough of this idle chatter! I will defeat you, Husk! I will take you down in the name of freedom and liberty for everyone across the land and liberate my country from your wicked grasp!"

Mr. Husk turns toward Adam, and staggers over to the author, saying, "You fool! You cannot simply defeat me and think that will free the land of tyranny! Me, Fump, the IKEBB, even *Kroshechnyy Von Chlen*; we are all but a very small few of the evil beings upon this planet. There are thousands, if not millions just like us; waiting for the day we are no more so they can take the people's trust and proceed to do just as we are doing now. Face it, there is no hope for this country or even for all of humanity."

Mr. Husk gets close to Adam, sniffing the air around the gagging author before continuing, "But you, Adam Ordell, you are of a higher intellect. You could be one of us – I sense that potential in you. You could live the so-called 'good life' – what every human wants. You could be rich, writing only what we allow you, yet just what the people want to hear. In fact I implore you now: join us. Let this battle be fought by lesser intellects and reap the rewards of having superior intelligence."

Mr. Husk is staring intently into Adam's eyes, grinning sinisterly and eagerly; awaiting the author's response. But Adam knows that is not what he wants out of life, and so he uses the incredible might of the Black Power Gauntlet to knock Mr. Husk off the roof.

"No!" the author shouts. "I don't give a damn about the wealth and power you and Fump have! I consider myself ten times more powerful than all of you bitches combined because I have what you never will: the unadulterated power of my literature and the truth I speak with it! That is something that can never be taken from me; not even death will stop my words from fighting evil forces such as yourself!"

Mr. Husk jumps back on top of the roof, his bottom lip torn open and secreting some sort of transparent-brown, oil-like fluid, and he screams, "Imbecile! This insignificant, microscopic movement you are bringing about won't change the way things really are! Someone like you could never save America from the doom which lurks just beneath its surface.

"So many of the people in this country are lazy and complacent. They would rather let their minds be ruled over by the same system which keeps them yearning for things they'll never have than to stand with you and fight this futile battle! They would rather go out and buy into the latest consumer craze and ignore their own empty bank accounts; their liberties and freedoms slipping away.

"As for some of the others, they've already sided with us you pathetic peon! Many of the ones we have under our control are even willing to destroy relationships with their own friends and family members just because they do not pledge their allegiance to us! These people won't listen to you! You are their enemy through their eyes. We have them believing it is people like you who are the enemies of their freedoms – all the while they worship us like gods and give their entire lives to us."

Adam thinks about Mr. Husk's words for a moment, then an idea comes to him as he says to the half-mechanical monster, "If they will not listen to me, fine. But they will listen to their precious Fump."

Before Mr. Husk can analyze in his computer-like brain what Adam had said, the author puts Husk into a chokehold and squeezes his neck until his bullfrog-human-hybrid head comes off.

His oil-like blood is pouring all over the White House roof, his big eyes flickering as he struggles to vocalize, "Y-y- you p-p- pathetic peo-o-onnnn."

The creature's head then makes an ear-piercing whirring noise before shutting down permanently along with its body. Adam throws the head down onto the partly cybernetic corpse and spits on both. He then jumps back down the hole in the roof which leads back into the Oval Office.

Inside the Oval Office, Adam finds Fump cowering in a corner, sobbing loudly and cradling his cellphone in his hands.

"Oh god, he's back inside!" Fump screams in high falsetto to his gay lover over the phone. "And now that he's killed Mr. Husk, he's going to kill me!"

Fump continues his blubbering as Adam approaches and snatches the phone out of the pathetic excuse for a world leader's hands.

Adam then says into the phone calmly, "You don't have to worry about your boyfriend right now – I will not be killing him. I only kill things that are a true threat to me; like a fly landing upon my turkey sandwich with only tomato on it. I can't speak for the lifers he'll soon be getting to know in prison, however."

The furious voice of *Kroshechnyy Von Chlen* shouts from the other side of the phone, "Who are you to tell me not to worry? Fuck you! I will have you killed! Do you fucking hear me? I–"

Adam hangs up the phone and tosses it across the room. He then breaks out in a fit of hysterical laughter as he watches the terrified Fump shaking on the floor, his pants soaked with urine.

Fump shrieks, "Oh god, please! Please don't hurt me!"

Adam picks Fump up by the lapels of his jacket and says, "God? Oh no, Fump, don't get all religious now. Because if she really existed, God wouldn't have let your parents reproduce.

"But besides that, didn't you hear me talking to your boyfriend just now? I'm *not* going to kill you. If I were stupid enough to kill you, then the history books of tomorrow would mark you as one of the greatest U.S. presidents to have ever lived. But *I'm* going to write this one, and I'm a damn good author and ain't a decent author alive or otherwise who don't write the truth."

Fump wipes the tears from his red eyes, and laughs a little before asking, "And how are you going to show this 'truth' to the people?"

"Through you," Adam quickly replies. "You will tell the people the truth about you and your fiendish plot."

The author then looks out the window and sees a large crowd gathered outside, with a reporter and news crew surrounding her. At this scene Adam smiles, thinking that the news would for once report the truth.

"But how do I get this motherfucker out there to tell them all the truth?" Adam asks himself silently.

Fump laughs more and he retorts, "Ha! You must think that you can get me to tell the truth out there, on the news! You dummy; I'll never tell the truth! And since you won't kill me, I've won! You idiot! You've lost because you don't have what it takes to defeat me! Hahahaha!"

Adam begins to contemplate knocking Fump unconscious while he thinks up a way to get the Emperor to tell the truth on television, and then D the fairy godfather appears once more to advise his godson on what he should do next:

"Damnit boy!" the fairy godfather exclaims. "How can't you figure this simple shit out?"

Adam looks at D and yells, "Motherfucker ain't a goddamn thing about none of this shit been simple! But I can tell by your appearing here you know what to do, so tell me: How the fuck do I get this sonofabitch to spill the beans to the people?"

"Did you forget about that gauntlet on your hand?" D asks in rebuttal. "Man, just grab that cracker by the nuts and use Black Power against him to make him tell only the truth! It's like Wonder Woman's whip or some shit."

Adam looks at his fairy godfather with a disgusted expression across his face as he retorts, "First off, I ain't grabbin' this sunburst-flavored-ass honkey by his nuts! Second, motherfucker what's simple about that? How the hell was I just supposed to know this Gauntlet is like the Lasso of Truth?"

D laughs a little and says, "A: Nigga, just grab him through his pants. And also I got some gloves for you."

The fairy godfather miraculously pulls a pair of black latex gloves from nowhere, and tosses them to the author before continuing, "B: Well, I guess that it wasn't really self explanatory now that I think about it – but you still shoulda seen some deus ex machina type shit comin' at you from a mile away! Sassafras!"

D the fairy godfather disappears in a puff of angel dust, and Adam looks at Fump, who's still on the floor, eyes now alert with a new sense of fear in them.

"Okay, wait," Fump stammers. "Maybe we can work something out! I can give you money, power whatever–"

Adam cuts the begging emperor off, shouting, "Oh no you little bitch! I heard once that you like to do this type of shit all the time anyway – so you oughtta like this shit you been dishing out."

The author puts the latex gloves on – the right glove almost ripping when being pulled over the Black Power Gauntlet – and grabs the would-be dictator by his testicles with the Black Power Gauntlet. Fump's testicles shrink down to the size of raisins, and all of a sudden, he can't help but begin compulsively telling the truth:

"I did it!" Fump cries. "I raped all those women! I killed 72 niggers with the kkk! In fact, I have my grand dragon robe in my closet back in my seaside home!"

Fump goes on to tell the truth about countless horrors and atrocities, many of which even Adam had not known about, and before long the author has to tell the Emperor to stop.

"Alright!" Adam exclaims. "Shut the fuck up for a moment! I want you to go out there to that news crew and tell America the truth about you and your evil ways! Or else I really will be forced to dispose of you."

The author breaks a window in the Oval Office, and says to the president, "Go on – the people want to know and they want to know now – so tell them." Fump helplessly squeezes his obese carcass out of the broken window.

The reporter, at the non-verbal cue of the cameraman, turns around and sees Fump staggering over to her.

"Um," the reporter stammers, "it appears President Fump is slowly walking over to us now... And it also appears that the president's pants are wet with what looks like urine."

Fump reaches the reporter and commands, "I demand you give me that microphone! I have something to tell America."

The reporter looks at the cameraman, who shrugs his shoulders and so she does as Fump instructed.

"I... I..." Fump stammers. "I have never had any of your interests in mind! I have only ever wanted to rule over you – all the while filling my pockets with your money. I have imposed these tariffs to aid in my rich buddies' plans to drive up the prices so they can get richer while all of you get poorer. I have single-handedly made our economy far worse than before I was elected. It was already in a bad way, but I made it even worse for profit and also for..."

Fump struggles not to say what the truth-telling effects of the Black Power Gauntlet are forcing him to say, before eventually succumbing: "And also for my secret lover, *Kroshechnyy Von Chlen*."

The whole crowd and the news crew around Fump gasps as he continues, "*Kroshechnyy Von Chlen* and I have been involved in a love affair for a number of years now. I have been secretly sending him classified Unites States documents as well as aiding him in his own evil plans for Europe.

"I am a racist and a grand dragon in the klu klux klan. I hate all brown people and am a supporter of white supremacy."

Fump once again tries not to tell the truth, before having to divulge even more information: "I have, in fact, defunded various public programs which help poor brown people as well as all poor people. I actually hate all people who aren't filthy rich like myself.

"I said in the past that these programs have been taking money away from your paychecks, which is technically true, but it is such a small amount of money that if it wasn't taken for those programs then we'd still take it from you anyway – which was also part of my plan. It has always been part of my plan to take all the money I've claimed to save Americans from spending and take it for myself.

"None of this is fake news… especially the fact that I am a womanizer and a rapist. I have groped, molested, and forcefully had sex with various women throughout my lifetime. In fact, most of the sexual encounters I've had were forced… the rest I paid for with money. I've spied on naked teenage girls, seen sexual potential in girls as young as 8 years old, and I have even groped my own daughter when she was underage.

"To cover all of these atrocities, my team and I have used various scapegoats such as Mexicans, middle-eastern people, black people, and all of the LGBT people across the country. I have a special hatred for the LGBT people because I secretly envy their self-sustained happiness. I'm just a fat, balding, ugly billionaire and I wish I could be like those LGBT people."

Then, The Offenders – having won each of their battles across Washington DC, appear surrounding Fump, with Adam blocking the camera's view of the Emperor.

The author thinks to himself, "Finally I was able to teleport like damn-near everyone else I've encountered!"

He then cracks his knuckles, facing Fump as he says, "Now, you're going to apologize to all of the people you've hurt."

Fump lowers the microphone and asks, "And how are you going to make me?"

Nico grabs Fump by the neck and says, "By giving you a simple choice: Either you apologize, or I kill you where you stand. You're fortunate that the rest of The Offenders have reason for keeping you alive – because I was going to kill you the moment I was able to get my hands on you."

Fump defecates in his pants as he whimpers, "O-okay! I'll apologize! I'm sorry!"

Nico puts the Emperor down and La Sirène says, "Not to us you moron; apologize to the cameras."

The Offenders clear away from the camera's view of Fump as he apologizes to America: "To everyone I've hurt, I have to apppp... apoooo... I apollll... I'm sorrr..."

As Fump struggles to find the words to apologize, Adam and the rest of The Offenders crack their knuckles, and Fump suddenly is able to say that he's sorry: "I'm sorry!"

The crowd once again gasps as Fump continues, "I have torn apart families, killed countless innocents, and sent many to their assured demise. I have even caused children to lose hope in humanity. I've caused many of them to attempt to kill themselves because of orders I've enacted against their parents' rights to allow them to be who they are.

"To all my supporters, constituents, followers, and die-hard fans – I'm sorry too. I know that many of you have blindly followed me; believing that I am not the piece of shit I really am. I have deceived you and made you believe in a false messiah."

Fump turns away from the camera, only to see the menacing glares of The Offenders, and so he turns back toward the camera and says, "And as of today, I am resigning as president of the United States of America." The entire crowd around Fump once again gasps.

Meanwhile across the United States, millions of Fump's believers sit or stand in shock – trying to come to terms with their former hero revealing himself to be the vile scumbag that he truly is. Some of them bawled their eyes out, some immediately tried to call relatives they had abandoned to try and rebuild the relationships they ruined while their minds were clouded.

Almost all of them denounced and rebuked Fump and all of his ways – if not aloud, then in their hearts. There were only a select few who wear white hoods and burn crosses who simply pumped their hands into the air and swore to follow their king to the bitter end.

Those watching who were opposed to Fump and his tyranny from the very beginning cheered as they watched the news reveal what they already knew to be the truth.

People across the entire globe cheered as well. They found solace in the fact that the plague in America – which was trying quickly to spread to their own countries – had been at least temporarily wiped out.

Adam then takes the microphone from Fump, steps in front of the camera and says, "We the People have sat back and awaited the lightning strike which would deliver us from the damnable throes of a tyrannical rule for far too long. This is why we have come together – the People and I – to form a supergroup I have named The Offenders."

Adam then names the members of The Offenders, pointing at each one as he calls their name: "We are The High Priestess of Soul, who represents all the black people of America. La Sirène, who represents all of the members of the LGBT people of America. Luis, a young and brilliant Latino law student who seeks liberty, equality, and freedom for his people: the Latin-American people as well as all immigrants across America who are currently facing injustice. And last but not least, me. My name is not important, I am just a writer who has been wronged by this unjust system a time too many and who sought his revenge against those who have wronged not only me, but all people across the globe: the greedy and vile, rich and powerful one percent.

"Today, we have defeated only one of their kind, but that is only a small battle won. Everyone across the country now has to join arms so we can finally liberate America from the rich and greedy: the enemies of the people. We all have to stop hating each other for our differences.

"No matter what religion you believe or don't believe in, no matter what the color of your skin is, no matter what country you came from, no matter whatever sexuality or gender you identify with – all of you are human. And if you cannot see it that way, so be it. If you can't all get along because of irrelevant differing beliefs or superfluous similar shades of your own skin, then so be it – I have already gotten my revenge today. I leave you all in the hands of The Offenders. They will not take your democracy from you, rather, they will help you to make the next few steps toward peace and true freedom."

Adam drops the microphone and walks away from the crowd. The Offenders stay in front of the cameras, shocked by the leader's apparent resignation from their group, yet answering questions from the crowd before them. The author returns to the pearl-white hog, gets in, buckles his seat belt, starts it up and drives it back to his apartment in River End to finally finish his upcoming book.

As Adam drives the hog at full speed down the highway, invigorated by his victory in Washington DC, D the fairy godfather appears sitting in the passenger seat, now a full-sized man, about 6 feet tall exactly. He still has his amazing black mohawk, his 18-millimeter earlobe gauges, his black leather trench coat, black Dickies and Doc Martins leather boots. The only difference now is his skin, which has turned reddish-brown instead of its former blue.

"Hey yo!" the godfather exclaims. "I'm back to my full size now! That prophesy shit musta been for real cause' it said that if you did the right thing then I'd return to my regular self!"

Adam stares at his godfather in amazement for a second, then looks back at the road and swerves back into his lane to avoid colliding with another car.

"Goddamn man!" the astounded author exclaims. "I thought you was just a pixie fairy all the time!"

D laughs and responds, "Hell no! I'm a full-grown-ass man! A couple months ago, my black ass was turned into a goddamn pixie by Lord Junkie's voodoo. I tried to kick his monkey ass the same way you did back at the start of this shit, but I found out the hard way that shit don't work with a junkie like him.

"That's when The Grandmaster's mysterious ass got with me and told me about that damn prophecy, and how at some point you'd be contacting me. He taught me how to use my powers and shit. But anyway, thanks man – for real. 'Cause now I can get back to really takin' care of my kids and shit. Maybe get some stuff done around the house, you know."

Adam laughs and replies, "Yeah, for sure. I was just doing anything I could to clear my name and then to get my revenge. But hey, if you ain't a pixie no more, then you ain't my fairy godfather no more either?"

"Oh don't worry about that," the former fairy godfather says. "I'ma still be your godfather from now on. I'll visit every now and then, you know, I ain't gon' treat you like a bald-headed stepchild or nothing like that. And as you can see, even though I ain't a pixie no more, I can still pop in on a motherfucker whenever I want! So I'll be around and I'll see you around my nigga – sassafras!"

With that, Derrick, the regular teleporting godfather, disappears in a puff of sugar and Adam finishes his drive in peace.

At home, the author finds that the Black Power Gauntlet is now able to be removed. So he takes it off and places it on his almost empty bookshelf.

"Kinda forgot about how most of my books got ruined the other day," the author says to himself. "Well, oh well; I'ma let it go now that I got my revenge and focus on rebuilding my collection."

The author manages to smile, then proceeds to open the blinds of the window just above his desk, letting in the dying light of the setting sun into his humble studio apartment.

He then sits down at his desk, opens up the document containing his upcoming book on his laptop, and asks himself, "Now, let's see where I left off last," before finding his footing and typing away – at last returning to what he loved doing most.

Epilogue

(As Told by D the Former Fairy Godfather)

At the end we find that all the shit has been laid out – and then again – we find that there ain't shit to be laid out in the first place.

Hello and goodbye. My name is Derrick White, but you know me better as D, the fairy godfather of the reluctant young hero of this little narrative: Adam Ordell. Now, you might be wondering to yourself, "Just why is the great, fantastic and incredible D doing the epilogue to the whole motherfuckin' story?" Well, it's really none of your goddamn business; but since you asked so kindly I'll tell you: I'm doing the shit because it's really *me* that was the central character this whole time.

Without me, this whole motherfucking shit wouldn't have even come together! Think about it! If my ingenious ass hadn't gave the boy the kick in the ass he needed to go out and do this ridiculous fuckin' quest, then he'd never done it and then what the hell would've you done with yourself for the past couple of hours? Woah woah woah! Yall freaks out there need to calm the hell down – I meant what other *constructive* thing would you have done.

But anyway, without any further ado, let me walk you on through the next couple of things that happened after ol' Fumpy was forced to tell America the truth about his ol' evil ass:

America went into some kind of damn hysteria after they heard their hero was actually one of the most evil supervillains America had in office since maybe Bush or Reagan or Nixon or, well, you get the point.

Fump supporters all over went all half crazy and shit; blaming themselves for all the fucked-up things Fump was doing behind the scenes. A lot of them tried hard to reconcile with people they'd hurt while brainwashed by Fump, but wasn't nobody trying to hear anything from any of the former Fump supporters.

A lot of people started riots and marches and shit like that; some of them even took all the madness as an excuse to start looting. Some people who already knew about Fump's crooked ass but couldn't do nothing about him before started saying they were going to run for office. And that pissed off people who though The Offenders should look after the country. Basically, motherfuckers all over was pissed off and doing everything about it except the right thing.

See, that's why Adam didn't want no part of the rest of what was to come. He knew goddamn well this is how America would react to their own hostile liberation. He was just hoping that it would all work out for the better while he finished up his book.

Eventually though, people did come together and an emergency election was held. Somehow, America ended up with a black, lesbian, female president. I know! That shit tripped me out too but hey, this is a fairytale we're talking about. The government was therefore put back into effect, Fump's ridiculous fucking tariffs and made-up laws and regulations and shit was all undone, and the new president started on fixing the rest of the problems with America. (It took both of the two terms she was in office, and she still didn't get to fix much really, but at least she tried.)

But enough of this political bullshit! Let's get down to what became of our colorful cast of characters:

Adam Ordell, of course, stepped away from politics entirely and went on to finish writing his next book. Even though he ended up being a little late getting it to his publishers, they knew it was him on the news with The Offenders, so they went ahead and published it anyway.

Now, I wouldn't want to ruin the surprise for yall and tell you just how that book went down and all that. But let's just say, Adam went on to write a whole slew of damn good books after that.

The boy ended up traveling the world, running into his old friend Stinkbug occasionally – seeing all kinds of things that I can't tell you about. (Maybe he even got himself into a few more Epic Quests and Spectacular Adventures; wink wink.)

Ol' Ronald Fump and his crew was all tried for treason and various human rights violations. Fump thought he could beat this case like he did the last one, but what he didn't count on was a country full of motherfuckers who no longer supported him.

Half felt betrayed, some just wanted to see him hung by his nuts, others thought he oughtta be exiled from America permanently. In the end though, Fump was sentenced to triple life in prison, without chance of parole, while his buddies were all exiled from America forever.

Now, Richard Pryor once made a joke about a triple life sentence, saying it meant if you die and come back then your ass got to go right back to penitentiary. I thought that's what it meant my goddamn self, but apparently it really means you're serving time for three different crimes all at once.

Fump's first crime, of course, was multiple counts of rape. The second crime was an amalgamation of all the human rights violations Fump committed while in office; such as the targeted mass deportation of brown-skinned people, executive orders which encouraged discriminatory hiring, and policies targeting people of the rainbow. The third crime was his attempt to take over America and rule it as some sort of king. Rumor says Fump's asshole been turned inside out in the joint, but those are only probably factual rumors – I ain't saying shit is a concrete fact.

Turned out Lord Junkie's crackhead ass wasn't killed by the collapse of his palace. Instead, he was only paralyzed from the neck down. He gave up his voodoo junkie king ways and went on to become some kind of discount amateur magician for hire at kids' birthday parties. The sonofabitch is actually pretty decent for only a crack rock per appearance – I'd never let him entertain at my kids' events though.

Now, remember little 13-year-old Lynne Brown: the middle-schooler pimp with the sweet-ass '64 Impala? Well, that boy didn't learn a goddamn thing from his encounter with Adam and the court. Boy went on to make pimping history; pimping girls all over the world from Australia to Greenland. He was the first ever pimp to have stables in multiple countries all at once. Lynne put great names like Iceberg Slim to shame and he aged like fine wine – getting better with age.

And as for his first horse, little 16-year-old Janie Fagen, she quit whorring after a false pregnancy scared her straight. She was then adopted by one of the members of the LGBT's, and began living the life of a normal teenage girl.

Judge Composé and the prosecuting lawyer, Dr. Hochstedler, from Chapter 2, was both thrown in prison for ten years for conspiring against and attempting to falsely imprison a citizen. The rent-a-lawyer, Jacob Browning, quit his job as a public defender and became a mortician.

The Grandmaster felt he didn't need to be a mysterious motherfucker anymore, so he decided to take up rapping. He's damn good too; spitting out better shit than any of these crap rappers we got nowadays. And recently, he got so pissed off at this record executive that was trying to fuck him on the back end of a deal that he found the strength to stand for the first time in over 3 decades! He almost didn't kick that cracker's ass he was so happy to be standing.

After being able to walk again, he took up extreme hiking. He toured some of the most crazy-ass terrains on Planet Earth. The Grandmaster climbed mountains, swam across alligator-infested rivers, lakes, and lagoons, walked across burning deserts, frozen tundras – anything and everything until the day he died.

The Count got himself a young apprentice, who he's teaching how to play the organ and the MPC the right way. They're both getting on pretty good. The Count and his apprentice aren't exactly going on Epic Quests and shit, but you know, the musical journey ain't no shit to scoff at – might even make a good book! (Wink wink.)

Jack Allen and Fresh Factory Fred continued to guard The Count's Castle for the rest of their lives. (And of course, Jack did get that rematch with Adam. I won't tell you who smoked who, but a motherfucker did get smoked that day I'll tell you that!)

The High Priestess of Soul went on the open the Secret Society of Black People to all black people across America. She's been taking in black people from all walks of life and building the world's greatest society with them all. It's really great, you know, seeing all those brothers and sisters come together and building something for the future. There's still the occasional fuck up, of course, like niggas just trying to be niggas; acting like they ain't got no common sense. But it's all to the good. And white folks still don't know about the Secret Society either. So if you's a white folks reading this, then pretend you ain't see nothing.

La Sirène guided her people out of the underground caverns they found themselves in and out into the light. She still governed over the LGBT's though, since a lot of them still felt they needed a leader. That's since just because a piece of paper says all people are equal, doesn't mean that all people see it that way.

She eventually passed the throne down to Prince Sebastian, the Royal Music Programmer. After she did that, La Sirène took a wife and together they traveled the world, giving refuge and a helping hand to LGBT's all over.

Eventually though, they both settled down in La Sirène second home country aside from the UK, France, and opened a school of music for all ages. They even had a kid of their own. (They didn't adopt, but La Sirène wife was a cisgender woman, and La Sirène never did get the old snip snip, if you get what I mean.)

Lily Green, the first of the LGBT Trialmasters, became an international sensation like Kurtis Blow! She was a real superstar, even in today's stick-up-the-ass world with hits like *Bring That Ass Over Here, Let's See How You Like THIS in Your Pussy*, and everybody's favorite: *The 24-Inch Strap*. I think the girl's hilarious myself, especially her entire album she call *Eat Me or Treat Me*.

Larray, the second Trialmaster, ended up getting with and marrying Recto-Verso, the third Trialmaster, and them two boring-ass niggas settled down into a life of domesticity and tranquility. Larray was still one for the dramatics, becoming a talk-show host on some local thing that eventually became a national thing. Recto-Verso, however, started going to therapy for his multiple personality and bipolar disorder. They both got along alright, I guess, just kind of fucking boring for this sort of tale is all.

Nico, the young Latino revolutionary finished law school and became Chief Justice and eventually Head of Immigration. He helped not only his own Latin people out in America, but any and all immigrants coming here looking for a better life. At the age of 55, in fact, he even became the motherfucking president of the United States. That's some real fairytale shit, I know, but don't forget what you reading now.

And now, for the moment you've all been waiting for; the question I know you've been asking since the end of Chapter 9: What ever became of that clever, witty, hilarious and talented brother Derrick White, otherwise known internationally as D?

Well, as you already know I grew back to my normal size after Fump was defeated and that voodoo curse was finally taken off my ass. What you don't know, however, is that I lost my motherfucking powers of teleporting and creating deus ex machinas shortly after telling Adam I got to keep them. That was alright with me though, because I was tired of being the color of a Smurf and the size of a damn hummingbird anyway – can't get no pussy like that. Speaking of pussy, no sooner did I grow back to 6 feet tall than I found me one fine-ass woman named Wanda.

Now, you know me; I was just cruising down the street in my sweet-ass '72 – bumping some new metal tunes I'd picked up at a little record store I been getting my CD's from forever now – straight macking you know, when I got to a red light. I stopped, of course, and then this blue, 1969 Camaro pulls up next to me. It happened to be a drop top and I got to see the driver inside: this beautiful, mocha-choco-latte supreme deluxe with extra sprinkles!

She had that pretty-ass hair and great big brown eyes and... well... fuck it I might as well keep it real; she had some big ol' titties and so I rolled down my window and I yell over, "Hey, my first-ever car was a '69 Camaro! Mines was the same color as yours too – except mines was a hard top!"

She smiles, her teeth looking all pearly and shit – and says back, "Oh that's a funny coincidence... That car you driving now is pretty loud. Is it fast too?"

Then, shit, you know I had to get my game going and shit so I said, "Let's race and you can find out! And *when* I win, you *have* to give me them digits."

She agreed and you already know I smoked that ass – then I ripped that ass the very next week! I been settled down with my baby for a little while now. She done moved into my place after I got it cleaned up, and I got plenty of room for me, her, and my sons and daughter whenever they come to visit. My ex wife be hating too. On the surface she be saying she happy for me and all that – but I can tell she's jealous of me and my happy life. But hell, I ain't bothered.

Anyway, I hope you enjoyed this little American Clustertruck we got here. I know everybody involved worked real hard so I know it means an awful lot to them that you're reading it and smiling right now. Maybe you even found it inspiring or some other shit like that. Until next time yall – *sassafras!*